THE MIDDLE AGES COME TO LIFE . . .
TO BRING US MURDER

THE SISTER FREVISSE MYSTERIES
by Margaret Frazer

THE NOVICE'S TALE

Among the nuns at St. Frideswide were piety, peace, and a little vial of poison . . .

"Frazer uses her extensive knowledge of the period to create an unusual plot . . . appealing characters and crisp writing."
—Los Angeles Times

THE SERVANT'S TALE
Nominated for the Edgar Award

A troupe of actors at a nunnery are harbingers of merriment—or murder . . .

"A good mystery . . . excellently drawn . . . very authentic . . . the essence of a truly historical story is that the people should feel and believe according to their times. Margaret Frazer has accomplished this extraordinarily well."

—Anne Perry

THE OUTLAW'S TALE

Sister Frevisse meets a long-lost blood relative—but the blood may be on his hands . . .

"A tale well told, filled with intrigue and spiced with romance and rogues."

—School Library Journal

"Very pleasant reading. May the series continue!"

—Kliatt

THE BISHOP'S TALE

The murder of a mourner means another funeral, and possibly more . . .

"Some truly shocking scenes and psychological twists."
—Mystery Loves Company

"Wonderful historical dark tapestry."

Minneapolis Star Tribune

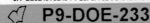
P9-DOE-233

MORE MYSTERIES FROM THE
BERKLEY PUBLISHING GROUP . . .

SISTER FREVISSE MYSTERIES: Medieval mystery in the tradition of Ellis Peters . . .

by Margaret Frazer
THE NOVICE'S TALE   THE BISHOP'S TALE
THE OUTLAW'S TALE   THE BOY'S TALE
THE SERVANT'S TALE

RENAISSANCE MYSTERIES: Sigismondo the sleuth courts danger—and sheds light on the darkest of deeds . . . "Most entertaining!" —*Chicago Tribune*

by Elizabeth Eyre
DEATH OF THE DUCHESS   CURTAINS FOR THE CARDINAL

PENNYFOOT HOTEL MYSTERIES: In Edwardian England, death takes a seaside holiday . . .

by Kate Kingsbury
ROOM WITH A CLUE   DO NOT DISTURB
SERVICE FOR TWO   EAT, DRINK, AND BE BURIED
CHECK-OUT TIME   GROUNDS FOR MURDER

GLYNIS TRYON MYSTERIES: The highly acclaimed series set in the early days of the women's rights movement . . . "Historically accurate and telling." —Sara Paretsky

by Miriam Grace Monfredo
SENECA FALLS INHERITANCE   NORTH STAR CONSPIRACY

THE BOY'S TALE

MARGARET FRAZER

BERKLEY PRIME CRIME, NEW YORK

If you purchased this book without a cover, you should be aware that this book is stolen property. It was reported as "unsold and destroyed" to the publisher, and neither the author nor the publisher has received any payment for this "stripped book."

THE BOY'S TALE

A Berkley Prime Crime Book / published by arrangement with the author

PRINTING HISTORY
Berkley Prime Crime edition / August 1995

All rights reserved.
Copyright © 1995 by Mary Monica Kuhfeld and Gail Bacon.
This book may not be reproduced in whole or in part,
by mimeograph or any other means, without permission.
For information address: The Berkley Publishing Group,
200 Madison Avenue, New York, NY 10016.

ISBN: 0-425-14899-8

Berkley Prime Crime Books are published by
The Berkley Publishing Group,
200 Madison Avenue, New York, NY 10016.
The name BERKLEY PRIME CRIME and the BERKLEY PRIME CRIME
design are trademarks belonging to Berkley Publishing Corporation.

PRINTED IN THE UNITED STATES OF AMERICA

10 9 8 7 6 5 4 3 2 1

Is this to yow a thyng that is honest,
That swich a boy shal walken as hym lest
In youre despit . . . ?

The Prioress's Tale
Geoffrey Chaucer

Chapter

◪ 1 ◪

THE WARM SUMMER'S afternoon was worn well away. They had been riding nearly without letup since there was light enough to see their way; the horses were tired, and so was Jasper, but he had little hope Sir Gawyn would let them stop soon. These June days the light bloomed early and lingered late, and if today went as yesterday and the day before had gone, Sir Gawyn would keep them a-horse until it was almost too dark to find their way. Then he would maybe make them sleep along a hedgerow as he had last night, instead of finding an inn or other sensible place to stay.

It had seemed such a great adventure when it began all unexpectedly two days ago. He and Edmund had been at afternoon lessons, with Master John intoning as usual over the endless declensions of Latin and Jenet sitting with her sewing across the room. Another hour and they would be loosed, Jasper had been thinking, watching a shadow not move across the windowsill.

Then Mistress Maryon had suddenly come in, followed by two servants. She oversaw their attendants, and no one had questioned her when she pointed to the boys' clothing chests against one wall and said, "Everything in those, and

1

be quick at it." Then she turned to Jenet and said, "Pack yourself a change of clothing and anything their graces may need on a few days' journey. I can give you a quarter hour, no more." And then to Master John, "You're dismissed. Their lessons are done."

Mistress Maryon had a brisk way with orders. Everyone was used to it, Jasper and Edmund especially, since they were ever and always in her charge because Mother and Father had a great many matters to see to and could not always have time for them. There were sometimes days on end when they and their little brother Owen, who was hardly more than a baby and had his own Mistress Geretrude, were taken right across the castle to a whole other set of rooms and kept there without seeing Mother or Father or anyone. Those times they were not allowed out at all, even to play in the gardens, because their parents were too busy and must not be distracted by so much as a glimpse of their children. They did not mind it so very much because when it was over and they were moved back to their own rooms, Mother and Father were always wonderfully glad, and there would be games together and especial things to eat and laughter— Mother was full of laughter—and singing—Father sang better than anyone—to make up for being shut up away from them.

But this time at Mistress Maryon's brisk instructions, Master John stared at her as if he had gone stupid, then said, "It hasn't happened."

"It has and why we should be surprised I don't know. Nor am I knowing how long we have, but we'd best be quick at it."

Master John had crossed himself, murmuring, "God have mercy."

But Mistress Maryon was already turning to snap at Jenet, who had the same stupid, disbelieving stare as Master John on her face. "Be moving! And don't cry. Or you two either," she had added, rounding on Jasper and Edmund. "We don't have time for crying, any of us."

Nor had there been. Not that he or Edmund had wanted to. It was quite clear they were to escape their lessons, and apparently they were going to journey somewhere. They had never been much of anywhere beyond the castle—a few times to the river meadows to watch their parents hawking; once to the wood edge just this May to bring the summer in—but from the way the servants were stuffing clothing into the bags, and Mistress Maryon was looking around the room as if unsure what could be taken, what would have to be left, this was going to be far more than a short jaunt out the gate, with them back home by nightfall.

He and Edmund had looked at each other, grinned, and gone to fetch their cloaks and a few necessary treasures from the little chest they kept under their bed. Edmund had taken the jesses he had demanded from the falconer in token of the peregrine he meant to have one day. Jasper took the embossed chape that had broken past repairing off Father's sword sheath; it was patterned with vines and leaves all wound around each other, and he had polished it as brightly as he could because, old and dented though it was, it was real silver—and had been Father's. Then, without asking permission, Edmund had strapped on the dagger that had been his birthday present from Father last winter. Jasper had looked at him doubtfully, but Edmund had set his hand firmly on its hilt and said, "If it's to be a real journey, we may need it."

Jasper rarely argued with Edmund and did not now, only regretted that he had no dagger of his own. They were so nearly alike in size as well as coloring, with their gray eyes, fair skin, and dusky red hair cut trimly about their ears, that they could easily be mistaken one for the other, when they were apart. When they were together, it was plain that Edmund was half a head the taller and more slenderly built than Jasper. He was quicker of movement and temper, too; and though, like Jasper, he never wavered in the certainty that they stood together in everything, he also never let loose of the advantage his six years gave him over Jasper's mere five. But the eleven months between them made all the difference in some things, including the fact that he had a dagger and Jasper had none.

If Mistress Maryon noted Edmund's dagger, she said nothing, only told Jenet and the two menservants to go down, that the horses were waiting in the fore yard, and then said to him and Edmund, "You'll make your farewells to your lady mother now. Quickly. It's a pity twice over your father is away."

As she led the way from the familiar chamber, Edmund eagerly at her heels and Jasper close on his, Jasper had looked back to Master John, still standing beside the lessons table. He was stern about their lessons but never more stern than he had to be and was often quite kind over any honest problem Jasper or Edmund had. Jasper raised his hand halfway in the beginning of a farewell to him, sorry the tutor had to stay behind with his books while they went adventuring. For surely the suddenness of this journey had to mean an adventure. But the sight of tears running down Master John's face had frozen Jasper's hand. Master John had never wept at their departure before, and Jasper had left the gesture half made as he turned and fled, unsettled by the sight.

And then, when they had come to Mother in her bedchamber, she had been alone, none of her ladies with her, and that was strange, too. So great a lady was never unattended. But she had been then, standing alone in the center of her chamber, and when he and Edmund had gone forward to make their low bows to her as always, she had not waited for them to finish but fallen to her knees and gathered them into her arms.

Edmund, always aware of proprieties even if he did not always choose to follow them, had gone momentarily rigid. Jasper, always ready to return affection for affection, had cuddled into her warmth without hesitation, loving the sweet smell of her.

"There, my darlings!" She had kissed one and then the other of them, and then kissed them the other way around, to keep it even. "And so again! You're going such a long way away with Mistress Maryon and Sir Gawyn now and you must do all as they tell you and be the brave chevaliers."

Jasper would have asked *why* they were going, but Edmund was their leader as usual and demanded, "Where?"

"Way away to where your father was born. Remember the stories he's told you? You're going there."

"To Wales?" Jasper said disbelievingly. Wales with its mountains and magics and dragons? Father's stories had made him want to go, but he had been told he would have to wait until he was grown.

"To Wales," Mother said. "But you mustn't say so to anyone, not even to each other, until you're safely there. Promise like brave chevaliers?"

It was a less strange oath than many they had heard in stories; they had promised vigorously, and she had kissed them again and stood up and said over their heads to Mistress Maryon, "Owen is already gone."

"Gone where?" Edmund had demanded jealously. How could Owen go adventuring like him and Jasper when he still had a nursemaid?

"To church," Mistress Maryon had said before their mother could answer. "To pray for you as you must pray for him."

"Are we going to have to pray before we leave?" It was a knightly thing to do, but Edmund had been impatient at the idea.

"No, but you must pray nonetheless," their mother had said. "For your brother and for me and for your father." Jasper had disbelievingly seen her eyes were sheened with tears as she said it. His mother, who was beautiful and merry and smelled always of summer flowers, could not be crying; it was wrong for her to cry. To keep from seeing it, lest he cry, too, and be sent to church with the baby, Jasper had burrowed his head against the warm curve of her neck, and she had hugged both him and Edmund tightly enough to hurt. And then she put them from her again and stood up, her eyes were dry and her voice her own as she said, "One last thing. You should have this, Jasper." She took from the table beside her a boy-sized dagger in a leather sheath already hung from a belt, ready to be worn. "We meant it for your birthday, but you had best take it now."

"My lady, there's little time," Mistress Maryon had said warningly.

Smiling down at Jasper's eager delight, his mother had bent to buckle the belt around his waist, saying, "God will give me time enough for this. Be thou a true, brave chevalier, my son."

The dagger had settled against his right hip as if it had always been there. Hand on its hilt, Jasper had smiled up at her and replied with due gravity, "I will, Madame." She kissed him swiftly on either cheek, and then Edmund, and said, "You're my brave and beautiful sons. God keep you in his love. Remember, remember that you're forever in mine. Remember."

"My lady," Mistress Maryon had said again, more warningly, and Mother had gestured hastily at them to go.

In the fore yard, Jenet and one of their mother's household knights, Sir Gawyn, and four other men were all waiting, mounted, with three saddled horses for Mistress Maryon and them. Proper horses too, not their usual ponies, Jasper had noted with joy. But then he realized he was unsure how to mount a saddle so high by himself.

He was saved by Sir Gawyn's squire Will coming to lift first him and then Edmund up. Will had then made sure of their girths and their stirrups for them, saying despite Mistress Maryon's impatience, "Better we see to it now so they can keep their seats than find out too late they can't." At Sir Gawyn's order then they had trotted out through the castle gates, and into a canter beyond the drawbridge.

They had slowed to a walk when they were away from anything Jasper was familiar with, and had ridden all the rest of that afternoon through the summer-lovely country-side. It had been exciting enough to be going along in a jingle of harness among men obviously set on covering as many miles as might be. They had kept to deep-hedged lanes, where flowers grew in the long grass of the banks and ditches. Blue, creeping mugwort here; a bold splash of scarlet pimpernel there; the scarlet and blue spires of Joseph-and-Mary sometimes; dog roses twining up the hedges toward the sun. There were glimpses of the green fields of grain through occasional gates in the hedges, and sometimes a long view across a swathe of common land where the hedges stopped. Sir Gawyn always raised them to a gallop across the openness and only slowed when they were back in a hedgerowed way.

In a while Jasper had realized that Sir Gawyn was indeed earnest about not being seen, that they were avoiding towns and villages and anywhere that people might be if they could. Once, ahead of them, Jasper had seen that their road ran right through a town, and he had thought with delight of the fairs Jenet had often talked of, where there were jugglers and music and games and sweetmeats. But they had turned

completely off the road and followed a band of woods that
led around and away from the town, to Jasper's great
disappointment.

That day they had ridden far past any hour Jasper had
ever been out before, far past supper time and well into
twilight. He had been nodding to sleep over his cantle when
a great cockchafer blundered into his nose, making him start
and startle his horse, who had jumped sideways suddenly.
Jasper might have fallen if Will had not been there beside
him with a steadying hand. He had been very glad when
soon after that they turned in under the gateway of a small
country monastery, and the day was over. There had been a
sort of supper, far plainer than he was used to, and then
beds, far harder ones, with rougher blankets, than any Jasper
had ever slept in. And oddly, as he was sinking into utter
sleep, he heard Mistress Maryon speaking to a servant about
"her sons," and dimly understood she meant him and
Edmund, which was not right at all.

At barely dawn Sir Gawyn had had them up and riding
again. There had been hills that day, and less choice of ways
to avoid what villages there were. Sir Gawyn refused them
any but the most necessary stops. They had even eaten—
mere cheese and bread—while they rode. And last night
they had slept not under any roof but on a dry bank below
a hedge in a field off the road, with only their cloaks for
bedding and he and Edmund crowded between Mistress
Maryon and plump Jenet for warmth because Sir Gawyn
would make no fire. There had been more cheese and bread
for supper and to wash it down only water from a stream,
and in the dew-damp dawn, more bread and cheese for
breakfast.

At midday Sir Gawyn had sent Will into a town they were
bypassing and he had brought back a pair of meat pies. They
had eaten sparingly of them then and he and Edmund were

promised some for supper, though it seemed everyone else would have to make do with what was left of the now hard cheese and bread.

But there was no promise of any bed better than last night's grass. And Jasper had begun to ache with all the riding. It was not fun anymore, and if this was an adventure, it had become a very dull one.

They were out of the hills; this was open countryside, all pastures and fields. Jasper knew Wales had mountains, but there were no mountains in sight even in the far distance when they would crest a rise in the road and have a long view ahead. He had not imagined it was this far to Wales and asked Mistress Maryon riding beside him, "Is it much farther? Are we almost there?"

"Not even half the way, I think," she said briskly. "You must set your mind to that, my lord. We have a ways and a ways to go yet."

"I want to do something else," Edmund announced from Jasper's other side. "I'm tired of riding."

"That's neither here nor there, my lord," Mistress Maryon said. "Your lady mother told us to journey and so we must."

"Why?" Edmund demanded, voicing the question he and Jasper had whispered between them in the brief moments before sleep last night, before Mistress Maryon had shushed them.

"That's not for me to say."

"Why not?" Edmund insisted.

"Because it's not my place."

"Whose place is it, then?" Edmund demanded. He had never been ill-kept and inconvenienced in his short life, and he did not like it. He had tolerated it at first as part of the adventure, but there had been no adventure except this riding for hours and hours and hours, with nothing good to eat at the end of it, nor any decent place to sleep.

Sir Gawyn rode up on Jasper's other side. He had always been a favorite with them among their mother's knights, ready with stories or a game or to show them swordwork when they asked, and was elegant in his dress and manners. It was strange to see him now in an old leathern doublet over a heavy shirt and rough breeches, with his curling brown hair barely combed and his beard coming in after these few unkempt days. Jasper noticed with surprise it was as much gray as brown. He had never thought of Sir Gawyn as any particular age. Was he old? Certainly he was different than he had been at home, with neither stories nor anything else for them, only orders.

Now he said over Jasper's head to Mistress Maryon, "I intend we'll press on until dark again. That will have us well past Banbury. We could be across the Severn sometime tomorrow maybe."

With a doubtful glance from Edmund to Jasper, Mistress Maryon said, "It might be better if we found somewhere for the night, rather than sleeping out again. There's a nunnery not far off this way we're going. It's a small place and nothing near it but a slight village. I think there'd be no harm in—"

"If it's known we're gone, scurriers will have ridden far faster than we've been able to. Warnings may have been sent ahead of us."

She pressed, "This isn't a place anyone will remember. And the boys need—"

"We're better to go on as far as may be. It's the only hope of outstripping anyone after us. We have to keep the good start we've made as long as we can. They're brave boys." He turned to Edmund and Jasper with his smile that invited them to join him in a sport. "Aren't you, my lords? You can ride on as long as need be, for your lady mother's sake?"

Not so readily as they would have done two days ago, but

for their mother's sake and to not be cowards in Sir Gawyn's eyes, Edmund and Jasper nodded. Edmund even asserted, "All night, if need be!"

Mistress Maryon began to say something else, but Sir Gawyn's squire Will, riding ahead with Hery Simon, said over his shoulder, "Riders ahead, sir. Beyond the ford."

The road had curved down into a broad, meadowed valley, to follow a willow-banked stream between fields where the tall bright grass, starred with buttercups, was nearly ready to be cut for hay. In the gap in the trees that marked its ford, the stream showed glittering in the late afternoon sunlight. It had been an empty, drowsing valley when they saw it from the road's crest, but now Jasper could see other riders halted off the road on the other side of the stream, five or six maybe, just visible through the screen of willows and alders.

Sir Gawyn drew rein, putting up his hand to halt the two men riding behind. Will and Hery had already stopped and were looking back and forth between the unknown riders and Sir Gawyn, waiting for orders. Mistress Maryon gestured Jasper back to ride beside Jenet and moved her own horse within reach of Edmund's reins. Jasper, suddenly aware that something was amiss, obeyed; Edmund, normally fierce in his independence, did not draw his horse away from Mistress Maryon's.

Sir Gawyn said with calm determination, "We'll go back behind the rise, then cut off the road to the river. We can hide in the trees. Perhaps they haven't seen us, and will pass without knowing we're here."

But they had barely turned in their tracks when Will said, "They're coming." Jasper looked over his shoulder to see that the other riders had come onto the road and had set their horses into a gallop, splitting into two groups, some of them following the stream to cut them off if they went that way, the rest crossing it, the water sheeting up around their horses.

Sir Gawyn kicked his horse in between Jasper and Jenet, dragged Jasper from his saddle and across his own horse to set him roughly in front of Jenet, braced between her and the high front of her saddle. "Hold on to him! Edmund, can you stay on that horse?"

Edmund nodded vigorously, his hand on his dagger's hilt. Jasper, trying to disentangle his arms from Jenet's to reach his own weapon, was strangling with the rage of being shoved into her keeping. He could sit a horse as well as Edmund did!

"Maryon, can you find that nunnery from here?"

"Yes." She had Edmund's horse by its rein.

"Then follow me. I think we can outride the men across the stream, and when we do, when we've crossed the stream, you and Jenet ride for the nunnery while we hold them back. Understand?"

"Yes."

"Then ride!" Sir Gawyn said and wheeled his horse back down the hill, toward the stream at an angle that cut them away from their nearer pursuers, driving his spurs into his bay's flanks so that it sprang forward into a full-out gallop. The rest of them followed in a desperate skein, his squire Will ranged in on Edmund's other side, and Hery Simon beside Jenet, the other two men behind them. Jasper clutched at the saddle, dagger and indignation forgotten.

There was no time to choose a crossing place; Gawyn rode straight for the line of trees along the stream. Jasper, looking around, saw that the other riders were riding to cut them off but would be too late: Sir Gawyn's change of direction had caught them by surprise. And then they were among the trees. Willow withies whipped at Jasper's face. He ducked them, bending to hide against Jenet's horse's mane that he was clinging to with both hands. His stomach lurched as the horse leaped. They jarred downward into the stream and water splashed up around him. Jenet screamed, and now Hery Simon had hold of her reins near the bit, forcing her horse along through the flurry of water flung up around them silver-and-diamond-sparkling in the sunlight.

Sir Gawyn reached the farther bank but not ahead of the riders coming to cut them off. They crashed down the bank through the trees to meet him. Swords were out on both sides, their brightness arcing in the sunlight. There were men yelling with a hoarse fierceness like nothing Jasper had ever heard on the practice field. Steel clashed and slithered down steel, and behind him were the shouts of the other riders closing on them, and Hamon and Colwin turning to meet them. He saw Hery Simon slice an unknown rider out of the saddle, had a glimpse of open mouth, wide-flung arms, a gaping redness before the man vanished into the water under horses' thrashing hooves. And then Hery was dragging Jenet's horse aside, spurring his own horse furiously after the gray haunches of Mistress Maryon's mount disappearing into the willows on the far bank, leaving the fight behind them.

Jasper ducked again, but lifted his head for breath as they galloped out the far side of the trees into an open field. Somehow Edmund was ahead of them all, clinging to a horse he probably no longer controlled but with Mistress Maryon close on his flank. Hery Simon was still beside Jenet, still holding her rein, and they were clear of the fight and away.

But behind them was the drum of other hooves. Hery looked back and swore. He had lost his sword somewhere, but he reached to snatch Jasper's dagger from its sheath, yelled at Jenet, "Ride, mistress!" and swung his horse back on their trail.

Jenet cried out, "Hery, no! Not alone!" But he was gone, and no one turned back after him.

Chapter

2

THE CLOISTER WALK was warm with the late afternoon sunlight. Frevisse, coming out of the church after making sure that all was in readiness for Vespers, walked along it slowly, head down as if in prayer. But she was watching the flick of her long skirts across the lines of paving stones as she walked, not thinking of very much at all. She was glad of the warmth and the quiet in this little while before the bell would be rung for the next-to-last office and all St. Frideswide's nuns would come from their afternoon tasks to the single task of prayer in the church.

Not all of the nuns, she corrected herself; and some of the pleasure of the day gone through in quietness and her tasks well done went from her with the thought. Domina Edith, their prioress, had not risen from her bed since Easter week. Only Sister Lucy among the nuns could remember a time when Domina Edith had not been St. Frideswide's prioress, and now Domina Edith was dying. Not of anything in particular or in pain but simply under the weight of her many years, in a fading whose end was sure and yet would leave an aching gap at the priory's heart.

But beyond the low inner wall of the cloister walk, in the

sunshine of the garth quartered by its four walks meeting where St. Frideswide's small bell was hung, the flowers—in blissful ignorance of their own and all the world's mortality—were bright with summer in this year of Our Lord's grace 1436. The daisies starred white in the thick grass, the columbine and flax and maiden pinks in their small plots, and soon the foxglove and valerian and lady's mantle.

Frevisse's long mouth curved slightly with amusement at herself. When had she learned to know them so well? So far as flowers went, she could appreciate them without a need to be bothered with their names. They were Sister Juliana's especial darlings; it had to be from so often hearing her go on about them during the brief hour of talk and recreation the Rule allowed each day that she had learned this much, whether she would or not.

What do we still find to say at recreation? Frevisse wondered. What is there to say we haven't said already? Do we even listen to each other anymore? St. Frideswide's was small; there were but ten nuns, and their last novice had taken her vows five years ago, with no expectation of another to take her place, unless little Lady Adela Warenne's father decided to give her up to the Church. Which was likely. The child was pretty, with pale skin and large blue eyes under dark, level brows, but with her malformed hip, she limped badly and always would; and with older brothers and another sister to inherit and carry on the blood, Adela's marrying, that might be difficult to accomplish, was not so necessary as it would have been if she had been Lord Warenne's only child.

He had probably given her into St. Frideswide's care with that in mind, and assuredly the nunnery could use the dowry that would come with her if he decided to benefit his soul that way. Not that Lady Adela had shown any inclination toward the religious life, but she was only seven, and a quiet, biddable child. Dame Perpetua, who had the teaching of her letters and numbers and beginnings of French was pleased with her and said she would do.

As if in answer to Frevisse's thought about her, Lady Adela came limping from the shadows along the far side of the cloister walk out into the sunlight of the garth with the servant woman whose duty it was this week to ring the bell for the seven daily offices. It was said that a misshapen child might be a sign of a parent's sinfulness—and Frevisse knew something of Lord Warenne that would warrant that—or a token of the child's own inclination of wickedness. There had been no sign of wickedness in Lady Adela that anyone at St. Frideswide's had ever seen, but despite her prettiness, the child walked with her head down, her shoulders slightly gathered in, perhaps because she knew what could be said of her. Or had been said of her, ofttimes in her little life. To Frevisse's mind, she was too quiet, too willing to go unnoticed, her one desire seeming to be to follow Dame Perpetua whenever she was allowed to, or to be with whatever servant she was told to, or else to sit mildly sewing in the garden or indoors.

But Frevisse had never been so willing to be quiet in her own childhood and maybe her doubts were simply from that. Assuredly Dame Perpetua was happy with the girl's demeanor, and Frevisse was willing to leave it at that, surely. She turned away from the pleasant picture of Lady Adela lifting a columbine's flower to look inside and the servant reaching for the bell rope. The nuns would come at the bell's summons; it was time she lighted the altar candles.

At the far end of the cloister the door into the courtyard slammed open, letting in an exclamation of shouts and the untoward clattering of horses in the cobbled yard along with one of the guesthall servant women clinging to the door as she cried, "Help, oh, help! Robbers! Murderers! At our gates! Help!"

With the immediate thought that opening the door to let them in was not the wisest of actions, Frevisse went quickly along the cloister, put aside the servant woman wailing and flustering in her way, and went out into the courtyard where there were neither robbers nor murderers, only a confusion of horses and riders and more priory servants than were likely to be of use.

In her first swift look around the chaos, Frevisse sorted out that there were five sweat-lathered, wild-eyed horses, two of them riderless, on the others only two women, a plump one clutching a child in front of her, the other holding the reins of a second child on his own horse. No armed men, no weapons. The worst danger was from the riderless horses; they were shoving and shying among the confusion, refusing to be caught. The plump woman holding the child on the saddle in front of her was crying and gabbling nonsense at the men who had caught her reins. Instead of listening to her they were giving each other orders and not listening to themselves either. Only the slender woman on the gray horse seemed certain what she was doing, forcing her horse and leading the other boy's among the servants toward the great door into the church to Frevisse's right along the cloister wall. Her wimple and veil were in disarray, her dark hair escaping in a tangle around her face. She was hampered by needing to manage two sets of reins, and when she saw Frevisse and the open door behind her, she brought her gray around to that nearer refuge, calling out, "You must help us!"

Frevisse jerked her head in a single sharp, agreeing nod. Whatever was happening, the woman's desperation was real. Whatever was happening, better she and the children and the other woman be brought out of the courtyard's chaos into the cloister's safety, where coherent questions and answers could be made.

Casting an anxious look over her shoulder toward the gateway behind her, the woman edged her frightened mare out from among the servants to a sidling halt beside the door. "The children," she said. "Take them inside. Jenet, here! Bring Jasper here!"

Frevisse sidestepped as the gray's haunches swung toward her and caught the reins of the boy's horse out of the woman's hand. Holding them near the bit, she soothed the horse with hand and voice, while the woman dismounted, jerking her skirts impatiently clear of the saddle and moving to lift the boy down. "Jenet!" she ordered again.

Frevisse, seeing Jenet still entangled with reins and child, other people's confusion, and her own crying, said, "I'll bring her. Go on in." She also saw, with relief, that Roger Naylor, the priory's steward, was coming through the gateway from the outer yard, with a look on his face that said he would put an end to whatever was happening. Knowing she could leave the handling of horses and settling of servants to him, she pushed her way to Jenet and curtly ordered the men clinging to her reins and bridle, "Hold the brute still." She had been hosteler a few years ago, charged with care of the priory's guests and visitors; the men had obeyed her then and did now as she pointed at one of them with her order and said to the other, "You help him down. No, not her, the child first. Give him to me. Jenet, let him go. It's all right."

Like the men, Jenet responded to the straightforward commands, surrendering the little boy to the man who easily lifted him down and handed him to Frevisse. The child squirmed in her hold, tearless and fierce despite everything around him, and demanded, "Put me down! I can walk!"

"Not here." Frevisse matched his preemptory tone. "At

the door." She set him firmly on her hip—he was small but nonetheless a solid weight resisting her hold—and turned to take him into safety, only to find that Dame Alys had come from somewhere and was blocking the doorway with both her bulk and considerable temper. Dame Alys was hosteler now, and clearly resentful at having no part in what was happening.

She had once been cellarer of the priory, second in authority only to the prioress herself, and at her best in the work of kitchener that had come with the office. She had been skillful at seeing the cooking was done well, and in the priory's kitchen there had been only servants to terrorize and unfeeling pots and utensils to batter, but when offices were changed, as changed they had to be, according to the Rule, she had done less well as sacrist. She had no delicacy of touch for the embroidered altar cloths; candles broke when she merely picked them up; goblet and paten and candlesticks had suffered from her harsh scrubbings. In a new shift of offices last winter she had been made hosteler, a duty she performed much as she did any duty she was given, with much vigor and no tact. As hosteler, she was in charge of the two guesthalls that flanked the gateway across the courtyard and—by her own officiousness if not according to the Rule—responsible for anything and everyone in the guesthalls' vicinity, which just now she apparently considered to include the courtyard and cloister door. A large, well-fleshed woman with far more vigor than sense, she was declaring over the heads of everyone in front of her, "What's all this about then? Just someone tell me that! What's this about?"

The first woman, the boy's hand firmly in hers, thrust a servant out of her way to come at the door and Dame Alys and said into her face, "Let us by at once. We're in danger!"

"Danger? The only danger here is from your mad horses!

There's no one coming in here until I know what's toward."

"We were attacked by men who may be just behind us. We want sanctuary! In God's name, you have to give it!"

"Just like that then?" Dame Alys scoffed. "This isn't a wayside tavern you can come tumbling into without a by-your-leave, no, it isn't."

Frevisse pushed between the desperate woman and Dame Alys and said, "She's asked for sanctuary. That puts them under my care, I'm sacrist." She was not sure how accurate that claim was, but she doubted Dame Alys knew any better; no one had ever claimed sanctuary at St. Frideswide's before. "Let them in."

"With who knows what at their heels? Without even knowing what they are?"

Behind Frevisse, Roger Naylor said, "I've had the outer gate shut and ordered men to guard it. No one else is coming in without we will it. What is all this?"

His question was to the woman but before she could answer, Dame Alys declared, "It's trouble, that's what it is. Bursting in here without so much as a crave-your-pardon or—"

"I think we had best have them inside, Master Naylor," Frevisse said firmly across Dame Alys's rising voice. "They've asked for sanctuary and I've given it. Anything they need to tell us is better heard with fewer ears about."

Master Naylor nodded brisk agreement. "Dame Alys understands that well enough, I'm sure," he said, his expectation that she would agree implicit in his voice. He was the priory's steward and no one had authority over him outside the cloister except Domina Edith herself. Besides that, he was a man, with a man's natural command. Dame Alys glared but with a stiff, grudging nod, she stood aside.

The slender, intense woman went first, leading the boy by his hand, saying over her shoulder, "Hurry, Jenet."

The other woman, still sniffling, obeyed, reaching to take the boy from Frevisse's arms with, "It's all right, M-Master Jasper. It's all right now. No need to be afraid anymore."

The boy cast her an indignant look and squirmed away from her hands. "I'm not afraid! I would have fought if you'd let me! I wouldn't have run! I would have stabbed them with my dagger!"

Frevisse set him down, said, "In! At once!" Janet snatched his hand and dragged him into hoped-for safety; and indeed it would be a godless pursuer who would follow them in there intending harm.

But Frevisse turned on the threshold to say, "Master Naylor, you'll tell us what is toward? If anyone—comes?"

"I've set men at the gates and sent warning to the village. I'll see to it none comes in but who belongs in here, and bring word when there's any to tell."

Frevisse nodded, satisfied he would do whatever needed to be done, and followed the others into the cloister as someone finally began to ring the bell for Vespers now that the trouble in the courtyard had quieted. The world's troubles, even when they came into the cloister itself, should not distract from the priory's purpose of prayer. Dame Alys slammed the door shut with thunderous force behind Frevisse and stalked away along the cloister walk toward the church. Frevisse called after her, despite the rule of silence that was supposed to prevail inside the cloister, "Will you light the altar candles, please you, Dame Alys?"

Dame Alys gave a curt nod without looking back. Frevisse turned toward the women and children who had, for at least the time being, somehow become her responsibility. She realized, finally having a clear look, that she knew the dark-haired woman who was in charge of them. Five years ago she had come to St. Frideswide's in service to—and a spy on—a lady who had then been murdered here.

Maryon. That was her name.

The woman met her look at that moment, saw the recognition in it, and slightly shook her head, a warning in her eyes. She did not want to be known. Before Frevisse could decide whether to heed the warning or not, the older of the two boys grabbed at Maryon's arm as if he had been trying less overtly to capture her attention for a long time and said in loud accusation, "You made me leave Sir Gawyn! You wouldn't let me help him!"

"You're not old enough to fight yet, Master Edmund, nor nearly big enough," Jenet interposed earnestly. "That's why the men were there. To protect you. So we could escape to here, away from the bad men. Mistress Maryon did what she was supposed to."

Edmund and Jasper gave her mutual, scornful glances. But Maryon said, "It was our duty. We had no choice. It's what we had to do. You understand?" Her tone indicated they had better, and like her look at Frevisse, it contained a hidden warning, too, one that both boys caught. They closed their mouths abruptly over something else they had been going to say, except the next moment Jasper burst out, aggrieved past silence, "Hery took my dagger!"

"Then he'll bring it back to you, surely," Maryon said. Before they could say more, she laid a hand on a shoulder of each of them in a firm grip and said to Frevisse, "My sons, Edmund and Jasper."

Edmund barely hesitated before bowing his head to her; the smaller boy, Jasper, sent a quick startled look at Maryon, then caught himself and echoed his brother's bow. Both straightened, their gazes on Frevisse as if expecting something from her, and she gave them a slight dip of her own veiled head. That seemed to surprise them, too.

They were so nearly alike except in height, with their dark red hair and gray eyes, that their identical stare could easily be disconcerting; but Frevisse was not easily disconcerted. She said briskly, "I'm Dame Frevisse, sacrist of St. Frideswide's. You're welcome to whatever shelter and comfort we can give," she added to the two women.

Jenet was mopping her face dry with the hem of her dress, still not recovered but better contained. Maryon, composed and steady-eyed, said, "We thank you."

While they had talked, the nuns had been gathering from whatever afternoon tasks they had been about, moving along the other sides of the cloister walk toward the church. There had been glances but no one had stopped, and now a few of the more devout layservants were hasting belatedly in their wake. "Maud," Frevisse called, and one of the women paused, questioning, then came eagerly, glad of a chance to see the strangers more closely, here where strangers so rarely came.

"Take our guests where they may wash and rest, and find them something to eat and drink perhaps," Frevisse ordered. "The warming room for now, I think. After Vespers we will consult Dame Claire about what might be best."

"I could take them to Domina Edith's parlor," Maud offered.

"No. No need to disturb her with this yet." Dame Claire was cellarer now and could make what decisions presently needed to be made and spare Domina Edith as much as might be. Especially until Frevisse had had time to learn more about whatever deception Maryon was involved in this time.

Chapter
🔳 3 🔳

St. Frideswide's had never grown much beyond its small
founding by a pious, wealthy widow on the last century, but
without greatly prospering, neither had it dwindled. Within
its outer wall were the ample barns, sheds, workshops, and
storehouses given over to the priory's worldly necessities,
and shut away from them by an inner wall and the cobbled
courtyard were the church and cloister that were the priory's
heart, where the nuns were supposed—according to the
holy Rule of St. Benedict—to live out their lives. Around
the four sides of the covered cloister walk were ranged the
church, their dormitory and refectory, small chapter and
warming room, kitchen, and all other rooms necessary to
their work and life. Beyond them was a walled garden
where the nuns could walk for recreation and, beyond that,
an orchard enclosed by an earthen bank and ditch where,
sometimes, they were also allowed to go.

The widow's endowment had been sufficient for all this,
but had allowed for no luxuries. Even the church itself had
kept within the modest bounds of the priory's resources,
boasting only a small, plain nave with a strong-beamed
wooden roof and clear-glassed windows. Before the altar

were choir stalls for twenty nuns, though St. Frideswide's had never grown to so many and now there were only nine besides their prioress.

Frevisse went to her place on the south side of the choir with Dame Perpetua, Dame Alys, Sister Lucy, and Sister Emma, facing Dame Claire, Sister Juliana, Sister Amicia, and Sister Thomasine across the way, knelt briefly and then settled herself into the familiar seat, ready to remove herself from the world's troubles into the intricacies and pleasures of Vespers.

The deep ways of prayer had saved her two years ago when she had had to come to terms with choices she had made that had led to deaths. She knew from bitter experience that prayer did not free one from the world; but it gave, at the least, respite from the world's troubles and, at best, led into the places where strength to face the power of the world could be found. In prayer when her need was greatest, she had found acceptance in herself of whom she was. And now, as so often, she found in the day's psalm something apt to her own feelings and need.

"Domine, non superbit cor meum, neque extolluntur oculi mei, Nec prosequor res grandes aut altiores me ipso . . ." they chanted. Lord, my heart is not proud, nor my eyes haughty. Nor do I pursue matters too great or high for me. No, I have quieted and subdued my soul . . .

Frevisse wove her voice among the other nuns' through the plainsong, all their voices familiar to her from so many other times through so many years. Consciously, she softened her own to allow Sister Thomasine's light, sweet certainty and joy to carry part of the psalm that Frevisse knew she particularly loved.

"Sicut parvulus in gremio matris suae: ita in me est anima mea." Like a child in its mother's lap; so in me is my soul.

Sister Thomasine had come to St. Frideswide's with a child's simplicity, and her wholehearted wish to be here had not diminished with time.

The psalm ended gently with the reassertion that their hearts were not proud, and in a whisper of skirts, the women sat for the scripture reading.

Quietly, out of nowhere, the thought slipped across Frevisse's mind: Maryon is not the mother of those children.

Distracted, she found herself following that idea away from the service. There had been no mention or hint of husband or children when Maryon was here five years ago, and the older boy was surely six or seven years old and the other very close to him in age. Of course Maryon might have married a widower and the children were his. But they had been surprised—the younger one obviously—when she claimed them. And Maryon's look at him had been a warning, one that he had readily heeded. Warning of what?

And if that claim of Maryon's was false, what about her story of being attacked on the road by outlaws? Something had happened, surely. The boys' indignation at being snatched from the fight had been real. But what exactly? Outlaws were a scattered menace and none had been reported near here in a long while. And when any such made brave to attack travelers, they usually chose a party rich enough to make it worth their while, which almost invariably meant upon a high road. Wealthy travelers rarely came the byways near here. And Maryon, though well-bred, was not noble or of a merchant family. At best she was gentry, and Welsh gentry at that. There was no indication of wealth enough to draw outlaws down on her. She and the boys were all plainly dressed, and Jenet was no more than a common servant. The horses were of good breeding, but there was nothing particular about them or their harness to indicate rich travelers. Nor could there have been many men in the party, or there would have been some to spare to ride away with the women. Or had their attackers been so many?

Master Naylor would know by now, or shortly. He would have sent out men to learn what had become of the rest of the party and whether there was still danger that might come their way. Could she find a way to talk to him before Compline?

Frevisse came to herself with a guilty start. None of that should be her concern. She was no longer hosteler; the women and the boys as guests of the priory were Dame Alys's concern.

Except Maryon had asked for sanctuary.

Not shelter or safety but sanctuary, which the church was required to give to those who asked for it. But why had she asked? Sanctuary was specifically for those in flight from the law.

Vespers ended on its sigh for those who were gone forever beyond worldly care. ". . . *requiescat in pace* . . ." Rest in peace. Amen.

The words sank to silence, and for a moment no one moved in the choir, all of them quiet in the moment of the peace that came with the words.

Then Dame Alys rose with her accustomed vigor, and Sister Emma and Sister Amicia unthinkingly rose with her. But Dame Claire was cellarer now, and held precedence in Domina Edith's absence; it was her place to signal when they all would rise. The more discreet—Frevisse and Dame Perpetua, Sister Lucy and Sister Thomasine—remained seated, their heads bowed, waiting Dame Claire's lead. Sister Juliana, less discreet, looked at Dame Alys with open indignation. Dame Claire, without apparent offense, merely raised her eyes to Dame Alys.

And Dame Alys, belatedly realizing her error, glared at Sister Emma and Sister Amicia as if they had caused it, and sat back down forcefully, enough the choir stall's wood groaned. Dame Claire waited a moment, then rose to lead them from the church.

The hour between Vespers and the day's last prayers at Compline was for recreation, when ordinary, even idle, talk was allowed. The anticipated ease was already in their movements as they came out the door into the cloister walk, and most of the women turned toward the slype, the narrow way that led out into the garden. But Frevisse, coming among the last, saw Ela, a servant from the guesthalls, slip among them to catch Sister Thomasine by the sleeve and draw her aside. The others went on but Frevisse slowed, and Dame Claire, waiting beside the slype to see everyone out, came back to see what the trouble was, since Sister Thomasine was infirmarian and if Ela wanted her, then someone was ill or hurt. Dame Claire had been infirmarian before Sister Thomasine and still cared more for those duties than any other ever given her in St. Frideswide's.

"It's those who were with the women," Ela was saying. "They've been brought in. Master Naylor's men found them and one of them's hurt, bad hurt by the look of him."

Sister Thomasine looked to Dame Claire. "I'll need your help if it's very bad," she said.

Dame Claire nodded. "Go see him. I'll fetch what we'll need and come after you. Dame Frevisse, will you go with her?"

"Assuredly," Frevisse said. Sister Thomasine had shown herself skilled and sympathetic as infirmarian on occasions of illness but no more than nervously competent when there were open wounds, as happened sometimes among the priory's villeins at their work or some village roughness. That after her first wince at some hurt, she then did the best that she was able, no matter how ill she looked while she did it, had given Frevisse respect for her. Now she smiled at

Frevisse with shy gratefulness as they turned to follow Ela out of the cloister.

Across the yard there was a cluster of men and servants at the foot of the steps to the new guesthall, in such excited talk among themselves they did not see the women coming until Frevisse was near enough to hear, ". . . like bloody hog-butchering it was, all across Lough Meadow. I'd not known a sword could let that much blood out of a man. You'd think—"

The man broke off with elbows digging into his ribs from both sides, and belatedly a way was made for the nuns. Frevisse glanced at Sister Thomasine, who was never comfortable outside the cloister and least comfortable among men, but though she was pale, she was unhesitating. Someone was hurt and she was needed and that mattered more than her feelings.

The hurt man had been laid on one of the beds in a side chamber off the main hall of the guesthouse. There were too many people in the room, and Ela, having done her duty, stepped aside, leaving it to Frevisse to order everyone out who was not needed there, only asking one of the men who by the blood of his hands had helped carry the victim in, "Where's Master Naylor?"

"Seeing to having the bodies brought in before dark."

"How many?"

"No idea. I saw three and there might be more than that. It was a nasty piece of business all around. He might know." He jerked his head at a man standing tautly at the foot of the bed, all his attention focused on the hurt man. "He's one of them."

Sister Thomasine was by the bed now, hands clasped to her breast, her head bent in prayer before she began. More practically, Frevisse ordered one of the servants hovering beyond the doorway, "Bring hot water, a basin, clean cloths, quickly," and moved to the hurt man's side.

He was an older man, somewhere in his middle age, roughly dressed for riding, his clothing ruined by a great stain of blood soaking his left shoulder and down his sleeve. He lay very still, eyes closed, the rigid set of his mouth betraying he was conscious and in pain. Someone had pulled his doublet open at the collar and wadded torn cloth inside his shirt to slow the bleeding. Along the bare side of his throat his pulse jerked as if his heart labored unsteadily. Carefully, knowing there was no way this was not going to hurt, Frevisse said, "We have to take off your clothing to tend your wound."

The man opened his eyes. They were dulled with his pain but he said coherently enough, "Someone said they reached here safely. The boys, the women."

"They're safe," Frevisse assured him. "They're here and safe."

He closed his eyes again. "Then do to me what you need to do."

A while later, Frevisse stood again beside his bed, looking down at him. His face was gray and sunken, drawn older than his years now, and he was no longer conscious, which was a mercy, considering what Dame Claire had had to do to his shoulder.

"But he'll mend well enough," she had said before she left, "if it doesn't infect. And if he will take nourishment enough when he recovers consciousness."

She had looked nearly as exhausted as he did. Beside her, Sister Thomasine had been blanched with the strain of suffering with him, but she had never faltered in wiping away blood or holding torn flesh while Dame Claire sewed it closed or anything else that had been asked of her through all of it, and at the end had gathered up the bloody clothes and instruments into a basin and said she would see to their being cleaned and put away so Dame Claire might go and have a belated supper.

"Mind you come eat, too, before you go to pray for him," Dame Claire had said firmly, and Sister Thomasine had bent her head in shy, quick agreement because the church was always her resort in any need, and with a man's life now the need, she was more likely than ever in the passion of her prayer to forget that the Rule bade there should be sufficient hours of sleep in each day as well as hours of work and prayer.

She and Dame Claire were gone now, and so were all the servants but Ela scrubbing the blood off the floor, and the man who had been at the foot of the bed when Frevisse first came. He had shared with her the task of holding Sir Gawyn as still as might be when Dame Claire began to work over his wound, until unconsciousness had ended the necessity. He was a lean man, solidly rather than heavily built, and almost as gray as his lord with exhaustion under his natural ruddiness. He had called the knight by name in that harrowed while and to judge by his care and distress was likely his squire.

"I don't know your name," Frevisse said to him.

He looked up from his lord's face with a vague surprise, as if he considered himself irrelevant, but recovered almost on the instant and bowed his head to her and said respectfully enough, "Will Tendril, my lady."

"You're unhurt? You weren't hurt in the fight?"

"No, my lady. Only bruised a bit, and a scratch." He showed the long tear in his sleeve, from elbow to shoulder, and the dried blood on the strong arm under it. He grimaced. "That will take some mending." He seemed to mean the shirt more than the arm.

"Someone here will do it for you gladly. You were lucky."

"And so was Colwin. But Hery, he's dead, and Hamon, too, and that's a pity. Your man said he'd see to their bodies?"

Frevisse reassured him, "If he said so, then he will. Where's Colwin?"

"Seeing to the horses, I suppose. He helped me bring Sir Gawyn off, but he had little stomach for seeing blood. He'd have been no use here."

"How did you come to be attacked? How many were there?"

"Five, I think." Will was doubtful. "There were trees and I didn't take time for a clear count. They'd split up and come on us from front and back."

"Were they outlaws? Thieves?"

Will shrugged. "What else would they be? We weren't doing anything but riding on our way when they saw us and though we'd have avoided them, they came at us. So we fought." He turned to look at Sir Gawyn again. "His shoulder won't be what it was, will it?"

"Dame Claire did what could be done."

"Oh, aye, there's no doubting that. I've seen many a man have worse care after a battle. But it's bad, isn't it?"

"Bad enough."

"But he'll live?"

"He looks to be strong, so likely he will. But it's unlikely he'll ever have full strength in his left arm again, and maybe not full movement."

Will dropped his head with troubled sadness and his forelock of bright hair fell forward. He pushed it back with a slow hand. "That's not good for him."

"No. But we can pray for better and maybe it will come," Frevisse said. "Now you look as if you need to eat and be off your feet. Ela, have you finished there? See to food being brought, and a mattress. You'll stay here?" she asked Will.

"Better me to watch him than anyone else," he answered, as she had thought he would.

Dame Alys had apparently not come to the guesthall to see if all was in order for their guests. Frevisse gave what orders she thought necessary for the night to various of the servants besides Ela and then went in search of Master Naylor, though by now it was well beyond the time she should have been inside the cloister.

Beyond the gateway, the long, soft light of the summer's evening filled the outer yard. The warm and quiet day was drawing to a warm and quiet close, as if there had been no panic and fear at the cloister door, or a badly hurt man in the guesthall, or dead men to be buried. None of that seemed any part of St. Frideswide's, but only an aberration of the moment now past and ready to be forgotten.

But it was not past. There was still much to be dealt with, and Frevisse was glad to see Master Naylor detach himself from a group of men talking beside the gate out to the road and start toward her across the outer yard. The gate, Frevisse noted, was closed and barred, a thing usually done only at the edge of full dark. And there was at least one man on the roof of the gatehouse over it, where there would be a long view of the countryside in most directions.

"Dame Frevisse," the steward said with an inclination of his head as they met near the middle of the yard. Through experiences neither of them had wanted to have, they had learned respect for each other, and he asked more directly than he might have any of the other nuns, "How does the knight? The wound looked bad."

"Dame Claire thinks he'll live if it doesn't infect. His squire could tell me almost nothing about what happened." Or had not chosen to. "What have you learned?"

"Only that they were traveling and were attacked by outlaws. The men fought while the women fled with the boys for safety. Two of the men were killed and five of their attackers."

"The man I talked to, Sir Gawyn's squire, thought only five attacked them."

"That's what the other man said, too, when I questioned him. If so, then this band of outlaws at least is finished."

"But you've seen fit to close the gates and set a guard."

"And have sent warning to the village to be on watch and a man to the sheriff and Master Montfort." The sheriff both for protection and to look into this breach of the King's peace; Master Montfort because he was crowner, with the duty to look into any violent or uncertain deaths and determine where the wrong lay and what was owed the King in fines and forfeitures.

"Have there been any reports of outlaws hereabouts?" Frevisse asked.

"None for years."

"Did Colwin have any idea why they were attacked?"

"None. He says they just attacked without any reason he knows of."

"And do you believe him?"

"No."

Frevisse waited but he went no further until she prodded, "Why not?"

Slowly, as if wishing to keep his thoughts to himself until he had had longer to think them over, Master Naylor said, "Any outlaws looking for prey worth their while around here would have to be on the foolish side of their work, and these men were too well dressed and well weaponed to have been fools."

Master Naylor was no more easy in his mind about the outlaws than she was about Maryon's claim to be the children's mother. And there was another thing. "Sir Gawyn was wearing a breastplate under his doublet. I think his squire is, too, from the way he moves."

Master Naylor frowned over that, following her thought. "The roads aren't so unsafe that men usually go armored. Or if they do, they wear it openly, to warn attackers that they're on guard and ready."

"So they were expecting they might be attacked, and at the same time wanted to seem like no more than plain travelers."

"And now neither of us thinks they are," Master Naylor said.

"No," Frevisse agreed. "We don't."

Chapter

⚜ 4 ⚜

IT WAS TOO late now to look to the kitchen for food, but fasting was familiar to her, and comfortable; the discipline freed the mind from the body's demands. And just now her mind needed freedom to think through what had happened— was happening—and how much trouble it might mean for St. Frideswide's if her suspicions were anywhere near the mark.

Her soft-soled shoes made almost no sound on the stone paving as she made her way around the cloister walk toward the door and stairs up to the dormitory. In the relative privacy of her bed there would be time for thinking.

But at the far corner of the cloister walk, someone rose from where she had been sitting on the low inner wall among the evening, flower-scented shadows and stood in her way. Maryon.

Frevisse stopped. They regarded each other in mutual silence. There was starlight enough to recognize one another, used as their eyes were to the darkness, but not enough for Frevisse to read Maryon's face in the moth-pale circle of her wimple and veil.

Not that Maryon's face had ever been easy to read,

Frevisse remembered. When she chose, she had the wide-eyed innocence of a considering cat, her manners smooth and bland as skimmed milk, even when in danger of being considered a murderess, as she had been when last at St. Frideswide's. Come in supposed service to the formidable and offensive Lady Ermentrude but actually a secret ward against that lady's indiscreet tongue, her anomalous position had become known when Lady Ermentrude had died precipitously of poison, and only Frevisse's refusal to be satisfied with the obvious had cleared her then.

Driven by urgent need this afternoon, she had not been calm, and that told Frevisse something about how deep the danger might be, and something about Maryon herself. Even driven and afraid, she had had her wits about her and kept control of her tears and temper.

In the hours since then, she had had time to recover her smooth calm. Her voice lilted softly with its Welsh inflections as she said gently, "I need to talk with you."

Her need matched Frevisse's desire. Without speaking, Frevisse beckoned her along the walk to the slype, the place within the cloister where conversation that could not be delayed was allowed. The narrow passage led from the cloister toward the garden and was shadowed to deep darkness. Maryon hesitated before entering, listening for betraying sounds, and glanced around to be sure there was no one else near, before she followed Frevisse in. With a caution come from Maryon's own wariness, Frevisse said barely above a whisper, "What do you want?"

"First, to thank you for not giving away you knew me."

Frevisse bent her head in acknowledgment, and waited. Maryon glanced over her shoulder again and said, "Will anyone else remember me, do you think?"

"Of the nuns, only Dame Claire and Sister Thomasine might."

"Dame Claire came to tell me of Sir Gawyn, that he'll likely live, God be thanked, and she didn't remember me then so that's all right. Will you tell Sister Thomasine to say nothing, please?"

"Sister Thomasine is so minded on otherworldly things that I doubt she'll even notice your presence unless you talk face-to-face, and if you come to that, you can tell her yourself. Some of the guesthall servants might remember you, but it's been five years since you were here, and a great many visitors have come this way since then."

"But we can stay in the cloister, can't we?" Maryon asked quickly.

"You still wish to claim sanctuary? Because that means that when the sheriff comes, he'll have to know and there'll be the question of why, and what law you broke and what king's officer you're fleeing."

"We're guilty of nothing," she said in a level voice.

"But are accused of something, and need protection until you can prove your innocence?"

Maryon hesitated before answering warily, "We're accused of nothing but we need safety until we can leave here."

"All the men who attacked you this afternoon were killed. There's nothing more to fear from them."

"No, not from them," Maryon agreed.

"From who then?"

Maryon did not answer.

Choosing her words carefully, Frevisse asked, "Do you still serve . . . the lady that you did?"

Somewhere among the stones a cricket was chirruping; there was no other sound in the quiet thick as the darkness around them except their own breathing for the betraying while until Maryon said, "Yes."

"And the boys are her children, not yours."

As if the word came between clenched teeth, Maryon answered, "Yes."

"God help us," Frevisse breathed fervently.

Maryon grasped her arm in the dark with fingers far stronger than their white slenderness suggested and said, as near to open desperation as Frevisse had ever heard her, "It's *your* help we need right now. For pity of the Virgin who suffered for her Child, hide these children here just this little while until we can go on our way. Help me to hide them."

"From whom? From what? Their mother is the queen dowager. Their half brother is the King of England." The words sounded unreal even as she said them. "Who threatens them?"

Maryon held silent.

Pushed by her own fear, Frevisse said harshly, "I need to know more before I can agree to anything."

"How much do you want to know? All of it?"

"No!" Frevisse exclaimed, with belated realization that she wanted to know only as much as necessary of the matter. What she did not know, she could not be held responsible for. But there was danger here beyond what had happened today. A danger she had helped to bring into St. Frideswide's, and she had to understand at least a little of it. "Are you in flight from . . . their mother? Is that it? If so—"

"She sent them away. We're all of her household. She entrusted them to us, to see them to safety with their father's folk in Wales."

"Why?"

A night bird in the garden and the cricket still chirruping filled the silence.

Frevisse put her hand over Maryon's still on her arm, gripping it as tightly as Maryon was holding to her, to make her understand the urgency of what she was asking. "Who wants these boys so badly and frightens her so much, their mother sent them in secret flight across the country? Not the King, surely."

King Henry was fourteen years old and still governed by his royal council, but by all reports he was a competent, clever youth, not someone his own mother would fear.

"Of course not! But he doesn't rule, does he? It's the lords around him who have power."

"And they've learned these children exist and want control of them."

Again rigidly, Maryon admitted, "Yes." But then as if that had freed something—with so much said, more might as well be—she added, "My lady kept them secret all these years because she was afraid of this. She wanted her marriage to be simply her marriage, not something talked over, considered, arranged by lords who cared nothing and knew nothing of her.

"So when she and Lord Owen fell in love, they both knew they had no right to but they were not able to help it. Truly they're lovely together, like a lord and lady of a romance, but she knew she could only marry him secretly. The lords of the Council had already cut her off from her own son. She's not allowed to live with him, nor have any say in his raising. Visit him sometimes and send him pretty presents but that's all, because she's a woman and would weaken his kingship by spoiling him." Maryon's rich contempt of the lords of the Council was plain in her voice. "They deny her the child she has and would have refused her any marriage or children more because that would all be complications for our lords of the Council. A stepfather and half brothers to the King, no, they'd not allow that."

"So she married secretly and had her children secretly," said Frevisse. And kept her secrets this long, which told a great deal about both her strength of will and courage and how beloved she must be by those who served in her household, that they had kept her secret as well.

"And lived away in the country as much as might be and made a happiness for her and Lord Owen. But now the lords of the Council know," Maryon said, "and there'll be no more peace for her, poor lady, or for Lord Owen. Or for the children."

The pity sounded real, and the affection, too, emotions Frevisse had never seen in Maryon before. They might be feigned; she did not doubt Maryon was capable of great deceit when it served her purpose or the purpose of those she served. But the danger to the children this afternoon had been real, and so had Maryon and Jenet's fear. Despite herself, Frevisse heard herself asking, "What lords?"

"My lady most fears Gloucester." The King's uncle, and, until such time as King Henry had a son of his own, the King's heir since the death of the duke of Bedford last year. "But there's the bishop of Winchester, too, and the lords that follow him against Gloucester. He'll not be behindhand in a matter like this."

Frevisse had occasion to know something of the bishop of Winchester firsthand and did not argue that but said instead, "Your lady lied to my uncle five years ago when he came to her with suspicion of what she'd done."

Maryon's tone went milk-smooth again. "She told him true that she was secretly wed and would have a child by spring."

"And left out that she had two sons already," Frevisse said tartly. "Couldn't she have trusted him even that far?"

"He trusted you with that knowledge," Maryon said with a trace of that edge again. "Whom have you trusted with it?"

"No one."

Maryon was silent while she tested that reply. Then with a little nod, she said, "That was well done. And as to the rest, what isn't known can't be told. Even now. We don't know how much is known or by whom for certain. Word simply came that the boys were known of and men were coming for them. We left within the hour after that."

"And hope to reach Wales."

"Their father's people will keep them safe there."

"Until—" Frevisse cut off the question abruptly; her curiosity was taking her too far into things she had no need to know. Instead she said, "We'll give you what protection we can." She heard Maryon's held breath go out of her in a long sigh. "But the sheriff and crowner have to come because of the deaths. There'll be questions asked and you'll have to answer. Your being in the cloister will be suspicious."

"Then I'll go to stay in the guesthall. That will make it simpler." And put her in more peril if her fears were real, and there were men dead to prove they were. "But let the boys, and Janet to care for them, stay in the cloister."

"There's a child here already. Lord Warenne's daughter. The boys can join her at her lessons, as if they're meant to be here, too. If no one mentions them as being with you, then it might be all right. And they'll be in the cloister and safe."

She could feel Maryon nodding vigorously. "That might work. It might. Did you try your theory of the boys' parentage on anyone before me?"

"No. But I'm going to have to tell Domina Edith what's toward and ask her approval for it."

"Why?"

"Because she is *my* lady," Frevisse said, "and she still guides St. Friedeswide's."

"They say she's dying."

"But neither dead nor witless yet," Frevisse said.

"And you trust her."

"More than I trust myself."

Maryon's fingers moved on Frevisse's arm as if counting possibilities in the dark, before she let go and said, "All right. But no one else."

"No one else," Frevisse agreed readily; and wondered how she had come to be—because she had assuredly not meant to be—in conspiracy with Maryon, who of all the people she had met in her life was among the most smoothly deceitful.

Chapter

◪ 5 ◪

THE PRIORY'S PEACE was undisturbed in the night, and the midnight office and the dawn's prayers and then breakfast gave no chance for talk among the nuns. Frevisse, for the sake of sleep and to give her full attendance to prayers in their time, had let yesterday's turmoil go from her mind until the problem of their guests needed to be dealt with again, but all through the nuns' light breakfast of yesterday's bread and a cup of flat ale in the refectory she was increasingly aware that Dame Alys must have used yesterday's recreation time to talk at large about what had happened. Under the overt obedience to the rule of silence, there was a tremble of excitement among the nuns, with many glances exchanged, raised eyebrows, and questioning looks. Changes in daily life were few at St. Frideswide's and excitements fewer. Frevisse knew the most would be made of this one, and they did not even know yet about the wounded man in the guesthouse and all the dead. She was not looking forward to chapter meeting this morning, their daily discussion of nunnery business, when they would all be free to ask questions. But at least through breakfast the Rule's injunction to silence held, for though Domina Edith was of necessity not there, Dame Claire was in her place with her authority and her keen eyes moved from nun to nun, reminding them of their duty to eat and be silent for now.

Breakfast was followed by Mass. Then from the church they went to chapter, following which, in the usual way of things, they would scatter to their morning's duties. These warm summer mornings it was usually a tedium to gather in the room that served as chapter house, to sit about on their stools while one and another piece of business was brought out for discussion, and accusations and admittance of misbehavior among themselves were made and disciplines given. But today most of them bustled briskly along the cloister walk, with Dame Alys nearly treading on Dame Claire's heels.

Frevisse, less eager, came last, in no hurry for what was to come. Ahead of her Sister Thomasine, too, walked at her usual measured pace, head down, hands folded into her opposite sleeves. Frevisse supposed it possible she was unaware there was any particular excitement today at all. Given a chance, Sister Thomasine had the admirable ability to lose herself so deeply in contemplation and prayer that she forgot where she was or what other task she was doing even while she went on doing it. There was almost unanimous agreement throughout the priory that she was on her way to sainthood. Assuredly she was the most devout person Frevisse had ever encountered and, unless Frevisse prayed very hard against her own inclination, also one of the most annoying.

Dame Claire waited outside the door while the nuns filed past her into the room and went to stand before their stools; then waited a little longer for Father Henry, the priory's priest, to come hasting from the vestry to join them. His naturally red face was brighter than usual from his hurry as he strode firmly into the room and took his place beside the prioress's high-backed chair. With everyone now in their places, Dame Claire crossed with her measured, quiet tread to Domina Edith's chair, faced them, and said in her deep, clear voice, *"Dominus vobiscum."* The Lord be with you.

"Et cum spiritu tuo," they responded. And with your spirit.

At Dame Claire's gesture, they all sat down together in a rustle of skirts and slight scraping of stool legs on the wooden floor but otherwise in scrupulous silence. Dame Claire's present authority was imposed on her, not desired, but that did not save her from her responsibilities nor excuse any of them from obedience to her. She regarded them wordlessly. Impatient to begin, they looked back at her, amusing Frevisse by how their faces gave away so much of who they were and what they were thinking. Or not thinking, as the case might be. Dame Alys was surly, ill-tempered as always against the world but more particularly today because of the present intrusion into the cloister. Sister Emma and Sister Amicia, shallow as a pair of plates, leaned toward one another, stifling nervous giggles of anticipation in their sleeves. Sister Lucy, Sister Juliana, and Dame Perpetua were on their dignity, attempting to show they were noticing neither the would-be gigglers nor Dame Alys's swelling ire. Only Sister Thomasine was, as usual, apparently oblivious, seated on her preferred stool well to one side and to the back, her hands folded in her lap, her eyes downcast, ready for whatever was to come.

"In nomine Patris, et Filii, et Spiritus Sancti. Amen." In the name of the Father, and of the Son, and of the Holy Spirit.

They crossed themselves and bowed their heads for the prayer to the Holy Spirit for guidance and blessing on the meeting. That done, Father Henry read the portion of St.

Benedict's Rule designated for the day, first in his halting Latin and then in English, followed it with a brief platitude meant to serve as commentary, blessed them, and left with rather more haste than dignity, probably sensing what was about to come.

But Dame Claire forestalled them all again by saying, "To calm and settle ourselves, unsettled as we are by these present matters, we will do a silent paternoster now."

Dame Alys visibly swelled with indignation. A fragment of a giggle escaped Sister Amicia despite herself. Without bothering to look at her, Dame Claire said, "A score of aves on your knees before the altar before Compline." Everyone's heads bent quickly and the room was quiet for a parternoster while until a tiny, uneven stir of fabric marked each of them crossing themselves as they finished.

Subdued but undeniable, expectation still showed on most of their faces.

"I suppose," Dame Claire said, "our first business must be the matter of our sudden guests and the satisfying of your curiosity over what happened yesterday."

Nods more eager than judicious agreed with her.

She turned her gaze on Frevisse. "You know as much of this as anyone, and I believe you spoke with Master Naylor at the end yesterday. There's been no word else since then, to change matters, so would you tell us what you understand happened and what Master Naylor had to say, Dame Frevisse?"

All their attention turned toward Frevisse who, keeping her tone and expression neutral, said, "A party of travelers was attacked near here, by outlaws it seems. The two women and two children among the travelers fled here and were so frightened of being followed they were given refuge in the cloister rather than the guesthall. Of the men with them, two were unscathed and one wounded. They're presently in the guesthall. Two others of their group were killed and so were all five of their attackers." Heads bowed and breasts were crossed among murmured prayers for their souls. Frevisse paused until everyone, except Sister Thomasine who was always longer at her prayers than anyone else, had looked up before she said, "With all their attackers dead, there is apparently no more need for alarm."

"Apparently?" squeaked Sister Amicia, unwilling to give up the exciting possibility of being frightened.

"Since all the outlaws are dead," Dame Claire said quellingly, "I think we can be said to be reasonably safe from them."

"And in any case Master Naylor has had the gates shut and a guard set, as well as sent for the sheriff and crowner," Frevisse said. "And the village has been warned of what happened. If there were still any danger, it would have no chance to come close to us. Master Naylor feels all is safe." Having made the point as clearly as she could, Frevisse sat down, indicating she was finished.

Dame Claire opened her mouth to say something, but Dame Alys pushed in with, "So that's all right. But how long are these folk going to be in the cloister? If they're not in danger anymore—if they ever were—" Dame Alys took a dim view of people feeling they were in danger. With her well-muscled arms and willingness to use anything at hand as a weapon, she had never felt in danger from anyone, nor ever expected to. "—then they can move into the guesthall where they belong, and save our folk some of the trouble of bed-nursing their man with the hurt shoulder." Dame Alys also had a low opinion of those who let themselves be incapacitated by injury.

But her basic conclusion was sensible; Frevisse had been afraid someone would bring it up, and now Dame Alys had, before Frevisse had had a chance to talk to Dame Claire privately about there being good reason Maryon and the children should stay in the relative safety of the cloister. Before the matter could open into a general discussion, or Dame Claire agree with Dame Alys, Frevisse moved her hand to draw attention to herself and at Dame Claire's nod said without time to plan what she was going to say, "They were very frightened. The women and the little boys."

"Boys!" Dame Alys said distastefully.

"Very little boys," Frevisse said. "Who probably saw men killed yesterday. Men they knew and men who were trying to kill them. It's not surprising the women wanted the extra safety of the cloister then, and surely if they still desire it today, we can't deny it. For the peace of their minds and the comforting of the children, until they feel safe again."

"Boys don't belong in the cloister!" Dame Alys insisted.

"It's long since been allowed by every bishop that boys less than eight years old are allowed in a nunnery when there is need," Frevisse said back.

"For schooling. For raising until they can go into someone's household or a monastery. That's not the case here!"

"They're allowed when there is need, and in this case there is need!"

"It would seem to me," Dame Claire put in moderately, "that there is some need, given what happened to them yesterday." Dame Alys snorted. Fixing her with a look but speaking to all of them, Dame Claire continued, "Could we agree it were better to err on the side of kindness rather than caution and let them stay at least for today?"

Dame Alys's face fully expressed her opinion of kindness as a reason for any action, but there was a general nodding of heads among the others.

"I think it would be sweet to have them in the cloister, even for a little while," Sister Emma said happily. "'Suffer the little children to come to me, for such is the kingdom of heaven.' "

"It would be pleasant for little Adela to have companionship, even for today," Dame Perpetua added. "She's been so alone since she came here."

A little more talk among themselves decided it, though Dame Alys had the next to final word with, "Say what you will, Domina Edith ought to be informed of what's toward."

Dame Claire agreed and said, "Dame Frevisse, will you see to it after chapter?"

Dame Alys bristled. As hosteler, the matter of guests was her concern and she should have been the one to advise Domina Edith. With the uncharitable thought that Dame Alys enjoyed disliking people and now had reason to dislike both Dame Claire and her at once, Frevisse bowed her head in agreement.

Dame Claire moved the meeting on to its everyday business and firmly held it there, at the end gave the benediction and sent them all about their day's duties without chance to bring up the matter of their guests again, except that she bid Dame Perpetua to inform them they might stay this day at least in the cloister and to ask the boys' companionship for Lady Adela. Frevisse noted Dame Perpetua was smiling happily as they all left the room.

The cloister was still in shadows, the morning was so young, though there was a gilt edge to the roof ridges where the sun was reaching now. Because it was the shortest way to the stairs to Domina Edith's chamber, Frevisse crossed the cloister garth rather than going around. The path was narrow; her skirts brushed dew from the grass on either side, and the smell of earth and growing things was pleasant in the warming morning. Beyond the roofed, open-sided pentise where the bell hung in the center of the garth, a small figure stood up hastily on the path and curtsied to her.

"Lady Adela," Frevisse said. Because children were presently on her mind, she made an effort she would not have otherwise and asked kindly, "What were you looking at?"

"The lady's mantle, if it please you," the child said softly, her eyes down.

Frevisse glanced down at the wide-leaved plant in its neatly turned bed. Each leaf was silvered with fine hairs that held the dew in separate droplets, fine as pale pearls. "They say that if you're looking into a dewdrop on a lady mantle's leaf when the sun first touches it, you can see your future in it," Frevisse said.

Lady Adela nodded. "I know. That's why I come."

"And have you seen your future?"

Lady Adela shook her head. "Not yet. Dame Perpetua always wants me for something before the sun is high enough."

"Well, today Dame Perpetua has something to do before she comes for you so maybe you'll have time."

Lady Adela considered the possibility—she was a quiet, considering child—before answering, "Thank you, Dame," as if Frevisse had given her some favor.

"You're quite welcome," Frevisse responded as solemnly, bowed her head to the child's slight curtsy and went on her way.

Because as prioress Domina Edith needed upon occasion to receive the priory's more important guests or conduct business requiring more privacy than the chapter meetings gave, her parlor was furnished with some degree more luxury than the rest of the nunnery. Its windows that looked out over the courtyard were glazed; a Spanish woven tapestry covered the table; there were two chairs and a fireplace, and even such small private comforts as the prioress's embroidery frame. As prioress, Domina Edith also had her own bedchamber, but this she had kept bare, with only her bed against one wall, a prie-dieu with a crucifix over it on another, and a plain rush mat for the floor. Since her illness, a table had been brought in where a candle or lamp could be set at night and her medicine kept. Through the day one small, unglazed window gave what light was needed.

Tibby came to the parlor door at Frevisse's knock. She was a village girl who had come in early spring asking if there was work she could do for money at the priory. Since there had been need then of someone who could watch by Domina Edith at night and during the days when everyone else was busy, she had been taken on and had proven to be both generous and gentle in her care. It was generally understood that she wanted to earn money to maybe buy her freedom because there was a young man in the matter somewhere, which was not surprising, she being a pretty thing and good-tempered, but in the meantime she had been an answer to prayers that had scarcely been offered and become a needed part of St. Frideswide's.

Now she smiled friendfully at Frevisse and made a low curtsy. Her curtsying had become more expert in her months in the priory, just as a natural neatness had likewise asserted itself in her clothing and manners. Frevisse smiled at her and asked, "How is it with her this morning? Could I talk with her, do you think?"

The nuns had come to depend on Tibby's assessment of Domina Edith's day-to-day health and strength, and Tibby now answered readily, "She'd like that, I think. She slept well last night so is feeling better than some mornings. Only mind if she starts to tire and don't go on if she does."

"I'll take care," Frevisse said, holding back her amusement at Tibby's young earnestness.

Domina Edith's bedchamber was soft with shadows. The

prioress lay in the narrow bed that was no better than those her nuns slept on, even to its straw-filled mattress. She could have had better, presuming on her office, but she never had. Now she lay in it with the same quiet dignity with which she had sat for so many prayers through so many years in her prioress's stall in the choir, apart from her nuns only so far as her duty as prioress required.

As the Rule required, she wore her undergown even in bed. A white linen coif, tied under her chin, securely covered her hair. Her hands where they lay on the blanket beyond her sleeves were simply thin skin over bones, and her face was almost as pale as her coif and the pillow behind her, featureless in the vague light until, aware of Frevisse's coming, she opened her eyes.

Their color had long since faded with age to clouded blue, but their intelligence was not dimmed. "Dame Frevisse," she said softly, and smiled.

Frevisse curtsied to her. "Tibby says you're better today."

"Tibby said I was better than I am some mornings, and that is true enough." Domina Edith let her eyelids drift down. For a few moments she breathed as evenly as if she slept and possibly she did; there was clearly little strength left in her body. Frevisse waited, and in a few moments she opened her eyes and asked as if there had been no pause, "What brings you to me? The matter of the folk we sheltered last night?"

Frevisse glanced around to find where Tibby was. The girl had discreetly gone to sit with some sewing on the bench below the windows on the far side of the parlor; if they spoke low, she would not hear them, and since with Domina Edith it was simply and invariably best to be direct, Frevisse said, "Yes. You know how they came to be here?"

"Tibby found out for me. There will be prayers said for

the dead. That much we can do for them, God rest them. And the man who was hurt, how does he this morning?"

"Dame Claire was going to see him directly after chapter. She has hopes he'll mend if the wound doesn't fester."

"I'll pray for him." Domina Edith's eyelids drifted again, this time not quite closing before she roused herself and said clearly, "But he is not your problem, is he?"

"No. There is the matter of the children. And the women with them. One of the women with them." Carefully, Frevisse told what she had suspected and now knew of Maryon and the children, and how that made their presence in St. Frideswide's a greater problem than it had first appeared.

Through all of it, Domina Edith occasionally, slightly, raised her eyebrows but held silent and did not drowse. Frevisse finished with report of what she had been charged to tell her from the chapter meeting, and at that Domina Edith nodded a little.

"That is as right. We cannot put them out so long as they ask our aid and do us no harm. Say in chapter tomorrow the women and boys are to be welcomed for as long as they feel the need."

"But the matter of who the boys are—" Frevisse hesitated. "The attack on them surely wasn't by chance. Someone wants them, possibly not dead but is willing to kill others in order to have them, and even Maryon isn't sure who or exactly why."

"Or so she says," Domina Edith said, summing up all of Frevisse's uncertainty, because when Maryon had last been here, she had proved herself an accomplished liar, and remembering that, Frevisse could not be sure how much truth or falsehood was in anything Maryon had said last night. Or would be today if questioned further.

But one thing at least was certain, and Frevisse said it as

plainly as she was able, so that Domina Edith would fully understand. "There's danger in their being here. Possibly great danger."

Domina Edith slowly closed her eyes, smiling gently, and slowly opened them. "Not to our souls," she said, as if that made the matter simple.

And after a moment Frevisse saw that it did. Let their souls be safely kept, then what dangers to the body that the world might offer were irrelevant. All that was needful was to do their duty, and presently duty required them to give the sanctuary for which Maryon had asked.

Frevisse bowed her head. All of her prayers, her devotions and contemplations had not yet brought her to Domina Edith's depth of faith that made such matters simple. "Thank you, my lady," she said, and meant it for more than this moment's advice.

Domina Edith's eyes had closed again. Frevisse stood still, waiting to see if she were fully asleep this time or if she should slip away. Just when the prioress's even breathing had convinced her she was asleep, Domina Edith said with dreamy slowness, "You have a cousin. I would write to her if I were you."

"Alice?" Frevisse asked blankly. She had last heard from her cousin months ago when her Aunt Matilda, Alice's mother, had died, and had sent her an answering letter of condolence. Since then there had been no word between them nor none particularly expected. Their lives had long since gone widely different ways and though there was fondness between them, there was little else. "You mean Alice?"

Domina Edith did not open her eyes. "Countess of Suffolk, isn't she?"

Indeed. With her husband the earl deep into every matter around the young King Henry. And a member of the royal

Council. If there were things to be known concerning the dowager queen and her children, Alice would know them, or be able to learn them.

"You need not say what is toward here, but that you have heard rumors and are curious. There are ink and parchment in my parlor. Tibby knows where," Domina Edith murmured. "Stay here to write it, and give it secretly to Master Naylor to send, so that no one knows about it who does not need to. It would be good to know . . . what someone else has to say about . . . the queen dowager just now."

Chapter
◪ 6 ◪

JASPER SAT ON the bed's edge, swinging his legs and kicking his toes at the rush matting on the small room's floor, bored. Sitting on the floor beside him, Edmund—equally bored— was lifting splinters from the bedstead's nearest leg with his dagger point.

They had been in this place for three days now and there was nothing interesting left to do. At first it had been another part of the adventure to be told they were going to stay here, where everything was so different from home. But the place was full of rules and demands for silence and not exciting at all or even interesting anymore. At home the castle had had rooms and more rooms, all of them full of furnishings and tapestries and paintings that covered whole walls in bright colors and pictures. There had been passage-ways and spiraling stairs for games of chase, and beyond those the yards and gardens and stables, with all manner of people everywhere.

But St. Frideswide's—especially the cloister, to which they were confined—was small. Let free, which they almost never were, they could have been into every corner of it their first day here. As it was, working around Jenet and others, it had taken them not quite these three days.

They had not known people would live so comfortless on purpose. There were so few rooms, and they were all cramped in around the little cloister walk and cloister garth, with few windows to the outside, and those mostly so high they were no use for looking out. And all the walls were plain plaster, without paintings or tapestries even in the church. And where the floors weren't bare boards or stone, there were only woven rush mats.

Their own room, where they were supposed to stay for most of each day, had only a table where their ewer and basin for washing sat, one joint stool, and the narrow bed. And on the bed were a straw-stuffed mattress, coarse linen sheets, and plain blankets, nothing like the wide, curtained bed that was theirs at home, with a deep feather mattress and soft, fine-woven sheets and blankets.

Their second morning here they had been taken to meet—"Be shown to, like curiosities," Edmund had said afterwards—the prioress, who had asked them their names and bid them kneel by her bed while she blessed them, her bone-ridged hand light as a leaf on their heads, first Edmund and then Jasper. She had a room that was better than the others they had seen, with glazed windows and even a fireplace, but it was quite clear they were not to go there again.

This morning, slipping away from Jenet, they had finally managed to creep up the stairs they had been strictly told to stay away from and peered around a door's edge into the nuns' dormitory. But they crept down disappointed because there had been nothing much there, either, only a high-roofed room divided by many head-tall walls into each nun's sleeping cell. Afterwards, in the cloister garden's bright sunlight, Edmund had said they should have gone right in since there weren't any nuns there then, and explored each cell, but Jasper pointed out that a nun could have come at any time and caught them. Edmund had said he didn't care, what could they do but give the two of them back to Jenet and *she* wouldn't do anything, all sopping with tears the way she was ever since they came here.

"Well," Jasper had felt obliged to say, because despite her crying Jenet had done what she could to make them feel better about being here, "she's sorry Hery Simon is dead."

"So am I, but he died fighting to save us," Edmund had said indignantly. "She ought to be glad he died that way."

"But they liked each other. She misses him, I think."

"We miss Mother and Father, but we're not weeping all over the place."

"Yes, but they're not *dead* and we *will* see them again," Jasper had answered; and then had had the awful thought, but what if we don't? And maybe the same thought went through Edmund's mind, too, because his face had twisted up with either anger or holding back tears and he had flung himself at Jasper. Jasper had grabbed at him gladly and they had gone down in a tangle of kicks and blows that drove out the urge to cry.

Unluckily it had not been Jenet who broke up their fight but the nun named Dame Frevisse. She had dragged them apart and upright by their doublets' necks and jarred them down onto their feet. Jasper had already noticed she had uncomfortable eyes; they seemed to see into a person more deeply than other people's did. She had fixed them with those eyes then, fierce as one of their mother's hunting hawks, and pointed toward their room, not speaking because mostly the nuns weren't supposed to. She hadn't needed to; they had scurried as if for shelter from a thunderstorm.

At first all the nuns had looked alike in their black Benedictine gowns and veils, with their white wimples around their faces and throats, but he and Edmund had quickly learned to know one from the other. They had learned to stay clear of large, loud Dame Alys, who was still angry at their being here at all and always seemed to have something in her hand to shake at them whenever they happened to come in her way. And they wished they could avoid soft, cushion-plump Sister Emma, who cooed every time she saw them, which was often, for she came twice a day to see if there was anything Jenet needed for them. She patted their heads and pinched their cheeks while she was there and offered tangled bits of advice. Once, while exclaiming over what handsome boys they were, she said dotingly, "There's many a fine colt come from an addled egg." And though Jasper guessed she had probably meant it well he had been offended anyway.

The nuns who only smiled at them and nodded and went on about their business were much less trouble, and Dame Claire in the kitchen had become by far their favorite. She did not dote or pat heads but smiled as if she thought it rather pleasant to see them, and when they had slipped in there yesterday afternoon, she had given them each a fat slice of buttered bread and let them eat it at their leisure before suggesting they had better go find Jenet, who must be worried about them.

They had found Jenet along the cloister walk that time, talking with bright-faced Sister Amicia, who had gestured eagerly for them to come be cuddled, just as she always did when she saw them. Edmund and Jasper had backed off with hasty bows and retreated to their room.

They were always having to go to their room. There was nowhere else for them to be, except when Jenet took them to Dame Perpetua to do lessons, or to prayers in the church. Praying was everyone's need and duty, but the nuns seemed to be forever going to prayers. Jenet thought it would be good for them to go, too, though not so often as the nuns. They were spared the midnight and dawn and bedtime offices but went to the other three and daily Mass, and that was altogether too much.

Mistress Maryon had said before she left them to Jenet's care, "You must pray for Sir Gawyn. For his own sake, and because the sooner he mends, the sooner we can go on to Wales." God knew how hard they had prayed at first after that, thanking God that Sir Gawyn was alive and not forgetting the souls of the men killed defending them. But this was the fourth day now, and their prayers were less eager. As Edmund put it, "We're not any less grateful. It's just they've either been saved or not, and Sir Gawyn looks as if he's going to live now, and I don't suppose God wants us going on at him more than we need to."

So now there was nothing interesting left to do. Even the lessons were of no use or interest. For an hour every morning and another hour every afternoon they had to sit in one of the bare nunnery rooms with Dame Perpetua and that useless girl Lady Adela and pretend to learn things. But they had had lessons enough in manners that they did not need Dame Perpetua teaching them. And they already knew French far better than Lady Adela, even though she was a year older than Edmund and half a head taller, which Edmund did not like and Jasper resented on behalf of both of them. In fact, their mother was French, so their French was better than Dame Perpetua's; though she did not know it because though she often said words wrongly, she thought Edmund and Jasper did not understand her because *their* French was poor and they must learn to speak it as well as Lady Adela did.

But nonetheless she would tell them how clever they were and how good it was for Lady Adela to have someone her own age here. Edmund and Jasper quite understood they were clever, but to their minds Lady Adela was *too* good. She sat with her eyes down and her hands in her lap and never said anything except to answer Dame Perpetua or read aloud in a soft, smothered voice when she was told to.

It didn't help that Dame Perpetua had found out early on that they knew Latin and so had set them to memorizing prayers from the Psalter while she taught Lady Adela her sewing.

At least they weren't expected to learn to sew. But that didn't change that there was nothing interesting to do and no one to talk to except each other, and that everything was discomfortable and strange. Though neither of them had said it aloud, they both wished they were home again.

Jasper stopped kicking the rush matting and kicked Edmund instead.

"Stop it," Edmund said. "I'm putting my name in this stupid bed leg."

"Jenet won't like it."

"Nobody will like it. Except me."

Jasper knew this mood of Edmund's. It meant somebody had better find some amusing task or game for him soon or there would be trouble. But Jasper had nothing to offer. In fact, if he had still had his dagger, he would have been carving his name on the other bed leg. Or maybe the table, just to be different. And maybe just his initial; he wasn't all that good with printing yet, usually blotting his letters when he struggled with pen and ink, so he might do even worse with wood and knife. He'd never had a chance to try his dagger even once before Hery Simon had taken it, and now Hery Simon and his dagger were both gone.

"I'll tell," he said. It was an idle threat; neither of them ever told anything on the other. Edmund went on carving. Jasper kicked him again.

Edmund shifted away to be out of reach without giving

up his work, and Jasper was considering shifting down the bed to be in reach when someone else said, "I shall tell."

He and Edmund both looked to see Lady Adela in her plain gray gown watching them from the doorway.

"I shall tell," she repeated.

"You won't," said Edmund definitely. He had discovered he could sometimes change people's minds if he said things definitely enough.

"Not if you come out to play," Lady Adela returned with equal assurance.

"There's no place to play here," Edmund said and went back to his carving.

"Outside the cloister there is."

"We can't go outside."

"Into the garden."

"That's outside."

"It isn't."

"It is."

"It isn't. The nuns go there all the time."

"They don't."

"They do. There's a passage right from the cloister into it. It's called the slype," she added, to give her assertion authority.

Jasper knew the passageway she probably meant, a dark, narrow opening on the far side of the cloister walk from their room. Jenet had said it was a back way to the kitchen and they should stay out of it. Since they knew the front way to the kitchen, it had been easy enough to agree to obey Jenet in this one thing at least and so they had never gone all the way to its farther end. But Jenet was one of those people who thought it all right to lie to children to make them do what she wanted, so maybe the slype did go where Lady Adela said it did.

But Edmund was shaping to quarrel about it just for the

pleasure of quarreling, and once he started they'd never be out of here. Jasper jumped to his feet. "Show us," he said, moving toward the door. Behind him, Edmund scrambled to his feet. If they were going instead of staying to quarrel with him, he might as well go with them. Lady Adela put her finger to her lips and led the way.

There was no one in the cloister walk. With the speed and silence of accomplished fugitives, they reached the slype without being seen and dodged into its shadows, Lady Adela still leading. Its far end opened into a wide walk between the back of the cloister buildings and a high wall running to the children's left. Rightward the nunnery thrust out a room's width further, with a door into it just beyond the slype's end.

Adela peeked out with elaborate care. Edmund demanded, "Where's that door go?"

"The stairs up to the necessarium."

"*Not* the kitchen? Jenet lied," Edmund said with great satisfaction.

"From the other end there are stairs down into the kitchen and others up into the dormitory," she said impatiently.

That would be why they had not been shown the necessarium; it went too many places they weren't supposed to go—including out. Adela led them leftward, away from the necessarium, toward a gate in the wall that blocked their view of what lay beyond. It was a wicker gate, chin-high on Jasper if he went on tiptoe to see over it, and as Lady Adela had promised, there was a garden beyond it. He could see at a glance there was no one there and that it was only an ordinary garden, with neat little paths and proper little flower beds, an arched green arbor along one side, and turf benches built against the tall stone wall that closed off all view of the world beyond. It was far smaller and plainer than any of his mother's gardens, without even a fountain.

Impatiently, Edmund reached for the gate's latch. Lady Adela said, "Oh, let's not go here. They'll find us too soon. I know something better."

Without waiting for their agreement or argument, she flitted away along the garden wall, quick on her feet despite her limp, to another gateway closed by a solid wooden door that gave no hint of what might be beyond. Beside it, Lady Adela squatted down on her heels to scrabble at a large stone beside the path. It was heavy, and Jasper crouched beside her to help. Over them Edmund reached to try the gate's handle.

"It's locked," he said indignantly.

"Of course it's locked," Lady Adela answered. To their pulling, the rock rolled up on one side and, quick with triumph, she snatched out a big, rusty key from underneath it. "This is a back gate to the cloister. People aren't supposed to just go in and out of a back gate. They have to use the ordinary gate."

"Then what are we doing?" Edmund demanded.

"Going out."

Edmund and Jasper looked at one another. They both knew the answer they had to make to that. But matters of conscience tended to weigh more heavily with Jasper than Edmund, and he said for both of them, "We aren't supposed to go out of the cloister. Mistress Maryon said so."

"Nuns aren't supposed to go out. Nuns aren't supposed to do *anything*. But we're not nuns."

Edmund and Jasper looked at each other again, unable to argue that.

Lady Adela elbowed Edmund aside to come at the lock. The key was very large; she needed both hands to manage it into the keyhole.

"We shouldn't," Jasper said doubtfully.

"No," Lady Adela agreed cheerfully, wrestling with the key to turn it. It yielded with a mild screech. "We shouldn't. But I'm going to anyway."

Chapter

⊠ 7 ⊠

IT WOULD SOON be time for the small service of None. Set between midday's Sext and late afternoon's Vespers, None's interruption of whatever work she had in hand had annoyed Frevisse in her early days at St. Frideswide's, but she had long since come to value it for its reminder that the heart of her life was here and not in whatever worldly duties each day required. Since she was presently sacrist, with her duties mostly confined to the care of the church and its furnishings, it was of late easier to hold to that knowledge.

Today, having already done what was needed to ready the church, she had come to sit in her choir stall for a quiet time of thought before the bell rang. This near midsummer the sun rode so high it only shone directly into the church at earliest morning and latest evening. In the early afternoon now, the church was gray with soft shadows and coolness, a world apart from the warm, busy day outside. A goodly place for thought as well as prayer, Frevisse felt, and she was in need of both.

What she truly wanted to do was go to Domina Edith and talk through again the problem of the boys. Not that there was anything new to say; she only wanted it for her own comfort, and that was hardly fair to Domina Edith, so deep in her own necessity now.

She had written the letter to Alice as Domina Edith had told her to, and given it over to Master Naylor the same day. It was gone by messenger to find Alice wherever she might be; and of course Frevisse could now, when there was no help for it, think of better, more subtle, more politic ways she should have asked about matters that ought to be none of her concern.

She tried to keep it from her mind. A more reasonable worry—and still nothing to talk to Domina Edith about—was that the sheriff and Master Montfort, the crowner, would be here sometime this afternoon, according to their forerider who had come this morning. It all went well, they would make their inquiries and simply go away, perhaps as soon as tomorrow. If things went ill—if servants were questioned too closely and mentioned the boys and if some word had reached the sheriff about certain boys being missing and sought . . . But there was no reason the sheriff or crowner should talk to any of the servants. They would speak to witnesses of the attack. That meant to Sir Gawyn, Mistress Maryon, the two men, and possibly Jenet. Frevisse hoped they would all tell the same story and, as planned, leave the children out of it. If they did not, there could well be trouble, but Frevisse could think of nothing more to protect against it than what had already been done.

At least the children had been no great bother so far. Or at least not so great a bother as they might have been. Even if they did not stay completely out of the way, their manners were charming, they were quiet, and among the nuns at recreation it was generally agreed they were very sweet, handsome little boys. Only Dame Alys professed to find their presence intolerable, but Dame Alys would have found the presence of the archangel Gabriel intolerable if it suited her.

Frevisse had noted that the boys found ways to avoid Dame Alys when they could, which showed they had intelligence as well as charm, and if she had had to choose, she preferred intelligence to both charm and handsomeness because more could be done with it in the long run.

None of that solved the problem of them, however. It was a problem that could not be solved, only gladly parted with when Sir Gawyn was well enough to ride on with them.

With her forehead laid on her clasped hands, Frevisse prayed for his continued swift healing.

And for Domina Edith's.

No, that was not fair. Domina Edith was turned willingly toward her end, and any prayer for her should be that she come to it gently, not that she be kept longer from where she was so ready to go.

That, Frevisse had found, was very hard. But if she cared as much for Domina Edith as she claimed, then her prayers had to be for Domina Edith, not for herself. The words from the hymn that was part of None came to her.

Largire lumen vespere, Quo vita nusquam decidat, Sed praemium mortis sacrae Perennis instet gloria. Give light at evening, So that life nowhere fails But goes to the reward of holy death With glory perpetual.

She tried to draw the words deep into herself, to give herself up to them, but when she had finished, she leaned her head more heavily on her hands, mentally sighing. It was no longer so consistently difficult for her to know what was the right thing to do—not as it had been in her younger days when so many decisions had been struggles not only between conscience and desire but, more basically, to grasp what the core of the struggle actually was. She was better now at perceiving right desire against wrong desire, but the effort to do what was right rather than what was easier and more comfortable was still not always the simple matter she wished it could be.

A hand hesitantly touched her shoulder. Startled, Frevisse jerked upright. Sister Thomasine stood in front of her, hands clasped to her breast, a worried expression on her usually serene face. She beckoned Frevisse to come with an urgency so unusual in her that Frevisse immediately stood up to follow her from the church, along the cloister walk and into the slype. Frevisse could not remember a single occasion since Sister Thomasine had entered St. Frideswide's when she had made use of the slype's privilege to impart urgent information and, thoroughly alarmed now, she said as soon as they were in it, "What is it? What's the matter?"

In a low-voiced rush, Sister Thomasine said, "I can't find the children. They're nowhere in the cloister."

"Nowhere? Are you sure?"

"The boys—I thought to give them some horehound drops for a treat. I thought it would make them feel better." Sister Thomasine twisted her hands together unhappily and added hurriedly, "They are last year's horehound drops. We didn't use them up through the winter. We have a plenty of them and I'll be making more—"

"I'm sure it's all right," Frevisse interrupted. "A very kind thought. But you can't find Edmund and Jasper?"

"Or Lady Adela."

"And Jenet doesn't know where they are?"

"I don't know where Jenet is." Sister Thomasine had stopped wringing her hands and was now crushing them against her breast again. "I mean, I think I know, but I doubt the little boys are with her, and she wouldn't take Lady Adela. I think she went to pray over the dead men again. She told me—I didn't speak to her, I never have, but I happened on her once, coming back into the cloister crying and she told me then—that she loved a man and he was dead. She said there's no one else to pray over him and I think she goes to do it sometimes."

"She isn't supposed to leave the children for more than a minute!" Frevisse said angrily. "Assuredly not long enough to go all the way to the village!" The seven dead men had been put in the village church to await the crowner's and sheriff's coming. In the warm weather, with no certainty how long it would take for the crown's officers to come, that had seemed better than having them in the priory's church. But the village was a quarter mile away. By the field path it took only a short while to go and come back, if one's business there was brief, not much longer if one took the road. "How long has she been gone?"

"I don't know. I've been in the infirmary since dinner."

"What of the children? When were they last seen?"

"I don't know. I haven't asked anyone. When I couldn't find them, I came to you."

"Jenet wouldn't have taken them with her. She knows they have to stay inside the cloister." Frevisse was thinking aloud, and asked the next thought that came to her. "Why did you come to me before anyone else?"

Sister Thomasine bit her lip, dropped her eyes, and said at the floor, "I've seen how you watch them, and how worried you've looked ever since they came. More worried than anyone else. More worried than seemed needed." She huddled her shoulders up a little, in echo of a gesture she had almost lost since taking her vows. "So . . . I thought that maybe you knew more than the others about something wrong in their coming and when I couldn't find them . . ."

Her words trailed off nervously. She looked worriedly up at Frevisse, who stared back at her with an unsettled mingling of surprise and dismay. She had been wrong to think that Sister Thomasine did not notice much of anything beyond her prayers and duties. To find that she noticed

Frevisse specifically enough to know she was worried over the boys when no one else was, was disconcerting in the extreme.

But that was not to the point just now. "Lady Adela is gone, too, you said?"

Sister Thomasine looked even more wretched. "Yes. I couldn't find her either. And . . . and the gate to the orchard is unlocked."

Frevisse found she was staring at the younger nun. "What brought you to try it and find out?"

"When I couldn't find any of them anywhere inside the cloister, I went to see if they were in the garden. Lady Adela has been there with us at recreation. I thought she might have taken the boys. The orchard gate is just beyond and so I tried it, just because that's what a child would do, you know, and it was unlocked. It isn't supposed to be unlocked!"

"No, it isn't. Come with me." Without knowing she had made up her mind, she hurried out of the slype and toward the orchard gate.

Sister Thomasine followed her but asked, "Shouldn't we tell someone if we're going out?"

Strictly, she was right. Someone should be told and permission granted before any nun left the cloister except on such business as the hosteler had and then only within set limits. But seeking permission would take time and Frevisse was afraid there was no time to spare. "The fewer people outside the nunnery who know the boys are here, the better. If we can find them before someone else does, that will be best."

Just as Sister Thomasine had said, the cloister gate was unlocked. Frevisse went out it unhesitatingly but Sister Thomasine hung back. "I can't go out," she said faintly.

Frevisse paused, understanding her scruples but without time for them. "Then I have to go alone."

She should not. If a nun absolutely had to go out of cloister for a real and weighty reason, not for whim or fancy, even then under no circumstances was she supposed to go alone but always accompanied by at least another nun. For Frevisse to go out alone would only compound her fault of going out at all, but that would be less wicked than trying to coax Sister Thomasine into coming along against her fine-edged conscience.

But to her surprise, Sister Thomasine lifted her head and said, "You have authority over me as sacrist of St. Frideswide's. Say I must come with you and I shall."

It was as neat a shifting of responsibility as Frevisse had ever encountered, though it was undoubtedly done in total innocence.

"Come then," Frevisse said, and Sister Thomasine came without hesitation. Stifling an irk she knew she should not feel, Frevisse shut the gate and directed briskly, "You take this half of the orchard and I'll take that. Call to them and look for them and we'll meet on the far side if we don't find them."

It was a fair-sized orchard, meant to meet the nunnery's needs. Planted when the nunnery was new, the trees were gnarled with age, their lower branches near the ground, spread wide and temptingly easy for a child to climb, with good hiding in the summer's thickness of leaves.

The long grass whispered at Frevisse's hem and gave softly under her foot, silencing her steps. She called, "Come out now!" and summoned the children by name, and listened for an answer, but there was not even a rustle in the leaves to betray where someone might be hiding. Out of sight among the trees, Sister Thomasine was cajoling the children to show themselves with no better luck. As she neared the orchard's far side, Frevisse said grimly to herself, "They'd best not be playing hide-and-seek with us."

She and Sister Thomasine met along the earthen bank that curved around the orchard's outer edge, drawn together by their own voices.

"Perhaps they never came this way," Sister Thomasine suggested.

"Someone unlocked the gate from the inside," Frevisse answered. She was eyeing the earthen bank. It was perhaps six feet high, grown over with long grass and steep enough that anyone would have to scramble to go up it. But the climb was far from impossible; the bank was meant more to set the orchard apart than serve as an impassable barrier. "They surely came this way, and can't have gone far. We might see them from up there." Frevisse gathered up her skirts in one hand, preparing to climb.

"Up there?" Sister Thomasine regarded the height doubtfully. "The bell for None will go at any moment."

But Frevisse could not stop the search now, having broken the rules to begin it. Going back would only give the children time to wander farther. "I'll take responsibility if we're late," she said and bent forward to climb the steep slope. After more hesitation, Sister Thomasine followed her.

At the top Frevisse sat down with a grateful exhale to catch her breath and look at what lay beyond. Perhaps fifty yards away a wide stream curved between the nunnery and the open fields of the village. It was heavily bordered with trees that were mostly willows and alders to hold the banks together and provide withies for making baskets and hurdles and even walls of houses, but with larger trees among them whose deadfalls could be gleaned for firewood in season. The earthen bank was too low to give a view beyond the trees, and between the bank and stream was only a narrow field, this year in pasture with a few milch cows grazing at their leisure. Angling across it was the broad ditch dug to divert water from the stream to the nunnery, first under the kitchen and then the necessarium before curving back to rejoin the stream below the pasture. Made when the priory was new, it was nearly hidden behind its own screen of brush and younger trees.

Sister Thomasine struggled up beside her, less out of breath but far more shaken, if her white face and wide eyes were anything to judge by. Since she had come to St. Frideswide's as a novice seven years ago, she had been no farther out of the cloister than the inner yard and the orchard, and those only rarely. Now, plumping down beside Frevisse, she straightened her wimple and veil and smoothed the front of her dress with habitual preciseness. Then she stared out at the wide world beyond the bank with gentle wonder, squinting against the sunlight glancing into her eyes.

"Oh how lovely," she breathed, and Frevisse felt a pang of mingled satisfaction and alarm. It was good to see Sister Thomasine startled out of her still-faced holiness; it was also disquieting. There was nothing unusual to see from here, certainly nothing that would imperil anyone's soul to gaze on it, but it had been in girlhood that Sister Thomasine had blithely given up the world. What effect would this glimpse of unrealized beauty have on her now?

Very little, it appeared, for after a moment Sister Thomasine dropped her hands into her lap and, smiling, said contentedly, "It's good to see, once in a while, how beautiful it is, so I can understand the ones who choose to stay in it and pray the better for them. I don't see the children."

There was indeed no one in sight but the milch cows, but Frevisse said, "Listen."

From somewhere among the trees along the ditch children's bright voices laughed and called. Sister Thomasine crossed herself with a great sigh of relief. Frevisse gathered herself to her feet. "I'll go for them. You stay here, and if you hear the bell, go back without us. I'll be as quick behind you as we can." There was no point in both of them being in more trouble than was necessary. Sister Thomasine nodded gratefully, and Frevisse set herself to slide down the outer side of the bank.

They had meant to go no farther than the orchard, but when trees had been climbed and tag had been played and Lady Adela refused to be tied to a tree to be a maiden in need of rescuing—with Jasper chosen to be the dragon so Edmund could slay him—there was nothing left to do except climb the sunlit slope of the earthen bank. Once they had done that and seen a whole new world to explore, going down the bank's far side was inevitable.

Jasper had momentarily hung back. "We shouldn't," he said. But Edmund was already going, arms spread out for balance while his feet ran away with him; and when Lady Adela lay down athwart the hill and rolled, laughing, her hair tangling around her head, it was too much to resist. Jasper flung himself down and rolled after her, finding too late there was no way to control how fast he went so that he bowled to the bottom to land sprawled and laughing almost on top of her, any idea that they shouldn't go at all quite gone.

Edmund, indignant at having missed that sport, was ready to climb up and take his turn at it, but Lady Adela was already clambering out of the dry ditch at the bottom to set off across the pasture. Giddy and not sure if he could walk straight, Jasper followed her. Edmund trotted after them with the idea it would be fun to chase the cows, but Lady Adela said, "No," with so firm an assurance that he dropped the idea without argument. She was limping a little more than before, Jasper noticed, as if maybe her leg were tired or hurting, but she didn't say so, just led them to the grave-bottomed stream flowing among the withies through the pasture.

There wasn't any need to talk about it. They all sat down, stripped off their shoes and hosen, and waded in, up to their knees in its cool joy.

Jasper wasn't sure exactly how it was decided it would be his shirt they used, but before long his doublet was on the bank and his shirt had been turned into a net to catch the minnows that darted among the green streamers of water plants wavering gently in the current. Lady Adela tried at first to keep her skirts out of the water, but being careful interfered with their sport and she gave it up in favor of swishing her hem through the water to herd the minnows toward Edmund and Jasper. It didn't matter that they were having no success at all; and they were all so thoroughly wet that by the time Jasper stumbled over something and sat down up to his chin in the stream all he could do was laugh.

He had never in all his life been so without people expecting him and his brother to behave with dignity and good manners—and seeing to it that they did. Here there were just themselves and Lady Adela and nobody telling them what to do and that they shouldn't do something they wanted badly to do. There was water and sunlight and splashing and minnows and laughter as loud as they wanted it to be.

Until Lady Adela's giggle broke off with a gulp, and Jasper and Edmund followed her frightened gaze upward to Dame Frevisse standing on the bank above them.

Chapter

⬛ 8 ⬛

THE BELL RANG for None as Frevisse and Sister Thomasine herded the wet, subdued children back through the orchard gate. "Go on. You go to None, I'll see to the children," Frevisse told Sister Thomasine, who nodded gratefully and hastened away; but by the time she had disposed of the children, Frevisse was late, as she had known she would be, and had to slip into her choir stall among disapproving glances. Tomorrow in chapter meeting she would have to confess to leaving the cloister and taking Sister Thomasine with her and then do whatever penance was given. For now, she joined in the office's second psalm even before she had found it in her prayer book, her head bent diligently to prayer. But only for a few lines. Then her mind slid away.

The children were safely back in their rooms, with one of the priory servants to see Lady Adela into dry clothing and Jenet tearfully setting Edmund and Jasper to rights. No harm had come of their disobedience, but she doubted this was the end of it. She had been above them on the bank for a time, watching their laughter and play, and it was plain that she—that everyone—had seriously misjudged Lady Adela. Assuredly she was a quiet, polite, attentive child, but that

77

was not all she was. And Edmund and Jasper were clearly not so biddable as they had seemed either.

Nor, Frevisse guessed, would the three of them go back to being as quiet as they had been, now that they had discovered the delight of each other's company. There was going to be need to supervise them more carefully, which was not going to be easy without it becoming obvious to the other nuns whose curiosity she did not want aroused.

At None's end, as the nuns left the church, Dame Claire waited beside the door with a gesture to Frevisse to stay with her. Head bowed, Frevisse stood beside her until everyone else was gone, then followed her around the cloister walk to the slype where Dame Claire said, "I suppose you had good reason to be late to the office?"

Dame Claire was as near to a friend as Frevisse had in the priory. They were alike in their reasons for choosing to become nuns, and had long since learned to respect and depend on each other's intelligence. But Dame Claire presently held the prioress's authority and to that authority instead of to her friend Frevisse respectfully said, "Yes, Dame."

"And you will explain yourself in chapter tomorrow?"

"Yes, Dame."

Dame Claire took a deep breath. "Good. I can tell Dame Alys so when she comes complaining to me about it at recreation."

Frevisse gave a small, tight smile. "As if no one had noticed I was late except her."

"And that there were grass stains on your gown and a smell of river mud on your shoes," Dame Claire said. "Why were you outside and what kept you late?"

"The children left the cloister and I had to go in search of them. They were playing in the stream at catching minnows. It was all three of them," she added.

"Lady Adela followed the boys? Why, to keep them from harm?"

"I rather gathered that she led them."

"Our Lady Adela?"

"Indeed. It seems to have been lack of opportunity rather than inclination that's kept her so quiet these months past."

"Oh dear."

"It was she who knew where the key to the orchard was hidden. That was the way they went out."

"How did she know about the key?"

"She wouldn't tell me. She was willing to admit how they went out but not how she knew where the key was. She'd only say she 'turned the rock over and there it was.' And maybe that's how it happened. They might have been playing and she found it by chance."

"Then likely she would have said so," Dame Claire said.

"I made her—made all three of them—promise not to go out again." There had not been time to scold them properly over what they had done, and aside from dragging that little about the key out of Lady Adela, Frevisse had settled for insisting at them that they had done wrong and that they must not, *must not*, go out alone again. At her angry demand, as she hurried them along the cloister walk toward their rooms, they had mumblingly given their word, but she did not for a moment believe that meant the end of problems with them.

"May I go across to the guesthall, to talk with Mistress Maryon? She may have an idea what would keep them occupied."

"We certainly have few ideas. But I wish I knew why we're keeping them at all—" Dame Claire broke off, perhaps because Frevisse's inadvertent expression gave away more than she meant it to. Dame Claire fixed her with a long and considering look before saying, "No, maybe I don't wish that. Domina Edith has agreed to it and with that I should be satisfied."

"It's best," Frevisse said. If anyone else had to be trusted with the secret of whom the boys were, she would choose Dame Claire first, but at present the fewer who knew, the safer all were.

And perhaps her face showed some of that, too, because Dame Claire nodded. "So be it then. Yes, of course you may go talk to this Mistress Maryon."

Dame Alys was at the guesthall before her. Frevisse heard her voice by the time she reached the top of the stairs from the yard, demanding why they were setting the table up so early and did they call it clean because she did not, when was the last time anyone had scrubbed it down properly, they could take it outside right now and do it, she cared not if it was still damp from its last scrubbing, they would do it again and thoroughly this time.

Coming into the hall, Frevisse stood aside as two of the serving men trudged past her on their way out, carrying the heavy tabletop between them.

"And so long as we're at it, we may as well look at all the others, too, and see how much else you've been slacking because you thought I wouldn't notice," Dame Alys declared at the servants left in the hall. "Go on. Stir yourselves."

She stood in the center of the hall, fists on her wide hips, glaring over her handful of minions as if she were a commander rallying particularly stupid troops for battle. It was Dame Alys's opinion that, generally speaking, everyone was more stupid than herself, and servants particularly so.

Nor was she pleased to see Frevisse, or interested in dissembling her displeasure. "What are you wanting here, Dame?" she demanded. "This isn't your place anymore."

Frevisse had long since learned that the best way to deal with Dame Alys was to say as little as possible and to say it very mildly. Now she bowed her head in acknowledgment of Dame Alys's blunt truth and said, "I've Dame Claire's permission to speak with Mistress Maryon."

"About having those whelps out of the cloister, I hope," Dame Alys snapped. "She's with that man." She jerked her head toward Sir Gawyn's room. "And he's as welcome to be out of here as those brats are."

Frevisse curtsied a small thanks and left her.

Sir Gawyn's room was one of the guesthall's smaller ones and plainly furnished. There was the bed, a crucifix hanging on the wall opposite its foot, a small table beside it, and a joint stool. The table was crowded with the clutter of necessities—a basin, a pottery jug, a roll of bandages, and various bowls and cups. Sir Gawyn lay as Frevisse had last seen him three days ago, his eyes closed and very still; but he was no longer sick-gray with pain, only pallid, and had been shaven and washed and his hair combed so that, even lying as he was, drawn and colorless, obviously worn with blood-loss and pain, Frevisse could see that though he was not handsome, there was an attractive strength in his face.

His squire, Will Tendril, was leaning against the wall beside the crucifix, arms crossed on his chest, his gaze on the floor in front of him. Maryon seated on the joint stool, in reach of both the table and Sir Gawyn, was telling her beads in her lap. She and Will both looked up as Frevisse paused in the doorway. Then Will straightened from the wall and Maryon rose to her feet, alarmed questioning in her face. Frevisse smiled reassurance that nothing was wrong and gestured for her to come out of the room.

"I'm awake," Sir Gawyn said. "You don't have to go." He turned his head on the pillow to see who was there, his eyes fever-bright but not burning. He frowned a little. "You were here at the first. When we came. I remember seeing you then."

"She's Dame Frevisse," Maryon offered.

Recognition sharpened his gaze. "Dame Frevisse," he repeated. "Yes, Maryon has talked about you. Will."

Will had come forward a step when Sir Gawyn first roused. Now, without needing further order, he bowed and went out of the room.

"He'll see that no one overhears us," Sir Gawyn said. "Is everything all right? The boys?"

"They're well. But they stole out of the cloister this afternoon—no, they came to no harm, only got themselves wet and happy playing in a stream and not so happy after I found them and brought them back inside."

"Where was Jenet?" Maryon demanded.

"Gone to the village church, I gather."

"To pray over Hery Simon's corpse."

"I suppose so," Frevisse agreed. If that was the name of the man she had loved.

At the man's name Sir Gawyn's mouth had tightened. Now he asked, "When will they be buried?"

"Tomorrow, if the sheriff and crowner are readily satisfied. They're to be here by this evening, had you heard?"

"Master Naylor sent word of it," Maryon said. "What's taken them so long?"

"I gather they had to finish sorting out the rights and wrongs of a quarrel broken into deadly violence at a village on the far side of the shire before they could come here."

"That's as well," Sir Gawyn said. "I've more of my wits about me now than I would have had if they'd come sooner, and more strength for it."

"You look far better than you did."

"It doesn't much feel better." His right hand went toward his left shoulder's bulk of bandages, but he did not touch it. "But I'm better than being dead like Hery and Hamon anyway." He laid his hand along his side again.

"And he's fevered no more than's to be expected," Maryon said. "Your Dame Claire is very good. If everything goes on as it is, we'll maybe be able to leave before the month is out."

Her soft Welsh voice lilted over the words, but Sir Gawyn, his eyes closed again, lay with his face rigidly still and no response. Pretending she did not see, Frevisse said, "Then we must find more for the children to do, if they're to be kept in the cloister so long a while."

"Jenet should see to them," Maryon said. "She'll have to stop so much grieving over Hery."

"She's doing as well as she's able, I think. It's mostly that we have so little to offer Edmund and Jasper here to entertain and occupy them. What I wanted to ask you was whether we might allow them to go outside the cloister, if someone was with them all the while and they stayed inside the walls? Not until the sheriff and crowner are gone, certainly, but afterwards? It would help them be quieter the rest of the time, I think."

"They might be less apt to go looking on their own if we allowed them that much," Maryon agreed thoughtfully.

"And I'll try to have someone besides Jenet to watch them, too." Perhaps Sister Amicia, who burbled like a never ending brook about how sweet and pretty and charming and witty they were.

Softly Maryon said, "He's sleeping again."

Her attention had never fully left Sir Gawyn. Now Frevisse saw that his breathing had evened, his face eased. Sleep was probably the best thing for him through these days, and in silent agreement, she and Maryon left the room.

Will stood a few feet beyond the doorway, in talk with a short, stocky man, rough-dressed as if he were a groom or man-at-arms; by the sword at his side, he was the latter. "Colwin," Maryon said to him. "Is everything well?"

"Aye, mistress," Colwin answered with a bow. "I've been out to exercise the horses is all, and Will and I are trading places now."

With Sir Gawyn ill, the men had apparently accepted that authority now centered on Maryon. From what Frevisse knew of her, she would handle it well, and woe to anyone who thought she could not. With glimmering amusement, Frevisse wondered what had passed between Maryon and Dame Alys here in the guesthall, with their very different ways and very similar wills.

A flurry and bustle of something out of the ordinary around the outer door made them look across the hall. "I think the sheriff and crowner are here," Frevisse said with sinking heart.

Maryon returned to Sir Gawyn without a word. Will and Colwin exchanged glances and moved to flank the room's door.

Frevisse wished there were some way to reach the cloister without encountering the crowner Master Montfort. The few times he had come here, he had never approved of her interference in his business. And she had never approved of either his arrogance or his ignorance. But he and a man she assumed was the sheriff were already entering the hall with perhaps half a dozen of their entourage behind them. Dame Alys was bearing down on them to make welcome, and there was no likelihood of avoiding any of them unless Frevisse chose to make an ignominious retreat to the kitchen and hope for a chance to slip out later.

She chose not to do that. Hands tucked into her sleeves and her gaze lowered, she started across the hall with the thought that if Dame Alys and Master Montfort would ignore her, she would willingly ignore them.

Probably Dame Alys gladly would have, but as Frevisse circled to pass them with no more than a respectful inclination of her head in their direction, Master Montfort said, "Dame Frevisse, is it not? You're no longer hosteler so what do you here? Interfering again? I won't have it. This is the one I warned you of, Master Worleston. Take heed, Dame Frevisse, he's been warned. He knows about you and won't have you interfering any more than I will."

Her expression carefully mild over the seethe Master Montfort always roused in her, Frevisse made curtsy to Master Worleston. He made bow back, and they both took the chance to look directly at one another. He was a well-fleshed man, with the high color of good living, dressed in a dark, calf-length houppelande cut sensibly for riding with none of the excess of sleeves that Master Montfort indulged in to show his importance. Frevisse saw that he was more amused than anything by Master Montfort's introduction of her as he said, "Dame Frevisse, my pleasure to meet you."

"God bless you in your duties," she responded.

"She was just leaving," Dame Alys declared. "She was only here on errand from Dame Claire and she's finished with it, aren't you, Dame?"

"Indeed," Frevisse agreed, bowed her head slightly to Master Worleston and Master Montfort, and left the guesthall with her temper nearly intact.

Chapter

9

THERE WAS A brief rain the next morning, pattering lightly away to nothing, and the sunlight breaking through by the time Frevisse came out of the church at mid-morning, that much of her day's duties completed and half her penance of five hundred paternosters and two hundred aves well begun. The other part of her penance—to drink neither ale nor wine but only water through the coming fortnight—was neither so easy nor so readily disposed of, but she was smiling inwardly—outwardly would have been unsuitable just now—because the great benefit of a penance was that it cleared the conscience. And she was free and clear from her responsibility for Sister Thomasine because her plea that Sister Thomasine had acted under her order in leaving the cloister had saved Sister Thomasine from any penance of her own.

In the cloister walk she paused to gaze into the garth where every leaf of grass and petal of flower was sparkling with crystal droplets. The air was rich with the smell of wet earth and growing things, and Frevisse drew a deep breath, letting everything but the moment's loveliness slip from her mind. She had learned the value of life's momentary beauties and to enjoy them when they came.

This one was ended by Dame Claire hurrying along the cloister walk toward her, a small, stoppered pottery jar in her hand. When she saw that Frevisse had seen her, she beckoned with her head for Frevisse to follow her into the slype. Gathering herself back to duty, Frevisse did, and there Dame Claire held out the jar to her, saying, "Would you take this to Mistress Maryon? I told Sister Thomasine that I'd do it today, she so hating to go among strangers and there being so many there just now, but there's a problem in the kitchen that I have to see to if we're to have dinner on time. Mistress Maryon can put it on the wound, that's not a problem, but I want to know how his hurt looks and would rather you told me than have it from a servant."

Though Frevisse had hoped to avoid both Master Montfort and Master Worleston, she understood both Dame Claire's needs and Sister Thomasine's and took the jar with a reassuring smile. "Willingly, Dame."

"Thank you," Dame Claire said and sped away toward the kitchen.

The rain had kept most of the sheriff's and crowner's entourages inside so far that morning, but, like the sun now, they were coming out, down the stairs from the guesthall to sit on the well curb in the courtyard or wander out the gate to see what there might be to do in the while until their masters were done here. Frevisse, her hands tucked up her opposite sleeves with the jar in one of them and her head bent down so the forward swing of her veil on either side obscured her face, passed among them and through the hall unnoticed, she thought, to Sir Gawyn's room.

Only Sir Gawyn and Maryon were there. He was raised a little higher on the pillows than yesterday and was not so pale, but the red across his cheeks made Frevisse ask without other greeting, "Are you fevered?" A fevered infection of the wound was the main thing to be feared in a wound like his.

"No," said Maryon too quickly, as if to avert the possibility by firm denial.

Tersely Sir Gawyn added, "I've just finished an unpleasant time with the sheriff and that idiot of a crowner."

Frevisse had had her lesson that a little while spent with Master Montfort usually raised a person's choler as well as color. "And did you satisfy them?"

"I think so. Montfort at least. The sheriff has more wit about him, but there was nothing he could particularly fault other than that this is an out-of-the-way place for outlaws, but that was hardly our fault. We were traveling and we were attacked." Sir Gawyn closed his eyes and with a heavy breath eased down farther in the bed. "But it wasn't as easy as I'd hoped."

"They're questioning Will and Colwin now," Maryon said. "We hope that will be the end of it and they'll go."

"They won't talk with you or Jenet?"

"They asked if I confirmed what Sir Gawyn said, and I did; and they don't seem interested in trying to learn anything from someone so shaken she's in the care of the nuns."

"And Edmund and Jasper?"

"None of us has mentioned them."

"What of the dead?"

"They went to see them yesterday, before supper, and have given permission they be buried. The funeral is this afternoon, with burial in the village churchyard."

"Even the outlaws?" Who should not be buried in consecrated ground.

"Not knowing who they were, no one can be sure they were actually outlawed, and so your priest has said they could be buried in the churchyard," said Mistress Maryon.

"I'll see the boys are watched so Jenet can go to the funeral Mass," Frevisse offered.

"That would be good of you."

Frevisse handed her the small jar. "Dame Claire sent me with this for the wound. She said you'd know what to do and that I was to see how the hurt looked."

Maryon turned toward Sir Gawyn. "Can you bear it now, or would you rather rest a time?"

Sir Gawyn's smile was bleak. "Best do it now and have it over."

Frevisse stood across the room while Maryon uncovered the wound. Sir Gawyn bore the necessary movement and pain in silence, but despite Maryon's great care, he was pale again when it was done, his mouth tightly shut, his chest rising and falling heavily with his effort to steady his breathing. Maryon looked around for Frevisse to come to the bedside.

Not given to squeamishness, Frevisse inspected the hurt closely. The flesh was still ugly around it but not red or swollen or streaked with discoloration nor smelling of rot. As nearly as Frevisse could judge it looked as well as could be hoped for, and far better than it had looked four days ago.

Sir Gawyn crooked his neck to see the gash and asked, "Does she know what she's doing? That mouse-meek nun that's come the other mornings says it's to heal from inside to out, rather than crusting over and healing to inward."

"There're arguments for both ways," Frevisse said, "but Dame Claire and Sister Thomasine have both had good fortune with this one."

Sir Gawyn gave a short laugh. "And how many sword gashes come your way in a nunnery?"

"Not swords but scythes and knives and carelessness

enough around the village that they've had their chance to deal with deep cuts and the like."

"This wasn't carelessness," Sir Gawyn said bitterly.

"It was," Maryon corrected. "The man meant to kill you and missed."

Sir Gawyn laughed. "True enough! Careless of him to miss and more careless of him to not stop my blow in return."

While they talked, Maryon had poured wine into one of the bowls on the table. Now, taking up the bowl and a sponge, she came back to the bedside. Sir Gawyn drew a deep breath, closed his eyes, and tensed for what was coming. Her own face set in a match to his, Maryon laid clean cloths along the wound and began with all the gentleness she could to soak it with wine. Despite the cost to them both, she did it thoroughly, then blotted it dry with a clean towel, put aside the bowl and sponge, and took up Dame Claire's jar of ointment. Gently, gently, her fingertips touching him as lightly as possible, she spread it over the wound, and as she set the jar aside said softly, "There. It's done for today. I only need to re-bandage it."

Sir Gawyn had shuddered soundlessly under her touch. Now he drew a deeper breath and his hands unclenched from the bedclothes, though sweat was beaded over his face. As Maryon began to bathe his face and neck with a clean cloth and water, he opened his eyes and smiled at her. "I'll be all right."

Maryon smiled back. "I intend you to be."

Something more than merely tending to his hurt was going on between them, Frevisse thought. Had it begun here, or existed before?

A sharp rap at the door was all the warning Master Montfort gave before entering the room. Without bother of greeting he stared assessingly at Sir Gawyn's shoulder and said, "There's a bad one, and you're lucky if it doesn't infect. I've seen a deal of wounds in my time, you know. I will say that one looks like it's healing, but you'll never have your strength in the arm again. In fact, I'd be very surprised if you even could lift your hand head-high when it's healed."

Before Sir Gawyn could answer, Maryon said with sharp scorn, "Time will tell. And the infirmarian here is very skilled. It's not for you to predict doom or joy."

"I deal in the truth, woman," Master Montfort returned, drawing up straight to display his dignity in the face of a mere woman's opinion. "I said it because I see it. People need to face the truth, no matter what it is."

But both Frevisse and Maryon had had experience with Master Montfort's idea of truth. For him, truth tended to be what he found most convenient or enhancing of his reputation. Because Maryon looked as if she were about to tell him so to his face, Frevisse said mildly, "Have you and Master Worleston come to a conclusion yet?"

Master Montfort swung his displeased attention to her. "That's what I came to tell these folks. That everything is settled as much to our satisfaction as we expect it to be. They were feloniously attacked by men bent on robbing them and who have paid for their stupidity with their lives. There's not even a fine in it for the Crown and probably not much profit from the felons' belongings when we sell them. A sorry business all around." He fixed a harder glare on Frevisse and added, "So I trust you don't think you've found a twist in the matter and are bent on making something other about it?"

But Frevisse bowed her head and said quite humbly, "No, I'm content with what you and Master Worleston have discovered and declared. We're all content with it, I'm sure."

"That's good then. That's very good." Master Montfort cast a sharp look at Sir Gawyn again. "That shoulder isn't going to do well at all, I should think," he asserted and left.

Maryon moved swiftly behind him, shutting the door with a force she only barely kept from a slam at the last moment. "Fool! Fool, fool, fool!" she raged.

"And that's to the good so far as we're concerned," Frevisse said. "I should be going." She had learned what Dame Claire had asked her to, and heard what she had hoped for from Master Montfort. The rest could be left between Maryon and Sir Gawyn; she wanted no part of it, and more especially since she feared—and thought Maryon did, too, by the intensity of her defending against it—that Master Montfort on one thing at least was right, that Sir Gawyn would be crippled no matter how well he healed.

They let her go with thanks, and she crossed the hall as she had come, avoiding notice of anyone, until outside the door, at the head of the stairs down to the yard, her way was blocked by Master Worleston. She inclined her head to him respectfully and would have gone around him, but he said, "Dame . . . Frevisse, isn't it?"

She stopped, perforce, acknowledging she was. "Is there anything you need that I can help you with?"

"We've been most well seen to and will be leaving after dinner. I knew your uncle. He spoke of you sometimes and I thought to take this chance to meet you."

Frevisse smiled at him. Now that the cruel early edge of grief that had come with her uncle's death was gone, it was good to hear him spoken of. But, "How did you know I was his niece?"

"Master Montfort spoke of it last night."

"Ah." Frevisse could imagine in what unflattering content Master Montfort had spoken of her.

Master Worleston had a straight-mouthed way of smiling,

as if he found amusement where he knew he should not but nevertheless could not resist. "He was warning me against you, of course."

"Of course," she agreed. "And whose opinion do you favor? My uncle's or Master Montfort's?"

Master Worleston drew in his brows in mock deep consideration and said solemnly, "On the whole, and weighing what I know of each man, what do you think?"

"That Master Montfort must be a severe trial to you."

"One might say so," the sheriff agreed.

"But at least you've concluded this trouble quickly enough."

"So it seems."

With a qualm, Frevisse heard a hint of qualification in Master Worleston's voice. "Seems?" she asked.

"A simple matter of failed robbery. Rather too many dead but that can happen. Everything explained and accounted for." Master Worleston rolled off the points as they would probably go in the record of the incident. But his tone was dissatisfied as he added, "And not so well accounted for."

"In what way?" Frevisse kept her own tone no more than casually interested.

"For such incompetent outlaws, they were very well accoutered. And there've been no reports of a band of outlaws anywhere near here."

"They could easily be from somewhere farther off, somewhere become too dangerous for them. Some other shire," Frevisse offered. "Or they might have lately been turned out of some lord's service and gone to robbery only now."

Master Worleston shook his head, not refusing her ideas but in dissatisfaction. "There are going to have to be more questions asked."

"You're not leaving then?"

"We're done here, right enough. I doubt there's more to be learned from these folk. But I'd like to know more about the men who were killed." He shook his head to clear his concerns away, smiled and slightly bowed to her. "My pleasure to meet you, Dame Frevisse. Your uncle always spoke praisingly of you."

Frevisse curtsied in reply. "My thanks for your kind words. I hope we meet again, sir. God be with you until then."

"And with you."

Another time, Frevisse would have been pleased to have made Master Worleston's acquaintance. He was both intelligent and personable. But just now Master Montfort's stupidity was more desirable, and Master Worleston's acuteness made her uncomfortably aware of how thin was the screen of untold truths she had agreed to help Maryon maintain.

And what other untold truths and possibly lies did Maryon have that Frevisse did not know of?

She did not like that thought, nor the fact that there was nothing she could do about it.

But because there was nothing to be done, she pushed it away and began to consider what the boys could do this afternoon while Jenet was gone to the burying of Hery and the others.

Chapter

◈ 10 ◈

MASTER WORLESTON, MASTER Montfort, and their entourage rode out of St. Frideswide's in early afternoon. From the cloister walk, Frevisse heard the clatter of their horses on the cobbles of the inner yard and then the quiet afterwards and drew a deep breath of relief. Master Worleston's inquiries, if he went on with them, might bring him back here later but for now the priory was clear of him and Master Montfort.

She went to the boys' room, knowing they and Lady Adela were at lessons with Dame Perpetua in the chapter house but in search of Jenet. As expected, she was there, sitting on a joint stool mending the torn heel of a boy's hose. When Frevisse knocked, she rose quickly to her feet with, "Come in, please you," and a curtsy. She was a plump young woman with a pleasant face and probably pretty enough when she was not red-eyed and tear-puffed from too much crying.

Nodding at the hose still in her hands, Frevisse said, "The children are hard on their clothing?"

Jenet twitched a small smile. "Not so very hard. They're good boys." She seemed unable to make up her mind whether to put the hose down or go on holding it. She dithered it from hand to hand instead, and when Frevisse asked, "You're going to the funeral this afternoon?" she pressed it over her mouth to stop a sob before gasping, "Yes, please you." She hiccuped on a dry sob despite her efforts and blurted, "He's to be buried this afternoon, Hery is, and someone ought to be there. He was a good man. I'm sorry about yesterday, about not being here." Tears brimmed in her eyes and started to spill over. "But I really must go this afternoon. I really must."

"Of course you must," Frevisse said soothingly, though she did not feel particularly soothing. She regretted the woman's grief but did not want to be soaked by it. "I've only come to tell you the boys will be seen to, you don't have to worry about them while you're away."

She had also come to make sure Jenet was still there and not so hopelessly unreliable as to have slipped away again even after yesterday's reprimand. It was all very well for her to be grieving, but it was Frevisse who would be doing a fortnight's penance on water for her carelessness.

Jenet, all gratitude and tears, sobbed, "You're kind. You're so very, very kind. Thank you. Thank you so much. Thank you . . ."

Frevisse left her gratefully weeping into the hose. She had arranged with Dame Claire that Dame Perpetua and Sister Lucy would spend much of the afternoon in the orchard with the children. They were Dame Claire's choice—Dame Perpetua because the children were most used to her, Sister Lucy because Dame Claire felt she needed respite from her almost constant care of Domina Edith. Though it was by her own wish and with her whole heart that she did it, Sister Lucy was not so very much younger than Domina Edith herself; the long effort was wearing on her, and an after-

noon's quiet in the orchard would be good for her. Frevisse
was to take her place with Domina Edith for the while.

She went now up the stairs to Domina Edith's rooms.
Sister Lucy was waiting at the parlor door, to forestall her
knocking. To Frevisse's inquiring look, she made gestures
that Domina Edith was sleeping and that all was well.
Frevisse nodded that she understood and, smiling, gestured
that Sister Lucy could go. After a last careful look into the
bedroom, she did, and when the shuffle of her slippers had
faded down the stairs, the pleasant quiet of the summer's
afternoon settled over the parlor.

Briefly, Frevisse went to the windows overlooking the
yard. It was too early in the afternoon for any new travelers
to come seeking the priory's hospitality for the night, and
with the sheriff and crowner gone with their men it was
presently a quiet scene. While Frevisse watched, Dame
Claire, recognizable even from the back and above by her
short height and firm step, appeared below and crossed to
enter the new guesthall. Going to look in on Sir Gawyn for
herself, Frevisse supposed.

She raised her gaze past the roofs to the sky, adrift with
white clouds across the blue of a perfect summer's afternoon that promised no more rain for a while. The haying
had begun this morning. After three famine years of
harvests spoiled by cold and wet, this looked to be a good
year.

But for St. Frideswide's there would be the sorrow of
losing their prioress.

Frevisse left the window and crossed the parlor to stand
in Domina Edith's bedroom doorway. The prioress lay small
beneath her sheet and so quiet that Frevisse took an anxious
step nearer, looking to be sure she still breathed.

Slightly, steadily, the sheet rose and fell. Obscurely
ashamed of the momentary clutch of fear around her heart,

Frevisse went silent-footed to kneel at the prie-dieu against the wall and pray, not for Domina Edith's continued life but for ease of passing when it had to come and, for herself, the grace to accept it. Willing acceptance of what had to be was among the lessons Frevisse had set herself to learn here in St. Frideswide's, but she was aware it was something in which she was as yet imperfect.

At least she had learned to go deeply into prayer, and as always when her praying went best, she lost awareness of time. It was Domina Edith who drew her back with a whispered, "Dame Frevisse?"

Frevisse hastily ended her prayer and rose to go to the bedside. "Yes, Domina. Dame Claire thought it would be well if Sister Lucy was outside awhile in the lovely day."

"That was good of her. I'm glad of it. And glad to see you." She lifted her hand off the sheet, barely. Frevisse reached out to take its age-thinned flesh and fragile bones gently in her own. Domina Edith's fingers closed around hers, and the prioress murmured, eyes shutting, "That's better." And after a pause, "I drift, and it helps to have someone to hold to." She opened her eyes and looked directly into Frevisse's face. "You won't be prioress after me, you know."

Without thought, Frevisse hurriedly crossed herself and fervently exclaimed, "God forfend I should be!"

Domina Edith smiled. "You would have been my choice, you know."

Frevisse did not try to hide how appalled she was at the idea. "No, I didn't know. I don't want the office."

"That is among the reasons that would make you best for it. But you won't be elected. Don't fear it."

Caught between the desire to ask why she would not be and the sudden confused realization that until this moment she had been refusing even to consider what would happen after Domina Edith's death, Frevisse held silent. Domina Edith's eyes closed again but she went on, "My hope is that it goes to Dame Claire. That's why I made her cellarer."

Because so many duties fell to the cellarer, it was usual for whoever had done well in the office to be elected the one step higher to prioress when the need came.

"I don't think she wants it either," Frevisse said.

Softly, from some distance of memory, Domina Edith said, "Nor did I. But one learns. God's will is wiser than ours, and one learns." She sighed and was silent. Frevisse waited, and in a while, as if unaware there had been a gap in their conversation, Domina Edith went on. "It's that you are so very much yourself. It makes you uncomfortable to so many people. You show too well how impatient you are of their silliness and carelessness and the lies they want to believe to make themselves comfortable. That's why they will not want you for their prioress. As if a prioress's purpose was to make them comfortable." The notion amused her. "But I'm sorry for it. You would do well."

There did not seem to be anything to say to that so Frevisse said nothing. The quiet drew out between them then. In the afternoon's pleasant warmth and the comfort of Domina Edith's presence, fading though it was, Frevisse came near to drowse herself and was unready when Domina Edith said, "It's quite all right, you know. It will be a great freedom. To be quit of the body."

Again without thinking, Frevisse said, "But not easy."

"Oh no, not easy." Domina Edith was gazing at the ceiling, serenity in her eyes, her voice soft with the drift of her thoughts. "Not easy at all. Nor as simple as it probably ought to be. But then nothing is so simple as it ought to be. Not love or hate or fear or even hope." She made a small, negative move of her head on the pillow. "No, hope is the least simple of all, I've sometimes thought. It requires so much of so many other things, including courage. And courage isn't simple either." Her eyes closed. The sheet rose slightly and fell deeply with the effort of her breathing; and in a while she said, quite clearly, "Only God is uncomplicated."

This time, after another while, it was Frevisse who broke the silence, not knowing if Domina Edith slept or not but needing to say aloud, "We'll miss you, my lady. Very much."

Eyes still closed and so softly Frevisse nearly did not hear her, Domina Edith murmured, "It won't be for a while yet. But only a little while." And the corners of her mouth lifted in the slightest of smiles.

Chapter

11

THE DAY FADED gently into evening. Within the garden's high walls the shadows had begun to lie long, but the day's pleasant warmth and the flowers' scents lingered, and overhead the sky bloomed with the rose light of the westering sun.

It was the hour for recreation and the nuns strolled the garden paths mostly in twos and threes, their voices cast low, as soft and easy as the evening. Even Dame Alys, talking at Sister Juliana, was audible over barely half the garden.

Frevisse walked at first with Sister Lucy, exchanging thoughts on how Domina Edith did, neither of them saying their foremost thought about her—that it could not be much longer—until there was nothing else to say but that and they fell silent. Sister Lucy paused over the promising buds of the Madonna lily in its tall jar at the opening of the arbor, leaving Frevisse to walk on alone, and at the next juncture of paths Dame Claire joined her. Frevisse knew her well enough to think it was not by chance, and as they fell into step beside each other, she asked, "What is it?"

Dame Claire did not immediately answer but finally said,

"Sir Gawyn asked to see me this afternoon. About his shoulder."

"It's worsened?" It was possible a wound could turn that suddenly, despite how well it had looked this morning.

"No. It will heal well enough, I think. But he's taken it into his head that even if it does, he'll not have full use of his arm again."

"That's Master Montfort's doing," Frevisse said. "He came in while the wound was uncovered this morning and said a wound like that would leave him crippled. I never thought—Sir Gawyn had taken his measure and I didn't think he'd heed aught Master Montfort had to say."

"I think Sir Gawyn half knew it anyway but was refusing the knowledge until forced to face it."

"You're sure he'll be crippled then, no matter how well it heals?" Frevisse realized her sick feeling at the thought could only be faint echo of what Sir Gawyn felt.

"I tried not to say it to him that plainly but, yes, that's what it comes to. I could be wrong. Folk have surprised me before. The body does things"—Dame Claire made a tense, frustrated gesture with both hands—"and we don't know why. But I think with him there's been hurt deep enough that the muscles will never have their cunning back. And there's nothing more I could have done or can do for him. There's so much hurt can be done to a body and so little—*so little*—we can do to mend it. It makes me angry!"

Familiar with Dame Claire's frustration when she could not heal as well as she wanted to, and with no comfort for it, Frevisse held silent. Her longer step measured to match to Dame Claire's, they walked on, and in a while, more quietly, Dame Claire sighed and said, "But what there's no help for there's no use weeping over, and I've been like this before, over other things I couldn't help, haven't I?"

"Often and often."

Dame Claire made a small, rueful laugh. "And I should be grateful for what skill God has given me instead of complaining over what I lack."

Too prone to that failure herself, Frevisse made no answer, and Dame Claire went on, "Mistress Maryon has asked if the boys might come this evening to spend some time with him. As diversion for both him and them."

"That's likely a good idea. Could Lady Adela go, too, do you think? To save jealousy."

Dame Claire smiled widely. "She's not the quiet child we thought she was, is she? What do you suppose she's been up to that we don't know about?"

"I've been wondering," Frevisse admitted.

"And there'll likely be trouble if she doesn't go with Jasper and Edmund this evening?"

"Possibly. If she sets her mind to it. And she might, if she feels the boys are being favored over her."

"We surely don't need more mischief." Dame Claire sounded more amused than annoyed. "You'd best take her, too, then."

"I'm taking them?"

"Directly after supper, if you will." Sensing Frevisse's unwillingness, she added, "Would you rather Dame Alys did it? Or Sister Amicia?"

"I thought—" Frevisse broke off. She had not thought about it at all. She knew Dame Claire was not serious about either Dame Alys or Sister Amicia but did not want her to be serious about her instead. "Jenet," she suggested.

"Jenet has collapsed. The funeral was too much for her. She came back in hysterics and is in the infirmary, asleep with something Sister Thomasine gave her. Tibby is watching after the boys. Do you want Tibby responsible for them outside the cloister?"

"I'll miss Compline. And be late to bed."

"I give you leave for it."

Frevisse realized that the objections she was making against going were out of proportion to the matter. She was trying, she realized, to stay as far as she could from a problem for which she had no solution and which worried her both because of her helplessness and the danger there was in it. But at least she knew the danger and no one else in the cloister did. She bent her head and said far more evenly than she felt, "I'll gladly do it."

The boys were undressed down to their shirts and hosen, enduring under protest Tibby's attempts to wash their necks. Unnoticed for the moment in the doorway, Frevisse watched Edmund duck grimacing away from the washcloth despite Tibby's grip on one ear and writhe as if the water running down his back was boiling oil until, exasperated, Tibby snapped, "You don't do this for your Jenet, do you? You stand still for her, I warrant, or she clouts you."

Edmund exclaimed indignantly, "Nobody ever clouts us!"

"And I'm sure I believe that, don't I? Not clout silly little boys? Who'd not?" Tibby said scornfully and pushed the back of his head, assuredly not as hard as she would have one of her brothers, but Edmund jerked away and rounded on her angrily.

"Don't you dare push me! Nobody pushes me like that! We're—"

"—very loud in a very quiet place," Frevisse said. And when all three looked at her, she added mildly, "Is this the way Mistress Maryon wants you to behave?"

Jasper, less angry than his brother, grasped her warning before Edmund did and looked instantly discomfited. Edmund, caught between his rage at Tibby and indignation at being interrupted, was less quick but caught her meaning soon enough to snap his mouth shut over whatever he had been going to say, flushing a red nearly as dark as his hair.

Pretending she noticed nothing of it, Frevisse said, "And now you have to dress again because I'm taking you both to see Sir Gawyn."

There was no trouble after that in their cooperating with Tibby. While Frevisse waited, they shrugged into their jerkins and found where they had kicked their shoes under the bed and let their hair be combed to tidiness with resolutely no fidgeting, then stood straight and still while Frevisse looked them over and pronounced them fit.

"And Lady Adela is to go with you, since she's become your friend," she added.

They had no objection to that either, so long as they were going to see Sir Gawyn and miss their bedtime in the bargain.

Dame Perpetua had Lady Adela tidy and waiting in the cloister. The girl curtsied prettily to Frevisse and then to Dame Perpetua, as mild-mannered as ever. But Frevisse caught the corner of a glance she gave Edmund and Jasper and knew the girl was as eager as they were.

The boys had not been in the yard since their precipitous arrival. Now, as they crossed it, Edmund swerved aside toward the well. Frevisse caught his arm, bringing him along with the rest.

"I only want to look down it," he protested.

"We're expected at the guesthall and it would be rude to be late."

"My looking down the well won't make us so much later," Edmund insisted. "Hardly later at all. Not so late that anyone would notice."

"People notice what you particularly don't want them to notice," Frevisse said. "That's something you'd best remember." She barely kept herself from adding, "my lord."

Their father might be a next-to-nobody, but it was clearly their mother's royal blood that told in both boys when they were crossed. "And besides, it's too late now, we're here," she added as she bustled them up the stairs into the guesthall.

Will rose from a joint stool outside Sir Gawyn's closed door as they approached. He bowed to Edmund and Jasper and then to Dame Frevisse and Lady Adela, before cocking a teasing eye at Jasper and saying, "I've something for you that you lost, my lord."

Jasper looked puzzled. Will reached behind his back, drew something from his belt, and held it out to him. Jasper exclaimed, "My dagger!" and took it from him eagerly. "Hery took it in the fight! I thought it was lost!"

Will laid a big hand over Jasper's on the hilt, making the boy look up at him. "I found it in Hery's hand, when he was dead," he said quietly. "Don't ever forget how he and Hamon died to keep you safe."

Solemnly Jasper met his look. "I won't forget."

"Was there blood on it?" Edmund asked. "Did he use it on anyone?"

Frevisse frowned, both at the question and at the eagerness on all three children's faces for the answer. But Will seemed only amused, taking their bloody-mindedness in good part. "Aye, there was blood enough. He'd done someone with it."

The dagger was clean now, but the children gazed on it with an awe more properly reserved to holy relics, and Frevisse said briskly, "I think we'd best go in now."

Will, taking the hint, rapped at the door and opened it for them. Edmund entered readily enough, and Lady Adela with him, but at the last moment Jasper hesitated, an odd expression on his face, as if he thought he might be sick but did not know for sure. Before Frevisse could urge him on,

Will leaned close and said to him, too low for anyone in the room to hear, "It's none too bad, my lord. He was up and walking a ways this afternoon. And the wound is bandaged. There's nought to be bothered over."

Jasper glanced at him with brimming gratitude and went in. Frevisse, ashamed of not having understood as quickly as Will had, murmured, "Thank you," and followed, Will bowing her through the doorway.

Because fresh air was known to be bad for any sickness or hurt, the room was shuttered and in shadow even on so fine an evening. A candle burning on the table beside the bed gave the only light, as well as a warm color to Sir Gawyn's face. He was sitting far more up against the pillows and looked marginally better than he had this morning, laughing at something Edmund had just said and chiding, "But you shouldn't say so, my lord. They've given us good shelter and comfort here."

"Dame Frevisse," Maryon said before Edmund could go farther about whatever he had complained.

Frevisse indicated with a silent movement of her hand and head that she could be ignored for this while, and went to stand in the shadows across the little room. The visit was for Sir Gawyn and the children; she did not need to be considered part of it.

Edmund had already climbed onto the bed to sit by Sir Gawyn. The knight now put out a hand and drew Jasper to the bedside. His hand on the boy's arm, his other hand on Edmund's knee, he smiled at Lady Adela and asked, "And who is this lovely lady come with you?"

"Lady Adela," Edmund said casually. "She's been here in the nunnery for years and years."

"She's Lord Warenne's younger daughter," Maryon said more formally.

Sir Gawyn bent his head to her as respectfully as if she

were a grown woman. "My lady. If ever I may serve you."

Lady Adela bent her head in return and said with equal courtesy, "I thank you, good sir."

Impatient with such courtesies, Edmund asked, "Does it hurt much? Your wound? Is it very bad? Where is it?"

"Here." Sir Gawyn indicated his left shoulder. "And no, it hardly hurts at all anymore, unless I forget and move the wrong way. But it's ill to talk of wounds around ladies. It distresses them."

Edmund scorned that. "Mistress Maryon has been tending you. She's not bothered."

"And Lady Adela doesn't care," Jasper put in. "She likes that sort of thing. We've told her all about the battle."

"It was a little small for a battle," Sir Gawyn said.

"A bloody skirmish!" Edmund enthused. "And more of them than of us!" He bounced to his knees on the bed and struck vigorously with an imaginary sword at an imaginary foe somewhere behind Sir Gawyn's head.

Sir Gawyn winced at the jerking of the mattress and loosed Jasper to take hold of his shoulder. Edmund, chagrined, immediately sank down to stillness beside him, eyes wide on his face. Jasper, pale as Sir Gawyn suddenly was, pressed closer to the bed, a frightened hand laid on the knight's thigh. Mistress Maryon started to say something angrily, but Sir Gawyn held up his hand enough to stop her.

"It's all right. He didn't mean it." He drew a deep, steadying breath and smiled at Edmund. "But don't bounce again, all right?"

Edmund shook his head. "I'll be still as anything. It really does hurt, doesn't it?"

"It really does hurt," Sir Gawyn agreed, then added with mock sternness, "but only sometimes. Like when you bounce."

Carefully, as if afraid the words might jar him too much,

too, Jasper asked, "When will you be better? When are we going to go? Tomorrow?"

A little shortly, Sir Gawyn said, "Not tomorrow."

From her place at the foot of the bed, Maryon put in, "Nor the next day even. Not until he's strong enough to ride. You'll have to go on being patient and doing what Dame Frevisse and the other nuns tell you for the while."

All three children made faces at that, and Lady Adela declared, "I want to come, too, when you go."

"You can't," Edmund said. "It's our adventure."

"It could be mine, too."

"No, it can't."

"It can!"

Into their escalating anger, Maryon said smoothly, "This was a quest laid on them by their—lord and they have to see it out as he wished, companioned with none but those he sent with them at the start."

"A quest," Lady Adela said, awed. "For what?"

"They're not allowed to say. That was laid on them with the quest itself."

A little silence at the burden of honor and duty that carried with it fell over all the children, until Jasper said wistfully, "Still, I'd like to go on with it instead of being here."

"When we do," Sir Gawyn said, "and the quest is complete"—he had quickly picked up Maryon's version of their journey—"I'll show you a cave where a dragon used to dwell."

"One of Merlin's dragons?" Edmund asked eagerly.

"Alas, not so grand, I fear. Only a common, cattle-eating dragon, but a dragon nonetheless."

"You've never killed a dragon, have you?" Jasper asked.

"I've never had occasion to, no," Sir Gawyn said.

"But you would have if you'd had the chance," Edmund said firmly.

"I would indeed," Sir Gawyn agreed.

"Just as you killed our enemies," Edmund declared. "Because you're a true knight." He looked at everyone else for their agreement. They all nodded, Jasper and Lady Adela vigorously, Mistress Maryon holding in a warm smile.

The expression on Sir Gawyn's face was less easily read, but Edmund suddenly said indignantly, "This shouldn't be your room. You shouldn't be here."

"No?" Sir Gawyn asked, bewildered.

Lady Adela understood and said eagerly, "You've been wounded on a quest. You're supposed to be in a fine room in a grand bed hung with tapestries, with fair ladies waiting on you. That's how it is in the stories. In all the stories."

"And this isn't fine at all," Edmund pointed out. "And you've only Mistress Maryon and Will to see to you."

Sir Gawyn shut his eyes, his face drawn taut with sudden pain. He reached toward his shoulder again, but Frevisse guessed that, vulnerable as Sir Gawyn now was, the pain came from somewhere deeper in him. In all likelihood, Sir Gawyn was what so many men were—a landless knight dependent for his living on his service in someone else's household, with his best hope for the future an annuity given for life by his lord. Or in Sir Gawyn's case, by Queen Katherine. But from what Maryon had said, it was unlikely that Queen Katherine was going to be in a position to be granting any such thing, now that her secret was betrayed. And anyone known to have served her would have difficulty taking service elsewhere, even if able of body, which Sir Gawyn was not likely ever to be again. He was very far from anything like the romances of adventure and chivalry that were clearly the boys' idea of knighthood, and the

children's blithe words had jarred his harsh reality against
what he would never have.

But Maryon with a forced lightness that betrayed how
much she understood—probably far more than Frevisse
did—said, "Then I suppose we should say he's in the Castle
of Cruel Duress, denied what should be his by right as a
brave knight."

That appealed readily to the children. Edmund and Jasper
nodded complete agreement and Lady Adela murmured
happily, "Cruel Duress. Cruuuel Duressss."

"And all we need now," said Maryon, "is the tale of how
he escapes from here."

She moved to stand at the foot of the bed, drawing
everyone's gaze to her. Frevisse knew, from other times,
how charming Maryon could be at need. Now she was
clearly set to charm not only the children but Sir Gawyn if
she could, and for that her Welsh imagination served her
well as she spun her story of his escape from St. Frideswide's and his adventures afterwards, making it more
fantastical as she went along by sometimes asking one of
the children, "And what do you think happened next?" and
weaving their wild and then wilder ideas into her telling.

In the candlelight, her eyes bright with the story, she
looked younger than her years that after all were not so very
many. Too plagued with the problems and possible trouble
she had brought into St. Frideswide's, Frevisse had stopped
seeing her as a person. Now she found herself acknowledging that in her narrow-boned, dark Welsh way Maryon was
lovely. Lovely enough to have married by now if she had
chosen to, even if she could manage only a small dowry.
How old was she really? What hopes did she have for her
life? How much was she in love with Sir Gawyn? And did
he love her? Frevisse could not tell, but relaxed deeply into
his pillows, he was mostly watching Maryon as she talked,

and the grimness—or was it only sadness?—that still
showed in the set of his mouth eased from time to time
when he smiled and once he even laughed at some particularly fantastical turn in his supposed adventures.

Will had left his watch and come to lean, arms crossed, in
the doorway, his deep-creased face eased with amusement,
the candlelight catching a gleam from his bright hair. The
children, all sitting on the bed now beside Sir Gawyn,
listened with glowing delight while the story came to a
castle high in the Welsh mountains, all in ruins except when
the full moon shone on it, and for that while, that little
while, it was whole and beautiful and full of lords and ladies
and great wealth. "But if you linger past that hour," Maryon
said, her voice throbbing deep and low, "or try to carry away
more gold and jewels than your cap can hold—you did
come wearing your caps, didn't you?" Three young hands
rose dismayed to their bare heads. "If you do that or stay too
long and the moon passes from full, the castle fades to ruins
again and you disappear forever from the earth."

"Not until just the next full moon?" Lady Adela asked.

"Forever," Maryon said, making the word toll doom.

"And what does Sir Gawyn do? He doesn't disappear
forever, does he?" Edmund asked.

"We'd have no more story then, would we? No, Sir
Gawyn . . ."

The story went on but Frevisse's attention strayed again.
She was tired. The nuns went to bed directly after Compline. In summer that was before the sun went down, which
had been difficult for her when she was a novice, but she
had long since grown used to it. She discreetly covered a
yawn. The candle was nearly burned out, puddling around
itself in the holder. When it began to gutter, she would tell
the children it was time to go.

She covered another yawn. Her mind completely drifted

from the story now, she watched as a long fragment of wax left standing up taller than the candle flame began to bend toward the heat. It had escaped its fate this long but no longer. Slow and slow it bowed over, wasting away in the candle flame . . .

"But in the next valley he found his home at last and all his people waiting for him and there was an end," Maryon said suddenly. "Now off Sir Gawyn's bed and away with Dame Frevisse to your own. That's all there is."

Even to Frevisse's lax attention, the ending had come abruptly. The children, vastly indignant, set up a clamor of protest. "You never said anything about valleys! What home? What people?"

"But the treasure! He hadn't found the treasure yet!"

"You didn't finish the part about—"

Maryon scooted them all off the bed. "Maybe there'll be more to tell another time but that's enough tonight. Go on. It's late. Away with you."

Will and Sir Gawyn were taken as much off guard as Frevisse and the children, but Will rallied, stepped aside from the doorway with a gesture that urged them through it, and said, "She's right, you know. Sir Gawyn is tired and so are the rest of us."

"*We're* not tired!" Edmund declared.

"You will be by the time you've reached bed," Frevisse said. "Will, pray you, see them to the yard. I need a word with Mistress Maryon."

That disconcerted Maryon, but she followed Frevisse from the room. As Will shepherded the children away across the hall, they moved away from the door to Sir Gawyn's room and Frevisse asked, low-voiced, "What happened? You're pale. Are you ill?" All that was needed now to make matters more difficult was for Maryon to sicken with something.

In the same near-whisper, Maryon answered, "No, I'm well enough. It was the candle." She shivered and wrapped her arms around herself even though there was no evening chill.

"The candle?" Frevisse asked, completely puzzled.

"You saw it. It made a winding sheet. Didn't you see? That bit of wax standing up beside the flame? A winding sheet."

Frevisse had never seen her so shaken. "I don't understand."

"Maybe it's only in Wales we remember. Maybe you've never heard. When a winding sheet standing up beside a candle flame begins to bend, the person it points to is marked for death."

Despite herself, Frevisse felt the creep of a small chill up her own spine. The "winding sheet" had been pointing toward the bed. Toward Sir Gawyn. And toward the children.

Chapter

12

By morning Frevisse knew how foolish her reaction had been to Maryon's fear. Assuredly Maryon had believed about the "winding sheet" of candle wax, but there were a great many such beliefs in the world, and very few of them proved true often enough to count for anything.

And any last thought she had about it disappeared in chapter meeting when Dame Claire asked for their especial prayers for Domina Edith after Sister Thomasine, as infirmarian, had explained in her soft voice, "It's not so much that Domina Edith is markedly worse as that she's simply . . . less here. She'll leave us soon. It could be any time."

Frevisse, in her own grief, had the comfort of the church itself, spending more than even her usual time there, doing again what was already done, cleaning into its far corners, dusting the choir stalls, polishing the altar steps to greater sheen, making more perfect the already shining altar furnishings, smoothing again and again the altar cloth as she prayed for the repose of Domina Edith's body and the safety of her soul.

She was rarely alone while she did. No one's duties around the nunnery were slacked; that would have been disrespect for all that Domina Edith had expected of them through her years; but the nuns came as they could, simply or in twos or threes, to kneel below the altar in prayer for however long they could spare from their other duties; and the cloister servants, kneeling farther from the altar but there in whatever brief moments they could take from their work; and even the boys and Lady Adela, brought by Dame Perpetua after their lessons.

A different hush than usual filled the cloister. Not the hush of work gone about in silence but a hush of waiting. And in that hush the burst of the boys' laughter and their sudden running in the cloister walk on their way to their afternoon lessons jarred beyond the usual. Jenet quickly shushed and curbed them, but Frevisse flinched at the broken silence and saw Sister Emma and Sister Juliana, just entering the church, look back into the cloister with resentful frowns. She considered a moment, then went to find Dame Claire, and when the children came out from their lessons, she was waiting for them with Sister Amicia.

Edmund stopped short at the sight of her. Behind him Jasper stopped, too, but Lady Adela bumped into Jasper and he lurched into his brother and they had to sort themselves out with an unnecessarily enthusiastic use of elbows before Edmund shook himself free and said with great and earnest innocence, "We weren't going to do anything!"

"I'm sure you were not," Frevisse agreed, and wondered what they had had in mind before her appearance forestalled them. "But Dame Claire has given permission, if Dame Perpetua agrees"—she emphasized that so they would understand this was no lightly given favor—"for Sister Amicia and I to take you out of cloister to see more of the nunnery than you have until now." As eagerness leaped up in the boys' faces, she saw Lady Adela's stricken face over

Jasper's shoulder and added, "And Lady Adela, too, of course."

Lady Adela swung around to Dame Perpetua behind her, caught her hand, and pleaded, "Please you, Dame, may we go? Please?"

Dame Perpetua looked surprised to see so much eagerness from so usually demure a child, but said with some hesitation, "I don't see why not, so long as you stay with Dame Frevisse and Sister Amicia and do what you're told."

"I will! I promise I will!"

"Then go on and be a good girl. And you be good boys."

Edmund and Jasper nodded unhesitating agreement. Frevisse suspected that all three of them would have agreed to anything for the chance of going out. She remembered too much of herself as a child and knew too much of other children to have any warmhearted notion that children were inherently innocent. Indeed, what she had seen of children seemed to support the doctrine of original sin.

Conversely, Sister Amicia had the notion that children were God's innocent lambs, and as they left the cloister to cross the yard toward the gateway to the outer yard, she was saying, "We're going to have a lovely time, aren't we? And you'll behave yourselves just as you promised Dame Perpetua because it's good little boys and girls who go to heaven, you know."

Sister Amicia always had all the obvious words for any occasion. But though Frevisse invariably found her tedious, she had chosen her as companion now precisely because she was not likely to notice if the boys inadvertently said or did anything that betrayed themselves. For the sake of that, she intended to endure Sister Amicia patiently, but intending was not the same as doing, and she barely held back a sigh as Sister Amicia pointed at the doves strutting on the cobbles near the well across the yard and exclaimed brightly, "See all the pretty doves? Don't they look pretty with the sunlight on them? All those pretty colors in their feathers! Aren't they pretty?"

A look passed among the three children, and with unspoken agreement and not an instant's hesitation Edmund and Jasper broke into a run toward the well. The doves burst up in a wildness of wings at their precipitous coming. Ignoring them, they leaped up the steps to the well and flung themselves belly-down over the coping to peer into its depths.

With distressed exclamations Sister Amicia scurried after them and caught hold of their belts as if they were sliding head down to destruction. Frevisse, with better opinion of their common sense, stayed where she was, looking at Lady Adela. The girl had run a few limping steps after the boys but stopped when the doves had flown and now stood with her head bent back to watch them as they swung high around the yard, rising and rising against the sky until they wheeled away over the wall and out of sight. She went on gazing after them into the empty sunlight, her look of longing so intense it told Frevisse more about her than any one thing else in all the months since she had come to St. Frideswide's. Lady Adela would never stay inside St. Frideswide's if ever she were given chance to go.

But meanwhile Sister Amicia was still clinging to the boys, trying to pull them back, which only meant they clung more tightly to the stones, squirming against her hold while she cried at them, "Come away before you fall! You'll fall in and drown!"

Lady Adela blinked, came back to herself, and ran to fling herself onto the coping next to Jasper.

In added agony, Sister Amicia cried, "Dame Frevisse, I've only two hands!"

Without raising her voice, Frevisse said, "We can stay

here until we're out of time or we can go on. The choice is yours to make."

The children glanced at each other and slid backward to their feet, Edmund and Jasper deftly twisting out of Sister Amicia's hold as they did.

"The stables," Edmund declared. "We want to go to the stables and see how our horses do."

That was reasonable enough. Frevisse led the way, the children behind her, and Sister Amicia last, telling the children they had to be more careful, not take foolish chances like that, she had heard of a boy who came to a terrible end at the bottom of a well. The only response among the children was Lady Adela complaining, "I didn't see any stars. They say you can see stars if you look down a well, but I didn't see any."

"It has to be a deep, deep well and this one isn't," Edmund said.

"It doesn't have to be a deep, *deep* well," Lady Adela retorted. "Only a deep one."

Before that could escalate into an argument over what was deep and what was very deep, Frevisse said, "Isn't that your man Colwin in the stable doorway?"

The outer yard of St. Frideswide's stretched to the outer gateway that opened onto the road. Around it, enclosed by the nunnery's outer wall, were the stables, byres, sheds, and a scattering of workshops needful to the nunnery's daily life. Just to the left outside the inner gateway were the long stables, and it was indeed sturdy Colwin standing in the doorway, talking with Master Naylor.

Edmund hullooed him and waved. "Our horses! We've come to see our horses."

Jasper turned to Lady Adela. "They're proper horses. Not ponies. We rode them all the way from home to here."

Edmund had not waited for Colwin's or anyone's response. He was running toward the stables. Jasper and Lady Adela paused long enough this time to ask Frevisse with a look if it was all right. She had meant to visit the stables anyway, and would welcome an inconspicuous chance to talk with Master Naylor, so she willingly nodded for them to go on. Jasper tempering his pace this time to Lady Adela's, they went on eagerly.

Frevisse and Sister Amicia followed more sedately. Though the children pelted straight on into the barn, Master Naylor and Colwin waited to bow to the approaching nuns before Colwin followed the children. From what little Frevisse had seen of him, she judged he had blunt good sense enough that the children would be safe in his care, but she said to Sister Amicia anyway, "You'd best go in, too, to be sure they keep out of the muck. I need to spend a word with Master Naylor."

"I haven't been in a barn since ever so long. I just love the smell of new hay!" Sister Amicia exclaimed and disappeared happily into the stable shadows.

To no one in particular Master Naylor said, "The new hay isn't in yet, we've only begun to cut it. There's only the last of last year's hay in there just now and it's gone musty."

"She'll probably not know the difference," Frevisse said.

Master Naylor was not given to showing much of his feelings on his face. He merely shook his head once and turned his attention fully to Frevisse. "May I help you, my lady?"

"I was wondering what you told the sheriff and crowner."

"No more than I had to."

"About the children?"

Master Naylor's brows drew down a little. "I had word from Dame Claire they weren't to be mentioned if it could be avoided. They weren't mentioned."

He fixed a look on her that said he was willing to have

that explained to him, but Frevisse slid away from it. "Have there been any . . . unusual . . . travelers of late, staying in the guesthalls, either one?"

"Won't Dame Alys tell you that?"

"Things seem to go better the less Dame Alys and I talk together," Frevisse said wryly.

With no hint of wryness in return, Master Naylor answered, "I could see how that might be." He had not enjoyed his necessary dealings with Dame Alys when she had been cellarer, and matters had not improved now she was hosteler. "There've only been the usual sort of traveler. None who've stayed more than a night." His gaze on her face sharpened. "And no one I've heard of asking questions out of the ordinary except you. What should I be looking for?"

"Anyone interested in the boys."

"Why would someone be interested in the boys?"

His direct, sharp question and her worry nearly drew the answer out of her. But though it might help for him to know, he was in the long run of it safer in ignorance. He could not be held accountable if he truly did not know who the children were. So against her inclination Frevisse shook her head and only answered, "I can't tell you. But there may be people who would think them . . . safer in their hands."

"Dame Claire knows this? Knows what you're about?"

"And Domina Edith." Who knew far more than Dame Claire and had surely given Dame Claire direction to order Master Naylor to silence. Or had she confided more than that to Dame Claire? Frevisse suddenly wondered.

Distant beyond the gateway and courtyard and cloister walls, the bell began to ring for Nones.

"Oh no!" Frevisse said. "I didn't know time had gone so far. The children have hardly been out at all. They're not going to be happy being taken back so soon."

"Leave them with me, if you like. Colwin and I will show them more. Between the two of us, we should manage well enough and bring them back to cloister."

It was a tempting possibility. Master Naylor had children of his own, Frevisse knew; and Colwin was one of their own people. But it was memory of Lady Adela's face, watching the doves soar away, that made up her mind. "Yes, that would be very good of you to do."

Sister Amicia burst out of the stable doorway, flustered near to tears. "They won't listen to me! They've climbed into the hay mow and it's all filthy up there, they're covered in dust and they won't come down and we're going to be late!"

"It's all right," Frevisse said. "Master Naylor and Colwin are going to see to them. We can go and we won't be late."

"Oh, Master Naylor, how kind of you. How very kind. Thank you, thank you so much. I promised they'd see the piglets. There are some piglets, aren't there? They might come down for you if you mentioned the piglets? And lambs?"

Sister Amicia's effusions backed Master Naylor away from her. Frevisse, not waiting for her to finish, simply walked away, forcing her to follow.

"There's Father Henry," Sister Amicia exclaimed, a little breathless in Frevisse's wake, as they reentered the inner yard. She waved happily to the nunnery's priest where he stood talking with Will at the foot of the guesthall stairs, and he waved back with a bemused look at seeing two nuns coming into the yard from outside. He was a burly young man, his tonsure almost hidden by unruly yellow curls, who looked as if he would be more skilled with a scythe in the field than cup and paten. Nor was he, to Frevisse's mind, among the clever people of the world, and his simplicity sometimes annoyed her; but it was a simplicity deeply given over to his faith and duties, and Frevisse feared the deeper fault lay in her pride rather than in his simplicity.

With a sudden thought, Frevisse said to Sister Amicia, "You go on. I'll be just a moment longer."

Drawn by the bell still clanging from the cloister, Sister Amicia hurried on without question. Frevisse turned aside toward the two men. They bowed to her and she quickly curtsied to Father Henry and bent her head to Will, following with, "Will, the children—the boys and Lady Adela—are with Colwin and Master Naylor in the stables. They're having an outing. Would you be free to join them, to keep watch over them until it's time they come in again?"

Will said, "Gladly, my lady."

"If it pleases you, I could go, too," Father Henry said. "There's safety in numbers when child-watching."

"That would do very well, if you would be so good and have the time." Knowing that Father Henry had a fondness for children and animals that went with his simplicity of heart, Frevisse accepted his offer with a curtsy of thanks and hastened after Sister Amicia. It would hardly do to be late again.

The office went its serene way to its end where Dame Claire said in her deep voice, *"Fidelium animae per misericordiam Dei requiescant in pace."* May the souls of the faithful, through the mercy of God, rest in peace. The nuns responded on one, low, long tone, "Amen," that sank away to silence.

Her mind eased away from one problem or another for the first time since Prime at dawn, Frevisse would willingly have stayed where she was but custom required she rise with the others and follow Dame Claire from the church. Quiet in her obedience, she did so, coming out into the warm afternoon shadows of the cloister walk in time to see

Ela from the guesthall and Father Henry coming along the cloister with the children in tow.

Frevisse's own intake of breath was covered by those of all the other nuns as they realized what they were looking at. Led by Ela, Lady Adela was crying aloud, tears pouring down her face, but she was the least of the trouble. Behind her, Father Henry led Edmund and Jasper by either hand and at his arms' length, well away from himself and anyone else because they were covered feet to waists and up their arms with black filth. And they smelled. Even before they were near, it was miserably obvious that they smelled and that they knew it, their faces screwed shut against breathing in any more than they had to.

It was also obvious that what they smelled of was pig-muck and, all propriety forgotten, Dame Alys bellowed, "What are you thinking of, bringing those filthy brats in here? They stink!"

"Dame Alys," Dame Claire said in mild rebuke.

"They do! You should have soused them off at the well before bringing them in here! Take 'em out and do it!"

"Dame Alys!" Dame Claire said more forcefully.

Dame Alys closed her mouth with an audible snap but nothing softened the glare she turned from Father Henry and the boys to Dame Claire. Ignoring her, Dame Claire held up her hand to stop Father Henry from coming any nearer and said, "Disaster overtook you, we can see that. We don't want them here. Take them to the laundry and have them cleaned, with my apologies to the laundrywomen. Dame Perpetua, take Lady Adela away. She isn't hurt or she'd not be howling so loud. Ela, find Jenet and tell her to take clean clothing to the boys. Dame Frevisse, you go with Father Henry and help."

Frevisse, remembering she had asked responsibility for

the children in their outing, smothered a protest, and followed Father Henry's hurried departure.

The laundry was with other work sheds and workshops directly needed by the nunnery, beyond a wall on the far side of the inner yard that could be reached by a back way beyond the kitchen or through a small gate from the yard. Father Henry chose the latter way, to be outside the cloister faster. Frevisse overtook him and the boys as they crossed the yard toward the gate, Edmund dragging back on his hand, protesting, "I don't want the laundry! I want a proper bath! They'll scrub too hard!"

"A proper bath is for proper dirt," Frevisse snapped. "You're filthy far beyond that. And you'll be scrubbed as much as needed no matter where it's done. Stop yammering. We're the ones who have to smell you." Edmund, startled at her sharpness, went silent, and she demanded of Father Henry, "What on earth were they doing in the pigsty?" That being the only place they were likely to have found that much pig-muck.

"They fell in," Father Henry answered, as embarrassed as if it had been his doing.

"They fell—or jumped?" Keeping her distance, Frevisse circled ahead of them to open the gate.

"Fell in. With the sow. And her piglets," Father Henry said, his voice shaking. He was distressed by more than the dirt and smell; under his tan he was white, and with good reason. A sow with piglets was vicious beyond any other yard-kept creature. If this one had reached either of the boys before someone grabbed them out, they would have been in need of far more than a scrubbing.

"Master Naylor and I snatched them out right enough," Father Henry hastened to assure her, as if she could not see for herself they were untouched except by filth. "But it was a near thing."

"She was grabbing for my foot," Edmund declared. "She didn't want Jasper. He doesn't taste good."

"Be quiet." Frevisse shut the gate behind them and led the way toward the laundry shed. "How did they come to fall?"

"They were on the top rail of the fence, sitting there and safe enough it seemed. They've the grip and balance of monkeys, or so I thought. But one of them fell and grabbed the other and in they both went."

"It wasn't that way at all," Edmund protested. "It wasn't our fault!"

"The rail rolled," Jasper said. "We couldn't stay on."

"The rail rolled?" Frevisse repeated blankly.

"The posts have holes through them." Father Henry let loose the boys to show with his hands. "The rails go through the holes. You know. Four rails up between each set of posts, and the ends of the next set of rails going through the same holes."

Like most of Father Henry's explanations, it was less than clear but Frevisse knew the sort of fence he meant. The rails rested in the holes in the posts without being fastened. They could roll, but not very readily. The boys must have been jostling them badly and someone should have stopped them.

"*We* didn't make it roll," Edmund insisted. "It wasn't our fault. It just did!"

"It doesn't matter whether you did it on purpose or not," Frevisse said unsympathetically. She was not sure at whom she was more angry: the boys for being so careless as to fall or the men for letting them sit there in the first place. Either way, the outcome was that they had to be cleansed of the dirt and stench when she would far rather have been praying for Domina Edith. Or seeing to almost anything else rather than them in their present state. Not bothering to temper her annoyance, she said, "What matters is that you're dirty and you have to be washed. And you're right. You *are* going to be scrubbed and very hard!"

Chapter

⊠ 13 ⊠

EDMUND, JASPER, AND Lady Adela sat on the low wall around the cloister garth, legs hanging over its grassy verge, brooding at a bright bed of gillyflowers in the morning sunshine. Except for the occasional thud of their heels against the stone, there was only the hum of bees among the flowers and the occasional whisper of skirts as a nun passed by.

They were bored. Again.

Lessons had been boring and Jenet was boring and St. Frideswide's was boring and, "I still have raw places where they scrubbed me too hard yesterday," Edmund muttered. He kicked a foot at a pale pink gillyflower just out of his reach and added for good measure, "I hate flowers."

The three of them considered that for a while, and then Jasper said, "Mother loves flowers." And after a while, wistfully, he added, "I wish Father would come for us."

Edmund punched him in the shoulder and said with a fierceness that threatened tears, "You be quiet!"

"I don't have to be!" Jasper's voice rose to match Edmund's and his temper with it. Anger was better than crying.

"If you fight," Lady Adela warned, "they'll send us all to our rooms!"

The threat made both boys hesitate. A fight would have made them both feel better, but to go back to their room meant going back to Jenet, who had finally stopped crying but now just sat, sighing and drooping, more boring than sitting on a wall. They both subsided, went back to staring at the garden and kicking the wall.

"I want to go *out*," Edmund muttered after a while. "There's nothing to do here."

"Nobody is going to take us out again, ever," Jasper replied sadly. "And it wasn't even our fault." He was still aggrieved about that.

"We could go just into the orchard," Edmund suggested. "Nobody would be very angry about that, if we didn't stay long. And nobody would miss us anyway." He swung around to hop off the wall but paused to see who was with him.

"They've moved the key," Lady Adela said, aggrieved in her turn. "I can't open the gate anymore."

"And we promised Dame Frevisse we wouldn't," Jasper said.

Edmund swung back, and the thud of their heels and the bees' hum were the only sounds for a while. And then Lady Adela said, "A forced oath isn't binding."

Edmund and Jasper looked at her.

"What?" Edmund asked.

Carefully, a little smugly, Adela explained, "If someone forces you to promise something, the promise doesn't count because they forced it from you. An oath made under . . . under duress . . . isn't binding."

Edmund and Jasper considered that. It made sense. Jasper saw his brother start to grin and felt obliged to point out, "But the gate is still locked."

"That one isn't." Edmund pointed to the door out of the cloister into the yard.

"We'll be seen."

"Maybe not. Come on."

"If we're seen, we'll be sent to our room forever."

"And if we're not seen, we'll be out and away. We'll go the way they took us to wash us yesterday. There's lots of places to hide and there has to be a back gate somewhere there. Adela will try it with me, won't you, Adela?"

Lady Adela had already swung her legs back over the wall and slid to her feet. "Come on, Jasper. It's better than sitting here," she urged.

That was true enough. And it was better to try and fail than to be a coward afraid to try at all. A true knight always dared, no matter how doomed a chance might be.

Jasper tended to consider matters a little longer than his brother did but, a decision made, he was as bold or bolder. As rear guard, he watched behind them for anyone coming as Edmund and Lady Adela opened the door the smallest possible crack to look out and survey the yard.

"There's nobody out there," Edmund said.

"All's right here," Jasper whispered.

"Then *go*," Lady Adela said, pushing at Edmund impatiently. "*Run*, before somebody comes."

Edmund ran, Lady Adela close behind him, and Jasper far last, having taken time to close the door to cover their escape. He followed Edmund's lead to the side gate Father Henry and Dame Frevisse had taken them through yesterday. Beyond it, they were among the side yard's clutter of small buildings. The only one they knew was the laundry, and that they gave a wide miss in memory of yesterday's indignities but found their way, unnoticed by anyone who thought to stop them, to the nunnery's postern gate.

It stood open. It was the common way in and out of the

nunnery for the servants coming or going to the kitchen gardens or farther away to the village. No one was there; they went through unchallenged, paused long enough to decide which way to turn, and with no need to argue over it, ran along the nunnery wall, ducked their way among the garden plots, and disappeared into the trees along the stream at the bottom of the slope.

Out of the sunlight there was sudden coolness. The sound of the water drew them, and they found it, running brown and clear between shallow banks, spangled with sunlight through the leaves overhead, rippling over smooth mud and rocky shoals.

Remembering the anger roused by their wet clothing last time, they were satisfied at first to throw twigs and drop leaves into the water and challenge each other over whose would be first out of sight around the stream's curve. But soon Edmund had a particularly fine twig and as it swung away on the current toward the bend, in danger of going out of sight forever, he stripped off his shoes and hosen and waded in after it.

"My leaf!" Jasper protested the swamping of his newest craft by Edmund's careless passing but Edmund ignored him, as was Edmund's usual way when he was set on something. And then he realized that what Edmund was doing was better than what he was doing and, forgetting his leaf, Jasper stripped off his shoes and hosen, too, and followed him into the water.

"That isn't fair!" Lady Adela protested from the bank. "I can't! My dress will get wet!"

"Too bad," Edmund called back without noticeable sympathy. "You're a girl and it can't be helped."

Jasper saw Lady Adela's eyes tighten with anger and said, "You can follow along the bank. Come on."

She stuck out her tongue at him, but she came, along the

narrow, deep-trodden path along the stream that showed other people came this way and often.

Around another bend the stream widened into a broad pool below steep banks. Edmund's twig had already drifted out toward the middle and he would have followed it but Lady Adela called, "You'd better see if it's too deep first."

Edmund looked as if he were about to say that was a girl-thing to do, but Jasper dragged a long stick from a flotsam along the bank and poked out into the water. Hardly beyond where they stood, the stick went deep and still did not touch bottom. He and Edmund exchanged looks. Edmund shrugged. "Maybe we can learn to swim. Will told me he learned by being thrown into deep water. We could, too."

"You'd better not," Lady Adela said.

"We're not girls. We won't get our dresses wet," Edmund taunted. But he went no farther. Instead, he took the stick from Jasper and hurled it out into the pool. The splash was very satisfying.

Adela in a temper at his taunt snatched up a short, heavy stick from the ground beside her and flung it into the water directly in front of him.

"He! That's not fair!" Edmund yelled, stumbling back but still being spattered.

"Good!" Adela yelled at him. "You're a boy and you're rotten!" She grabbed up and threw another stick, splashing him even more satisfactorily.

"You're getting me wet!"

"I mean to!"

"Stop it!"

She did not. Her third stick splashed between him and Jasper.

"Come on," said Edmund. "Let's push her in."

He waded to the bank, Jasper after him, and scrambled out.

"You wouldn't dare!" Lady Adela said, backing away.

"Yes, we would."

She hesitated, decided he meant it, and turned and ran, off the path into the underbrush, almost instantly out of sight.

Edmund, still in a temper, would have gone after her, but Jasper stopped and called after him, "We don't have our shoes."

Edmund pulled up, thought about it, then shrugged it all away as a waste of time, settling for saying loudly at the woods, "We're well rid of her anyway! And she'd better not tell anybody where we are either." Then he added to Jasper, "Come on. I bet I can throw farther than you can."

It was more fun to throw sticks from the top of the bank, and watch the ripple patterns break against each other and make little dazzles of sunlight over the water. They came, of course, to tussling and then to daring each other to jump off the bank into the water, but they both knew neither of them dared to do it, Will's story notwithstanding. Their cheerful arguing had come down to, "I will if you will."—"You go first."—when Jasper, knowing it was not going to happen, moved away to find another stick. He was saying, "Not until you do," when Edmund's shocked yell spun him around.

He was in time to see his brother pitch sprawling into the water. As Jasper stared, he disappeared in a great splash, surfaced flailing desperately, too choked to cry out again, and Jasper realized he had to do something. But before he could, he was hit a great blow in his back by two hands, sending him over the edge after his brother.

Once she had determined the children were nowhere in the cloister and made sure the gate into the orchard was locked and the key still hidden and had snapped at Jenet for being useless and set her to look through the cloister all over again, Frevisse crossed the yard to the guesthall, learned by quiet questioning of one of the servants that the children were not with Sir Gawyn or Maryon, and returned to stand angrily at the top of the guesthall steps while trying to decide what best to do next.

They were not in the cloister, she was sure of that, and they had not gone out the orchard gate. They were unlikely to have all three fallen down the well together and made no sound while they did it, and someone would have seen them if they had gone out the kitchen door or gotten as far as the outer yard. That left only the side yard and the postern gate. It was quite possible that three small, determined children could have skulked out that way unnoticed.

She should go back to Dame Claire for permission to go out, Frevisse knew, but that would take time and the sooner and more quietly the children could be brought back, the better. If she did not find them very soon, then Master Naylor would have to be asked for men to look for them, but it was too soon to raise that much alarm. She doubted they had gone far.

At the postern, looking out over the gardens and sun-bright fields, her hand shading her eyes, she tried to guess where the children might have gone; and saw the trees along the stream and knew where, as a child, she would have gone on such a warm afternoon.

The two servant women hoeing in the kitchen garden straightened as she passed them but to her question said they had only just now come out and had seen no children go by. Frevisse went on, still sure of where they most likely were, and at the wood edge came on Lady Adela sitting in the long grass trying to weave fading sweet cecily flowers into a wreath.

Relieved to see her, certain Edmund and Jasper must be nearby, Frevisse said, "Their stalks are too stiff to work well for that."

Unaware of her until then, Lady Adela dropped her work and scrambled to her feet to curtsy and gasp, "I didn't hear you come, Dame."

"I could tell that," Frevisse said, standing very straight and staring down at her sternly.

Lady Adela gulped, scooped the ragged wreath from the ground, and held it out to her. "For you, Dame," she suggested hopefully.

"I don't think so. Where are Edmund and Jasper?"

Lady Adela dropped the wreath again and pointed into the trees. "There. At the stream. They were mean to me," she added.

"Show me where."

Lady Adela hesitated. "Are we in trouble?"

"You know the answer to that. And in worse trouble the longer people are worried over you. Show me where they are."

Lady Adela sighed at the inevitable and turned to lead the way in among the trees.

From somewhere not far away there was a cry and a great splash, followed an instant later by another splash.

"They've fallen in!" Lady Adela exclaimed. "Into the pool, and it's deep!"

Frevisse pushed her aside and ran. Hampered by the underbrush and her skirts and veil, she fought her way through and, following the sounds, came out onto a path above the wide curve of a pool. Well out in the water, beating madly at it, sinking and fighting their way to air again, were Edmund and Jasper. There was no hope at all that they could reach the bank on their own, and Frevisse looked desperately around for a stick large enough to thrust out to them. There was nothing and with no choice she moved to where the bank was less steep, reached down to grab the back hem of her gown and pull it forward and up between her legs, bundling the skirts to above her knees. There was too much of it to tuck under her belt, she was forced to hold it with one hand, leaving her other hand free for balance as she waded into the water.

The bottom dropped steeply and was breast-high on her by the time she was in reach of Jasper. Stretching, she grabbed his out-flung hand and dragged him toward her, ordering, "Don't kick, don't fight me, or we'll both drown!"

She did not expect him, in his terror, to understand her but he did; he went limp and let her pull him to her. She swung him around to behind her, ordering, "Hold on to me!" and reached for Edmund just sinking out of sight. Only barely she managed to clutch his hair before he disappeared. Ruthlessly she dragged his head back up out of the water and toward her. He was conscious but gagging for air. He had swallowed too much water and needed help, but there was nothing she could do for him here. Shifting her hold to under his chin to pull him through the water with his face above it, and weighed down now with Jasper clinging to her gown in the back, she struggled back toward the bank.

Halfway there, she was unsure that she would make it. Her soaked clothing and the children were too heavy. They dragged her down and her legs no longer wanted to hold her up. But Lady Adela was weeping on the bank hard enough to break her own heart and anyone's who heard her, and Jasper was gasping his way through every prayer he had ever learned in English and French and Latin, and Edmund was so utterly at the mercy of her strength that she struggled against her own aching need to collapse the few yards more to water shallow enough that Jasper's trailing legs touched bottom and he stood up, releasing her from his weight. From there she was able to wrestle Edmund and her skirts to the bank, Jasper splashing beside her.

Ignoring Lady Adela's sobbing and leaving Jasper to help

himself, she pulled Edmund out of the water, rolled him onto his belly, and pounded on his back. He retched and gagged, water came out of his mouth, and he began to cry. Satisfied he was breathing sufficiently, Frevisse sank down in the soaking mess of her gown, fixed her gaze on Jasper's white but unwailing face, and demanded, "How could you be such fools as to both fall in?"

He began to shudder, sank down on the ground, drew his knees up against his chest, and wrapped his arms around them, holding tightly to himself. "We didn't fall," he whispered. "Someone pushed us."

Chapter

◣ 14 ◢

THE TWO WOMEN working in the kitchen garden spied them as they straggled out from among the trees and came running with exclaims to help. Without answering their questions, Frevisse ordered, "Take the boys to Jenet. I'll bring Lady Adela."

She had already told Jasper and then Edmund when he was more recovered that they were not to say to anyone else that they had been pushed. "Nor you either, my lady," she had added fiercely to Lady Adela, goaded by fear as much as by anger. "And after this when you're told to stay where you've been put, maybe you'll do it!"

Edmund and Jasper had nodded miserable, dripping agreement. Now they clung to her hands, one on either side of her, resisting being given over to the women, but Frevisse handed them firmly away. "You need to be dry and put to bed as soon as may be." And inside the cloister walls in safety. "I can't walk fast with these soaked skirts. Go on. I'll be there when I may."

They let the women pick them up then, Edmund's head drooping down onto Joan's shoulder.

With a belated thought, Frevisse asked the women, "Have

you seen anybody else while you've been out here? Has anyone else come by?"

"No, my lady. There's been no one, not nearby, save you. Most everyone's gone to the haying," Joan said readily. The other woman nodded agreement.

Frevisse gestured them to go on. Edmund had closed his eyes, but Jasper looked back at Frevisse all the way out of sight.

Seeming not to notice but with a small ache for him in her heart where she did not want it to be, Frevisse took Lady Adela's hand, kicked her soaked skirts away from her legs—even wrung out, they were a burden and bother— and followed, wishing there were someone to carry *her*, she was so exhausted. But there was not and she said a prayer for strength and kept on, one bare foot after another. Her shoes were somewhere in the bottom of the pool. One each in exchange for the boys' lives, she reminded herself, but the charity of the thought was forced. What she wanted was to spank them and Lady Adela very hard for their foolishness, and she dwelt on that thought because until she had them all, including herself, back inside the nunnery walls, she did not want to think about the possibility that whoever had pushed them into the water had almost surely still been there, hidden among the trees, watching, while she dragged them out.

But he was surely gone now, knowing the alarm would be raised. He would be somewhere else long before she could tell Master Naylor to send searchers. All the same, some sort of search would have to be made and soon. She would have to talk to Master Naylor quickly. No, she would have to talk to Dame Claire first. To explain what had happened, and to consult over what had to be done both to better protect the boys and to find whomever had attacked them.

No, she amended, pulling her skirts away from her legs again; first she had to change into dry clothing.

By St. Benedict's Rule, the dorter was supposed to be a large room where all the nuns slept communally, but in the centuries since St. Benedict wrote it, the Rule had eased in certain areas. The large dorter was divided into wooden-walled cells for each nun, where she slept and kept her personal belongings.

The curtain drawn across her cell's open end, Frevisse took off her wet, muddy gown and undergown and from the chest beside her bed took her only change of clothing, a gown and undergown identical to the first except they were clean and dry. She had meant to put them on after her weekly bath but there was no help for it now.

She concentrated on drying herself and re-dressing, but her mind was not interested in that problem. As she fussed at the row of buttons from the black undergown's elbow to wrist, the one thought that pushed at her was that someone wanted the boys dead.

A chance attempt against them by a killer passing casually by? Too unlikely to bother considering. There had to be a particular reason someone wanted them dead. Who? And for what reason?

It was hard to imagine it was someone of the nunnery or the village. So far as nearly everyone knew, they were only boys who had had misfortune on a journey. One of their own people? Why? Or someone else, from outside, who knew who they were and had somehow found them here? But again, why kill them?

Their mother was in danger, not of death but certainly censure and probably polite but ruthless imprisonment, for her imprudent marriage. The late king had imprisoned his stepmother for years for no better reason than that he disliked her. But how did their mother's indiscretion put Edmund and Jasper in danger?

Did someone want revenge against Queen Katherine and was willing to take her sons' lives to have it? There was a possibility, Frevisse supposed. Or it could even be revenge against their father. A Welsh feud and nothing to do with royalty at all?

No. If it had been as simple as that, Maryon would have said so.

Frevisse tugged impatiently at her sleeve, fighting the last button closed.

So suppose it was not against anyone else but simply a direct desire to have them dead. Because on their mother's side at least they were of royal blood? But not full blood. They were young King Henry's half brothers, and what royal blood they had was French, not English; they were no threat to his throne.

She slipped her gown over her head, with its open-hanging sleeves and full fall of black fabric from her shoulders to her feet, shook it straight, and reached for her belt; and stopped, the belt in her hands, as another thought came to her.

Young King Henry, their half brother and almost all of fifteen years old, was king of France as well as king of England. He held England by right of blood through his father. He held France through his mother, through the treaty her French royal father had made with England, naming her his last legitimate child and her husband and their children heirs of the French throne.

Did that mean that somehow Edmund and Jasper could be used as pawns against their brother, could be made to serve in some sort of French claim against England's hold on France?

Frevisse did not see how, but that did not mean it was not

possible. St. Frideswide's was too removed from the world
in general by site and purpose and inclination—rumors
from Banbury sometimes seemed as remote as anything
heard from London or France—for her to be able to
accurately judge what might or might not be likely in that
regard. There was no way she could hope to understand the
intricacies of court politics. And this particular guess might
be wide of the mark. But somebody, for some reason,
wanted possession of the boys very badly. That was why
they had been sent on their way to Wales: to keep them out
of someone's hands. And now it was certain that someone
wanted them dead. The same someone? Another someone?

She buckled the belt into place around her waist and took
up her wimple and veil. They at least had stayed dry enough
to be put back on, and she did so absently, feeling to make
sure her hair was completely covered by the white wimple
before pinning the black veil into place over it while her
mind went on with her questions.

Someone wanted the boys, either alive and in his power
or else dead and beyond anyone's use. Of that much she
could be sure. As for who that someone could be . . . She
stood completely still, staring at the floor without seeing it,
frozen by the certainty of her thought. It was said King
Henry would come of age this year, be given his royal
power, and the men who had formed factions around him all
these years of his minority would now have to contend not
only with each other but for the King's favor if they hoped
to share in power. And of those men the two greatest were
Henry Beaufort, Bishop of Winchester, and Humphrey
Plantagenet, Duke of Gloucester. The King's great-uncle
and uncle, both ambitious men who had believed all through
the royal minority that each should have had more power
in the government than they did. Who knew what either of
them might make of such untoward inconveniences as royal

half brothers with a putative claim to the French throne? For a surety, either of them could make something of it; they had the necessary power.

Frevisse had briefly had—much against her will—some dealings with the bishop of Winchester. He had not seemed the sort of man who would order children killed. He would undoubtedly be willing to have them in his power, yes, but dead? She did not believe that of him.

The duke of Gloucester, on the other hand, was said to be out of all proportion ambitious, proud even beyond his exalted place. And if King Henry died without fathering a child, the duke would succeed him on the throne.

Her legs gone weak, Frevisse sank down to sit on the edge of her bed. What sort of power could a man like that turn against St. Frideswide's if he chose? She slid forward onto her knees on the floor below the crucifix hung on her wall. *Kyrie, eleison, Christe, eleison* . . . Lord, have mercy, Christ, have mercy . . .

She wished her uncle Thomas Chaucer were still alive. He had known both how to use power and how to protect himself from it. But he was dead and she had already written to his daughter Alice, which now seemed as if it might have been a foolish thing to do for the same reason it had seemed sensible before: her husband was one of the men maneuvering for power around the young King, the men among whom almost certainly was someone who wanted Edmund and Jasper dead.

Agnus dei, eleison . . . Lamb of god, have mercy . . .

Frevisse's breath caught. Lambs were what they were here in St. Frideswide's. Not simply the boys but everyone. Innocent lambs who had no way to struggle against the kind of power that might be turned against them.

But not lambs for the slaughter. Not if they were innocent enough. So long as no one of the priory knew who the boys were, so long as everyone here could claim they had not known the boys were sought by powerful men, then even if the boys were eventually discovered and retribution was demanded for having sheltered them, Dame Claire could claim on the priory's behalf that it had been done in innocence, in simple obedience to the Rule to give shelter and comfort to those in need. So long as that were true, the chance was very good that no punishment would fall on St. Frideswide's.

Only on Frevisse, if her part in it were known.

But better on only her than on everyone. What mattered was to keep both the boys and the priory safe, and therefore the boys' secret to herself alone so that whatever the cost might eventually be, it would fall on only her.

She raised her head from her clasped hands, drew a deep, steadying breath, and stood up to go in search of Dame Claire.

When she understood that Frevisse's matter was urgent beyond the ordinary, Dame Claire brought her into the infirmary for greater privacy, and though the infirmary was no longer her domain, she went to the shelves of herbs, her hands moving among them familiarly because Sister Thomasine had changed nothing she could help changing since she became infirmarian, until she found what she wanted, took a few sprigs of last summer's dried lavender from one of the boxes, and handed it to Frevisse, saying, "Smell them. They'll quiet your nerves."

Frevisse had hoped she was not that obvious and bent her head obediently over the lavender, inhaling deeply.

As calmly as if they were discussing a simple kitchen matter, Dame Claire said, "So there's a dark secret concerning these children that you and Domina Edith feel it better I do not know."

"Best that no one knows," Frevisse said evenly, keeping

her voice both firm and calm. "Or if that can't be managed, then as few as possible."

"But they're in some sort of danger, you believe."

"Yes."

"You're certain, then, they weren't just claiming to have been pushed to avoid admitting they'd fallen in by carelessness?"

"They were too honestly terrified. Jasper especially." She had belatedly had another thought. "And they said yesterday that their fall into the pigsty was no accident either. No one paid them any heed, but maybe they were right. I need to talk to Master Naylor. Someone should look through the woods around the pool to see if there's any trace of who was there."

"And Maryon should be told. She's obviously not their mother—" Dame Claire made it a question but fixed her eyes on Frevisse, expecting confirmation. Frevisse nodded wryly, accepting that Dame Claire had already guessed more than Frevisse wished she had. "—but they're in her care so she should know," Dame Claire finished. "Is the lavender helping?"

Frevisse had gone on unthinkingly inhaling its slightly musty sweetness the while. Now, at Dame Claire's question, she realized her knots of keyed-up intensity had eased and left her mind more clear on what had to be done. "Yes," she said in surprise.

"That's good then." Dame Claire turned from the shelves to face her fully. "If I trusted no one else in all the world, I trust Domina Edith and she's depended on you in other matters like this. I'll accept I should not know why the boys are in danger, and you have my leave to do what you think needs to be done, and to come and go as you see fit, until this trouble is settled. Is that sufficient?"

"Very sufficient," Frevisse said. The matter was now

fully in her hands. Come of it what might, it would be on her head. "I'll go about it then."

The bell began to ring to None.

"Prayers first," Dame Claire said. "Those always first."

Frevisse opened her mouth to protest that the sooner the woods were searched the better, then closed it. Whoever had been there was long gone, and anything he had left behind would still be there when prayers were over. Obediently, she bowed her head and folded her hands into her sleeves, ready to follow Dame Claire to the church.

"And afterwards have Sister Juliana give you a new pair of shoes before you go out again," Dame Claire added.

Later, in the shadow of the gateway to the outer yard, Master Naylor eyed Frevisse with extreme disfavor. "And you're sure of this? They're not lying to save themselves a smacking?"

Frevisse wondered in passing if Edmund and Jasper had ever had a smacking, and doubted it, even as she said, "They're due for one anyway, leaving the cloister as they did. And, no, I don't think they're lying. You know a child who's only pretending to be frightened looks different from one who really is."

What might have been a smile lifted one corner of Master Naylor's mouth. "My boy has tried that fooling a time or two, yes. Good enough then." The brief amusement was gone from Master Naylor's face. "I'll go myself to see what I can find around the pool."

"Would you try to find out, too, if anyone unfamiliar was seen around here today? Or anyone not where they should have been?"

"With the haying started, most everyone that can be spared is in the fields. They'll know if anyone wasn't there who should be, and the same with the few left to usual tasks. But by the same hand, with nigh everyone in the fields, someone could come and go around the priory and not be noticed so long as they kept clear of the hay field."

"I know. But ask anyway, on the chance someone was seen, something noticed."

"Aye, Dame. But you'd best tell the boys' own folk what's toward."

"That's where I'm bound for next." Little though she liked the idea of telling Maryon about this.

Master Naylor, straightening from his bow, fixed her with the demand, "Why would anyone be trying to kill these boys?"

Taken unready by his bluntness, Frevisse took too long to finally say, "I don't know."

"But you have ideas."

"Yes." She forestalled his next question by saying, "I can't tell them to you."

He stared at her an uncomfortable time more, and she met his look with her own, until he nodded impassive acceptance, bowed again, and left her.

Satisfied that he would do all that she had asked and regretting what next she had to do, Frevisse turned toward the guesthall.

As Frevisse explained yet again what had happened, Maryon rose from where she had been sitting on the foot of Sir Gawyn's bed and, twisting her hands around each other, paced the narrow width of the room and back again. Frevisse finished, "They're safe now, tucked into bed and Tibby and Jenet both watching them."

Maryon snapped, "Jenet is useless!"

Frevisse silently agreed but only said, "They won't be left to just her care anymore."

"They should be brought here," Sir Gawyn said from the bed. He had been standing, holding to the bedpost but on his own feet, when Frevisse entered, and though he had lain down again, he was markedly better than yesterday, pale but no longer the ill gray that he had been. He seemed stronger, too, but Frevisse wondered how much of his strength came from his will to have it and not because he was actually that much better.

Now she countered his suggestion with, "I don't think so. They'll be far more vulnerable here than in the cloister."

"But they don't stay in the cloister!" Maryon pointed out. "This is the second time they've slipped out."

"We'll keep better watch on them after this."

"Not so well as we would." Sir Gawyn shifted himself higher against the head of the bed; he was becoming more adroit at managing with only his unhurt arm. "Mistress Maryon and I know them and they're used to us. And to Will and Colwin, too. The four of us know what's at stake. No one could guard them better the little while we'll still be here."

"It will be some while yet before you can leave," Frevisse said.

"Not very long." He ignored Maryon's protesting gesture. "Now that we've been found, we have to leave as soon as may be. Tomorrow if I could."

"You can't!" Maryon said. "Not so soon with your shoulder."

"No," Sir Gawyn agreed bitterly. "Not as soon as that. But soon. Two days or three."

Maryon bit down on another protest. Her face smoothed into the blandness of a cat convincing someone it was not eyeing the cream, and she said reasonably, "But whatever we decide, for now at least they're in bed and sleeping and we'll not disturb them. There's nothing can be done before tomorrow, come what may."

"No," Sir Gawyn broodingly agreed. "Not before tomorrow."

Will had entered while they talked and remained standing

just inside the door. Now, very quietly, he said, "You can't ride before another week is out, sire. Not without risk of opening your wound."

"We'll be risking more if I don't ride!" Sir Gawyn snapped.

Will opened his mouth to say something else, but Maryon interposed, "Did you find someone to mend your shirt?"

"Aye, one of the women here will do it." Will shrugged the question away.

Maryon, intent on diverting him from Sir Gawyn's shoulder, cut off whatever next he meant to say with, "And did you tell someone that Sir Gawyn can eat a heavier meal tonight than he has been?"

"I've told the cook that, yes," Will said.

"And—"

He cut her off impatiently. "I've seen to it all. Sire—"

Sir Gawyn cut them both off with a small sound of annoyance. "Enough, the both of you. I won't be worried over." And added, more to Will than Maryon, "I'm not your bone."

Will's expression shut abruptly down to the blank obedience of a servant. He bowed silently and fixed his look somewhere on the far wall. Sir Gawyn gave his attention over to Frevisse, saying, "Let things stay as they are for today. But tomorrow I think there's changes to be made. Our thanks for what you did. It will be remembered."

Recognizing dismissal, Frevisse curtsied, said, "Their safety is thanks enough. No other remembrance is necessary," matching his manner, and gladly left him to Maryon and Will. He had her prayers. She wished him well, both for his own sake and because the sooner he was gone the better; the boys would go with him, cease to be so direct a threat to St. Frideswide's and no longer her concern.

But until then they were, and she needed to find what else could be done to keep them safe.

Chapter

🔳 15 🔳

FREVISSE RETURNED TO the cloister and went into the church. Neglect of her duties as sacrist had not been included in Dame Claire's permission to see to the matter of the boys. In the sacristy she took out the third best silver-plated candlesticks and set to polishing them. With even the least diligence, she should be able to occupy her mind with the necessities of duty—when silver polishing was done, there was always the need to inspect the altar cloths for frays or tears—until Vespers, unless Master Naylor sent to say he had word of something.

What the something might be she supposed she could speculate on to no profit. Whoever had shoved Edmund and Jasper into the pool had taken care the boys not see him, even though he had not intended they live long enough for it to matter if they had. So he was probably careful enough to have left no footprints worth mentioning unless the attacker was phenomenally careless enough to walk in the mud somewhere, and even then soft shoe soles would leave nothing but an undistinguished foot-shape good only for determining if he had been generally large or small or medium.

It would be convenient if he had left a torn bit of his

clothing on a rough branch somewhere. She supposed she could hope for that much anyway. And there was still the chance he had been seen going to or coming from the woods, but there were hedges and walls enough, and nearly everyone gone to the haying anyway, that he would have to be either a dolt or unlucky to have been seen except by unlikely accident.

Except that if he were a stranger, he would not know his way around well enough to make such good use of walls and hedges.

But if he were a stranger, he would be more likely to be noticed even when he was well away from the stream and not bothering with concealment anymore.

But why had he been by the stream, in the woods, at all? Surely not in the specific hope of having a chance against the boys. Their coming there by chance would have seemed too unlikely. But then again, had their going there been only chance? Was there something the children had not told her? There could in fact be a great deal they had not told her; she had given them no chance to tell her much of anything. She could talk to Lady Adela this evening and the boys tomorrow.

But that did not solve the problem of who had lain in wait in the woods for them. Or not lain in wait? Suppose it had just been someone wanting to harm anyone who happened along and Edmund and Jasper had happened to hand. That kind of madness was not impossible. And ugly though it was, it would be less complicated than the other possibilities she had been considering.

She wanted very much to hear that a stranger had been seen somewhere near today. Preferably a disreputable hedge-crawler who looked the sort to be up to anything mean and hurtful.

She realized she had been polishing the same curve of

candlestick past any need, and turned it over to come at a different place but found she was finished with it, so set it back into its aumbry, folded her polishing cloth, and decided she would be better off in her choir stall praying until Vespers. But as she left the sacristy, Sister Juliana approached her and gestured that she was wanted at the cloister door. Frevisse silently indicated her thanks and went.

As she came out into the warm sunshine of the yard from the cool cloister shadows, Master Naylor stood up from where he had been sitting on the well edge and came down the steps toward her, his face, even for Master Naylor, grim.

"You found something?" she asked.

"More than you asked for. A dead man floating facedown in the pool."

Frevisse gasped and had to draw in new breath before she could force out, "Who?"

"The man Colwin. Drowned, by the look of him."

"Colwin?" The boys' Colwin who had cheerfully taken them into the stable yesterday? "In the pool? Drowned?" she repeated blankly.

"Unless he drowned elsewhere and then walked himself there. He didn't wash down that babbling stream in any flood, that's sure."

"But the pool isn't that deep. Not over his head if he stood up."

"Then obviously he didn't stand up," Master Naylor snapped.

Frevisse sat down on one of the well steps. "This isn't what I expected."

"Nor did he, I suppose," Master Naylor said acidly. But his anger was cover for his own dismay and, relenting, he said more reasonably, "But we're maybe making too much of it. His clothing was on the bank. He might have been in to swim, had a cramp and drowned."

Her wits beginning to gather back, Frevisse said, "How did he happen to know about the pool? Had someone told him about it or did he happen on it himself?" And then drown there the same afternoon the boys nearly did? She could not make that seem likely.

"The man who found him said he wondered how he came to be there," Master Naylor said. "He wasn't given to wandering around since he came here, apparently."

"Has Father Henry been told? Where's the body now?"

"He's been told. He's gone with the men I've sent to bring it in."

Frevisse stood up. "I want to see it."

Master Naylor hesitated. "It won't be a goodly sight."

"He can't have been in the water so long the corpse has turned awful," Frevisse said bluntly. "It's barely been half the afternoon since I was there."

At this evidence of a strong stomach, Master Naylor— who should have known better about Frevisse—closed his mouth to a tight line. He turned on his heel and walked away toward the gate to the side yard. Frevisse, assuming that was as near to agreement as she was going to have from him, rose and followed.

The four men sent to bring Colwin in were just at the postern gate as Master Naylor and Frevisse came out, the body on a hurdle carried between them and Father Henry walking alongside, praying aloud from his prayer book. He and Latin were not so comfortable together as they might have been, but he made up for his inaccuracies with intensity, and a soul cast unexpectedly from a body was in even worse peril than usually came at the moment of death; prayers as many and rapid as possible were needed to save it and, hopefully, ease its passing. Father Henry neither paused nor glanced up from his work as Master Naylor ordered, "Bring it this way," and the men shifted course to follow him aside to the open-sided shed where the hanks of wool were hung to dry after dying. No one was there today, nor any wool hanging, but there was a rough worktable and the men gratefully slid the piece of fencing onto it; Colwin had not been a small man.

Frevisse was grateful that the haying had nearly everyone out to the fields. Besides herself and Master Naylor, there were only the four men curious but saying nothing as Master Naylor ordered them to stand back, and Father Henry across the table from her, still intent in his prayers as she came near for her first clear look at the body.

Colwin's clothing was in a folded pile at his side, except that he still wore his short breech covering his loins, as men often did when they went in swimming. A single long look told Frevisse there were no wounds on the body's front.

"Turn him over, please," she said.

The men gave Master Naylor quick, questioning looks. He twitched his hand, bidding one of them obey her, and the fellow reluctantly did, heaving Colwin's flaccid body onto its side, then to its belly. Water came out of the mouth. An arm flopped over the table edge. Frevisse lifted it back to beside the body. The flesh was unnaturally cool but still soft to the touch, he had been dead so little a while.

There was no wounds on his back either.

"Was there more water come out of him when you picked him up?" she asked.

"Much more, my lady," the man said.

"So he was alive when he went into the water," Master Naylor said.

"Alive enough to breathe awhile," Frevisse agreed.

She touched his head, feeling to be sure the skull was intact. It was; no bones shifted under her probing. But . . .

She hesitated, felt again along the back curve of the skull, and then asked Master Naylor, "Do you feel anything here?"

Master Naylor felt, felt again, and said, "There's a lump." He parted Colwin's dark hair. "A large lump and new, I'd guess, but the skin wasn't broken. It didn't bleed."

"Big enough he could have been knocked unconscious by it?" Frevisse asked.

"He might have been," Master Naylor agreed. "He fell, likely."

But where in the pool or beside the pool could he have fallen hard enough to knock himself out? There were no rocks that Frevisse remembered. A heavy tree branch? Not overhanging the pool so that he would have fallen after striking it. And besides . . . She felt the lump again. It was a round lump, very localized, not oblong as it would have been if he had fallen against a branch or anything more than a small, round rock.

"When was he last seen?" she asked.

The men looked among themselves. The one who had rolled the body over suggested, "Dinner maybe? Midday?" There were nods of vague agreement from the others. "Then he went off. Don't know where?" he asked and the others shook their heads, agreeing they did not know.

"Will you ask around, to see if anyone saw him after that?" she requested Master Naylor.

"There're not many others here just now. All we can spare are out to the haying. But I'll ask."

Frevisse nodded. It was the same in the guesthalls and in the cloister itself. Only the most absolutely needed servants remained; this time of year the needs of haying came first in almost everything.

"Roll him back over," she said. The man did and she stood looking into the dead face. Someone had closed his eyes but with the handling his jaw had dropped in death's slackness. His hair had begun to dry on the way up from the stream but lay lank and formless around his head. He had not been particularly prepossessing in life and was less so now; but he had been alive and someone had taken his life from him, without chance of confession or absolution. Had taken more than his life: had taken his surety of salvation. For what?

She prodded through his clothing and pulled out his belt with his purse and dagger still hanging from it. The dagger was not especially fine but good enough to steal if one was out for theft. She looked in the purse. A silver penny, a bent halfpenny, and a well-used pair of dice. His money, such as it was, had not been wanted, either.

She put money and dice back into the purse and gathered up it and the belt and dagger. "I'll take these to his knight," she said.

"Is there anything more?" Master Naylor asked.

"No."

He told the men to go on with the body. They went, Father Henry with them still audibly praying, but Frevisse stayed where she was. She had more to ask Master Naylor, but he asked first, "So it looks like a drowning. Was it?"

"He drowned," Frevisse agreed. "But I'd guess he was hit on the head first and dumped in to drown afterward."

"Unless he was already in the water, swimming, when he was struck."

"The effect was the same," Frevisse said. "Was he the sort to go off by himself?"

"No. He settled himself among our folk almost as soon as he came here and has been fellow-well-met ever since. Generally liked so far as I could tell. The only reason he wasn't to the haying with most of the rest was he'd been told to keep close here in case he was needed."

"Needed? For what?"

"You're the one who knows what's toward here, not I," Master Naylor said. "You tell me."

"Apparently I don't know as much of what's toward as I need to," Frevisse returned. "I can't even guess whether he was more likely to have been killed by chance or to a purpose, by a stranger or someone here who knew him. Had he had quarrels since he came here with anyone at all?"

"So near as I could tell, he was easy tempered and easily gotten on with. No, that's not all true. He was in heavy words this morning sometime with that other fellow who came with him. The squire."

"Will? Sir Gawyn's squire? They were quarreling?" That might make things simpler, though she had not thought Will the ill-tempered sort to quarrel and then stalk and kill a man.

But Master Naylor shook his head. "Not an outright argument, I'd judge. A disagreement maybe, with Will— that's the name?—frowning and trying to make a point that Colwin just grinned at and shook his head against."

"But you don't know what it was about?"

"It was no concern of mine. I didn't ask. Maybe someone else knows."

"Was Colwin after women any?"

"Not that I saw or heard of."

"Could you ask around and see what's said of him? And if anyone knows what he and Will talked of that time?"

"That I'll do. And send a man I shouldn't have to spare this time of year to Montfort again. And tell people to keep an eye out for strangers. And hope this is the end of it. Is there aught else I should see to?"

"No. I'll go myself to tell Sir Gawyn and Mistress Maryon about this." The bell began to ring inside the wall. "After Vespers," she added with resignation.

"I'll go tell them, if you like. They should know as soon as may be."

"I'd be grateful if you did," she said. And then changed her mind. "No, I'd rather do it myself." To see their reactions as they heard of the death. "So I should do it now."

Chapter

🖅 16 🖅

When Frevisse came in, Sir Gawyn was across the room from his bed, leaning on Will, Maryon close on his other side in case of need, but upright and walking. Barely walking and obviously weak but moving mostly on his own.

The window, kept so definitely closed until now, was open, letting in the warm day's fresh air and the late afternoon sunlight to shine high against the wall above the bed.

They all looked up as Frevisse paused in the open doorway, their expressions glad with Sir Gawyn's triumph changing to surprise. Maryon glanced toward the sound of the bell as if it were something she could see and started to say, "Shouldn't you—" then froze, the gladness of the moment going out of her. "The boys. What's happened?"

"Nothing to them. They're in bed and probably sleeping. It's Colwin. He's dead."

She wanted particularly Will's reaction, but at her words he bent his head until his bright hair fell like a curtain, and she could not see his face. Letting loose of Sir Gawyn with his right hand, he crossed himself as Maryon and Sir

Gawyn, their expressions stricken, also did, Sir Gawyn asking as he did, "How?"

"Drowned in the stream below the nunnery. There's a pool there in the woods. He was found in the water."

"Drowned?" Sir Gawyn repeated. "How? Why didn't someone help him?"

"Apparently he was swimming alone. Was that usual for him?"

"Not Colwin," Sir Gawyn said. "He liked companions, whatever he did."

Will nodded agreement.

"Or he may not have been swimming," Frevisse said. "There's evidence he was struck on the back of the head. He was maybe unconscious when he went into the water."

Sir Gawyn made a wide gesture of a grief stronger than Frevisse had yet seen in him. And with the frustration of helplessness and anger.

But it was Maryon who put into words the fear surely growing in all of them. "They've found us and they won't stop until there are none of us left! Until there's no one to come between them and the children!"

Will raised his head, color flooding his cheeks. "No one is going to hurt the children," he said. "We swore it to their lady mother."

He looked at Sir Gawyn, and the knight met his gaze, their faces matched in rigid determination.

"We can't keep our oaths if we're dead!" Maryon said with angry fear.

"So we must stay alive," Sir Gawyn answered. A sweat was breaking out over his pallor. He sagged on his squire's arm. "I have to lie down again."

Maryon caught him around the waist, careful of his hurt shoulder, but it was on sturdy Will that most of his weight leaned as they helped him back to bed and laid him down on it, Will lifting his feet up and swinging them around to stretch him out flat. Sir Gawyn lay with his eyes closed, breathing as if after great effort; but when he had steadied, he said, eyes still closed, "We have to bring the children here. Where we can guard them."

"They're better kept in the nunnery," Will said flatly. "They're harder to come at there."

Sir Gawyn made a derogatory sound. "Simple walls, unguarded doors, no men—" he started, but Maryon interrupted. With a sharp look meant to silence both men, she said, "We can talk of it in a while. Dame Frevisse needs to go to Vespers."

It was direction to Frevisse as well as them, but the bell had long since ceased to ring; Frevisse was hopelessly late and she wanted to ask her questions now, before they had more time to think. "When was the last time any of you saw Colwin?"

The three of them looked among themselves, then Maryon answered, "This afternoon sometime. After Sext?" she asked Sir Gawyn and Will.

"I think so, yes," Sir Gawyn said. Will nodded agreement.

"Where?"

"Here. He came to ask if there was any chance the horses could be put out to pasture for just an afternoon. He thought they were going stale, kept so much in the stables."

"I wish they could be turned out," Sir Gawyn said, his eyes closed again. "But we need them sure to hand if we have to . . . depart suddenly."

"So you told him he couldn't," Frevisse said. "And that was the last you saw of him?"

"Yes."

Despite her now calm voice, Maryon stood with her hands clutched rigidly together. "Where is he? What's been done with him?"

"Master Naylor had some of the men bring him in. I don't know where he is now or what's to be done."

Will straightened from where he had slumped against a bedpost. "I'll go see to him. It should be . . . one of us . . . sees to him."

Sir Gawyn moved a hand, bidding him go, and he left the room.

"Were you here all the afternoon?" Frevisse asked Maryon.

"Most of it. I went to lie down awhile sometime. Around None, I think."

"And Will? Was he here all the while?"

"In and out, as always." Maryon sharpened to the questions. "Why are you asking?" she demanded.

"The crowner has to be summoned back for this. We'd best think about what questions he'll be asking and what we'll answer."

"God's nails!" said Sir Gawyn from the bed. His good arm was now across his eyes, his body slack; but his tone hardened. "We have to be out of here before he comes."

"Gawyn, you can't," Maryon protested.

"I have to. We can't expect the luck we had last time he was here. He's a fool but even a fool can see things eventually. I can ride if need be. Tomorrow I'll ride."

With a slight curtsy that no one heeded, Frevisse left them to argue it between them, with mental note to herself to tell Dame Claire what he intended. Dame Claire would surely have something to say about it, though whether she were heeded was another matter.

Like everywhere else, most of the guesthall servants were gone to the hay fields, but Ela came limping to intercept Frevisse as she crossed toward the outer door. "He's out there," Ela said, pointing to the door. "I thought I'd warn you."

"Warn me? Who's out there?"

"Will. The squire. He was going somewhere, I passed him going out as I was coming in, and then when I turned in the doorway because I'd heard something odd, he'd just sat down on the steps out there with his head in his hands and was crying. Still is, I think. I thought I'd warn you. What'd he be crying for?"

"Another of the men he came with is dead. Drowned. The one called Colwin."

Ela clicked her tongue in shock and sympathy. "Poor man. Poor, poor man. He was a good one, too. No trouble to anyone. And drowned. That's a pity, isn't it?"

"Was he in here at all today?"

"About Sext, I recall seeing him."

"And Mistress Maryon and Will, did they come and go at all this afternoon?"

"Will did. I saw him go out at least once, maybe twice. I didn't see the lady at all. But I wasn't here the whole time and couldn't say for certain about any of them, except the knight. He's kept in. Not strong enough to go anywhere, poor man."

"Thank you," Frevisse said and went on. As Ela had said, Will was sitting on the guesthall steps, halfway down to the yard, his elbows on his knees and his face in his hands, and by the shiver of his shoulders he was indeed crying.

Softly but not trying to hide that she was coming, Frevisse went down and stood a few steps below him. "Will," she said, and her own gentleness surprised her.

He raised his head. His cheeks were wet, his eyes tear-brimmed, and he made no attempt to conceal it; for sufficient reason the strongest man cried and it was no shame. Seeing her, he said, "My lady," and started to rise, but Frevisse gestured for him to stay seated.

"I didn't know you and Colwin were such near friends," she said.

"We weren't. There wasn't what could be called friendship between us. But he was—" He did not have the words for what he wanted to say, and shrugged his broad shoulders.

"But you were used to him. He was familiar," Frevisse offered sympathetically.

"That's it," Will said. "You grow used to people, and he was none so bad. You could depend on him. He was a cheery sort. And—" Will fought the grief tightening his face. "And he had hopes. Things he wanted to do. It's not right for him to be dead."

Inwardly Frevisse wholeheartedly and bitterly agreed that it was not right, that things were very wrong and Colwin's death was only part of it.

Drying his face on his shirtsleeve, Will said, "It's all come too fast. Hery and the others and now him. And Sir Gawyn hurt, so there's only me."

"What happened to your other shirt?" Frevisse asked.

Will looked at his sleeve as if surprised to find it on his arm. "What? Oh. My other shirt. I tore it, exercising the horses this afternoon. One of the women in the hall says she'll mend it. I've not the knack and surely Mistress Maryon won't do it for me."

Following an earlier guess and the slight edge to his voice, Frevisse said, "She would if it were for Sir Gawyn though."

"Oh, aye, she'd do that right enough," Will agreed. "She's set for him and means to have him if she can."

"And you're not pleased at the idea."

Warming to Frevisse's sympathy, he said, "She's butter and cream when she talks, and there's no denying she's pretty enough to look on, though not so young as she might be. But her mind is like a whip, and when she's not pleased her tongue matches it."

"You don't like her."

"Like or not doesn't matter. She does her duties as well or

better than anyone else could. I'll grant her that free and clear. But she's set herself for Sir Gawyn and she'd be no good for him."

"Why not? They seem fond of one another."

"Fond doesn't fill the belly. He needs to wed money, especially now he's—" Will shied away from saying it. "And so does she, come to that, having none of her own. So I don't know what she's playing at with him now."

"They're mayhap in love."

"That's a fool's game," Will said. "Love is no use if you've not the wherewithal to clothe your back, and if things have gone as wrong with her grace as they look to have—" He froze, realizing he was saying what he should not, then looked around to be sure no one had been near enough to hear, before fixing a sharp look on Frevisse. "You know about that. Mistress Maryon said you knew."

"I know." She prompted him to go on. "'If things have gone as wrong with her grace . . .'"

"Then there's no livelihood for either of them anymore, and they'd best be looking for what they can do next."

"But only after they've run the risk of taking Edmund and Jasper on to Wales. Why are you staying with them if it's all so bad? Shouldn't you be looking for your own gain, too?"

"I'm Sir Gawyn's squire," Will said, "and glad on it. There's been no one I'd rather serve, and have done most of my life. It's not my place to leave him, come what may. And I'm the queen's man, too." His voice warmed. "She's as fine a lady as ever was. And she loves her boys. I've seen her with them. If the only thing there's left for me to do in service to her is see them safe away, then that's what I'll do. For my lady's sake."

His words and warmth showed his grief had a core of gladness because it was grown around that most chivalrous of loves—love for a lady unattainable but seen as everything that could be desired and admired in a woman. For just the moment his face shone with it.

How old was he? Frevisse wondered. In his thirties somewhere, near her age, she would have guessed. But with his gladness on him, he looked younger, more as he must have been when his life was new and there was more hope in it than now.

But that was not what she was here for, and she asked, "What did you do all this afternoon?"

The gladness faded, lost again behind present needs. As if those were a burden becoming too heavy to lift, Will said, "I was here and there. In and out, as need be. Mostly in."

"Except for exercising the horses."

"Except for that," he agreed. He stood up. "I have to see to Colwin."

Frevisse did not move out of his way. "You were in heavy talk with Colwin this morning. What was that about?"

Will dropped his gaze toward his feet, paused before he answered from behind his forelock, "The horses, that would have been. They didn't look like they were being ridden enough. If we have to go on the sudden, we need them sharp. Colwin said they were fine, I said they weren't." Will shrugged. "That's all it was."

"He wasn't worried or frightened over anything? Over anyone?"

"No more than the rest of us are and probably not that much. So long as Colwin's skin was whole and his belly full, he was satisfied with whatever came his way."

The words brought up the reality that what had come Colwin's way was death. For a long moment, Frevisse and Will looked deep at each other, each of their faces very still and dark with the thought. Then Frevisse stepped aside to let him pass, and he bowed to her and went his way.

Chapter

⊠ 17 ⊠

VESPERS HAD ENDED and the nuns were coming from the church as Frevisse returned to the cloister. Seeing her, they stopped, united in their disapproval. Under their silent, accusing stares and knowing her fault in missing the office was the more grievous because she had gone directly against what Dame Claire had told her to do, Frevisse stopped a few yards short of them, in front of Dame Claire, and went down onto her knees. Head bent over her clasped hands, she said, "I am in fault and know it, confess it, beg pardon for it from you all."

The words fell into the deep well of the nuns' silence and lay there awhile before Dame Claire said, "Your fault is acknowledged and your confession accepted. You will go now into the church and stay there on your knees until Compline, without supper or recreation. We will deal with this matter at chapter tomorrow."

Frevisse bent her head lower. "Thank you, Dame," she said. And then, although the shorter way to the refectory for their supper would have been to turn and go away from her along the cloister walk, Dame Claire led the nuns past her, flowing to either side of her in a whispering of black skirts and accusing silence. It was permitted that someone in such disgrace could be kicked by her sisters as they passed; but there was strong chance that someone so indulging her disapproval might be in like position all too soon and the kick remembered when the time came, and only Sister Thomasine, for whom it was obligation not indulgence, and for the good of her soul, to punish someone, struck Frevisse's ankle with one foot as she passed, very lightly.

Knowing the others would appreciate the sight of her humility, Frevisse stayed where she was until certain they were all in the refectory. Only then did she rise unsteadily from her knees—she had gone down onto the stone flags without sufficient care—and go on along the cloister walk. No food until breakfast tomorrow. Her stomach was already beginning to rebuke her, and less gently than Dame Claire had.

But there was no help for it. She must not negate her penance and humility by resentment or regret. And she had fasted before; it was a matter of the mind accepting so that the body would, too.

With nonetheless a sigh, she entered the church, passed the choir stalls to the altar, and knelt down on the floor in front of it. Drawing her back up straight, she bowed her head. Two years ago she had spent every moment she was free to do so here, praying for peace for herself and another, both of them bound by decisions she had made to lies they could never be rid of until their deathbeds. The peace of acceptance and forgiveness for at least herself had finally come; and now, in a new and lesser need, the prayers came back to her in a rush of familiarity and comfort.

Miserere mei, Deus, secundum misericordiam tuam; secundum multitudinem miserationum tuarum dele iniquitatem meam. Penitus lava me a culpa mea, et a peccato meo

munda me. Nam iniquitatem meam ego agnosco, et pecca-
tum meum coram me est semper.

Have pity on me, God, according to your mercy; according to the greatness of your mercy wipe out my iniquity. From deep in me wash my fault, and from my sin cleanse me. For I recognize my iniquity, and my sin is in me always.

The psalm was from the Office of the Dead. She had felt dead in soul when she had turned to it that while ago and it had helped bring her back to her life. Now it was meet not so much for herself as for the dead man who was her new burden—this time, at least, through no fault of her own.

How had Colwin come to be killed?

How had he come to be along the stream at all, come to that? By chance, out walking for the simple pleasure of it? Or to some purpose—to meet someone? And met instead whoever had tried to kill the boys and been killed instead, to leave them one less protector when the next attempt was made against their lives?

She had probably been spared when she came to the boys' rescue because killing a nun was something almost anyone balked at. But Colwin would have been fair game.

But still, why had Colwin been there at all? To keep watch on the boys? No, he would have saved them if that was why he was there.

Or had it been Colwin who pushed them into the water?

Frevisse lingered over that ugly possibility. But if he had, then who had murdered *him*? To suppose he had shoved the boys in and then that someone had killed him meant supposing there had been two murderers lurking along the stream with separate purposes. She found that unlikely.

What had she missed in this? What didn't she know yet about Colwin? And about the others?

Or was she assuming too much where there was really less? Maybe Colwin's death had been an accident. Maybe he had only chanced to be there not long after the boys, had meant to swim but fallen somehow, knocked himself senseless, and drowned.

But she could not make herself believe it. Someone had tried to drown Edmund and Jasper. Someone had succeeded in drowning Colwin.

Where had Will exercised the horses this afternoon? Master Naylor would know or could find out. And she wanted to see his ripped shirt. How had it come to be ripped? Had it also perhaps been wet? It would not be wet by now. In this weather, it would have dried long since, and he could have easily had it dry before he gave it to anyone to mend. If it was ripped at all. She would have to find that out, too.

But this was not what she was supposed to be doing now. She was supposed to be praying for God's mercy for her disobedience, and if she could not pray for herself, she could at least pray for Colwin. *A porta inferi erue, Domine, animam eius.* From the gate of hell rescue, Lord, his soul.

And she should pray for Domina Edith, too, that her passing be as peaceful as her life had been, for though she was surely safe from hell, she was not bound to this world for much longer. And who knew which prayers were most needed? Everyone was in need of all the mercy God could give. Brought back to duty by her thoughts, Frevisse set herself to pray not only for them but for herself and her corrupting pride, and from there went deeper into prayer until in the freedom of it she gradually lost all sense of anything else.

The bell for Compline roused her. A little dazed with the intensity of where she had been, she gathered herself and rose stiffly to her feet. Her knees hurt but they eased as she left the church to join the others going to the chapter house for Compline, the day's quiet ending.

Nunc dimittis servum tuum, Domine, secundum verbum

tuum in pace . . . Now you dismiss your servant, Lord, according to your word in peace . . .

The words wove their rich, familiar way through the warm evening air that smelled of drying hay and sunshine and the mingled scents of flowers in the cloister garth. A late-wandering fly buzzed in through the chapter house door and out again. Like troubles, it came and went, Frevisse thought, and the flow of prayers went on as ever, a comfort and a surety beyond the griefs and alterings of every day.

Divinum auxilium maneat semper nobiscum. Divine help stay always with us.

Amen, amen, and amen again, Frevisse thought.

But tonight, instead of a moment of silence before Dame Claire dismissed them to their beds, she said, "We should pray especially now for Domina Edith. And anyone who chooses to spend the night or part of it in prayer for her in the church is free to do so."

A startled sob escaped Sister Amicia. Dame Perpetua, with tears in her own voice though she was not yet giving way to them, asked, "Could we pray beside her instead?"

"She's asked that we not. That only Sister Lucy and Sister Thomasine attend on her."

Drawn from her own concerns, Frevisse noticed for the first time that Sister Thomasine was not there, though Sister Lucy was, pallid and drawn, the only color in her face the bright pink of weeping around her eyes.

"Why only them?" Dame Alys demanded.

"Because Sister Lucy has known her longest and Sister Thomasine is infirmarian."

"What if we want to be there?" Dame Alys insisted.

"What we want isn't what matters here. For now, for this while still, Domina Edith's word is what holds highest sway."

"But what if she says who is to succeed—"

Dame Claire cut her off sharply. "If she says anything we

need to hear, Sister Lucy and Sister Thomasine will tell us."

Dame Alys gave Sister Lucy a grim glance and closed her mouth tightly over whatever else she wanted to say.

In the miserable silence Sister Emma gulped, sniffed, and asked tremulously, "It won't be long—?" She could not say the words.

"Perhaps by morning," Dame Claire said. "Perhaps another day. Hardly more." She concluded gently, firmly, "God's blessing on us all now and forever. Go in peace," dismissing them to bed or the church or—for Sister Lucy—Domina Edith's chamber. But with a small lifting of her hand, she bade Frevisse linger behind the rest, and when they were alone in the room said, "I directed some bread be left for you in the refectory. And you had best go to bed afterwards."

"I'd thought to go back to the church."

"I know, but your day hasn't been easy. You're tired and it shows. Eat and go to bed until Matins. There'll be prayings in plenty now but the flesh's willingness to bear more will wane with the hours. You'll be most in need between Matins and dawn. Go on and eat and take your turn then."

Frevisse curtsied her obedience and did not ask what Dame Claire intended to do through the night. Dame Claire's willingness to pray would not wane with the hours. But she could not help asking, "Has Domina Edith . . . Is she still conscious?"

Dame Claire shook her head. "Just before Compline she drifted into a sleep I don't think she'll awaken from."

In the refectory Frevisse found the bread, with a piece of cheese and a mug of water beside it at the end of one of the long tables. It was strange to sit alone in the bare-raftered room and eat in solitude. She gave thanks and ate because she had been told to, but her hunger was gone. No matter what had happened in her time in St. Frideswide's, there had always been the certainty of Domina Edith. Now that certainty was ending. Even with Dame Claire as prioress— for surely the election would follow Domina Edith's clear wish—things would be different, and there had been comfort in the sameness all these years.

Grief for the loss of someone most dear and unease at the unknown that must come kept her thoughts from other things until she had taken off her outer gown and veil and wimple, washed her face and hands, and lain down in bed in her cell in the dormitory with a sigh of gratefulness for the ease she had not known her body so much wanted.

The late light still lingered beyond the unshuttered windows, and a distant cheerfulness of voices told her the hayers were only now coming home from the fields. Make hay while the sun shines, as Sister Emma was far too wont to say. But the dormitory was darkening in soft blue shadows, and as nearly as Frevisse could tell, she was alone here, as she had been in the refectory. The others were in the church, praying for Domina Edith, with herself left out of everyone else's pattern yet again. And pattern was so much a part of the nunnery's life. A sameness from day to day that freed the mind to concentrate on prayer.

Not that prayer was the center of some lives, nuns though they were. Frevisse suspected prayer beyond the appointed hours received short shrift from Dame Alys, for instance. Or Sister Amicia, poor thing, who had only the barest idea of what even the offices were for and would have been happier as a gossiping housewife in some market town than as a cloister nun. And Sister Emma—

Frevisse cut off the thought. It was not her place to judge her fellow nuns, and to do it so uncharitably made it the worse. And she was falling asleep. Aware of her mind drifting wide and gently away, she let it go, and only at the very last thought, who was at the pigsty when the boys fell in?

Chapter

◪ 18 ◪

DAWN CAME WITH slow golden glory through the church's east window, the roof beams gilding first, then the church filling with light; and Frevisse in her choir stall, weary and rich with prayer from all the hours spent there since Matins, thought that now would be the moment for Domina Edith's soul to leave them, to rise toward heaven through the golden light in company with the glad, day-greeting prayers of Prime.

But when the nuns came out of the church, it was Ela from the guesthouse hovering in the cloister walk, uneasy on her feet and worried over something other than Domina Edith. Dame Claire looked at her questioningly and she pointed at Frevisse. "Master Naylor wants her to come soon as may be. Now, if she can," Ela said.

Dame Claire turned her look to Frevisse, gestured to ask if she wanted to eat first. Her own alarm rising with Ela's agitation, Frevisse shook her head, and Dame Claire gestured permission for her to go.

Not waiting, Ela hobbled away at her best pace, to be outside where she could more freely talk. The courtyard was still cool in shadows, even the doves not come yet; but there was a hurrying of folk who had no need to be there through the gateway from the outer yard, and as Frevisse closed the cloister door behind her, Ela burst out, "It's that Will, my lady. Sir Gawyn's squire. He's been stabbed dead, they say."

Nothing seemed to move in Frevisse's mind. She could only see Will as he had been yesterday on the guesthall steps, mourning for Colwin's death. He could as well have been mourning for his own.

"Dead?" she heard herself stupidly say. "Murdered?"

"And Master Naylor wants you as soon as may be. Now, please you!"

Frevisse grabbed at what would have to pass for her wits and walked away so rapidly that Ela was left behind. "Move!" she snapped at the men blocking the guesthall steps in front of her.

They pushed one another aside and called warning to the others ahead of them so that she had clear passage into the hall. A servant woman stood in its middle, wringing her hands in her apron and answering the questions being pressed at her with, "I don't know. They just say he's dead. He's been stabbed. I don't know by who."

She interrupted herself long enough to curtsy to Frevisse who demanded, "Where is he?"

The woman untangled her hands from her apron and pointed. "The back passage, just where it turns to the necessarium."

Frevisse left her to dither and the crowd to its useless curiosity. The back passage led to the necessarium beyond the smaller guest rooms, including those given to Sir Gawyn and Mistress Maryon. One of Master Naylor's more burly men from the stables was keeping anyone from entering, but stood aside readily and with a bow to let her pass.

Beyond him, after perhaps twelve feet, the passage doglegged to the right. As she went toward the turn Frevisse could just see Master Naylor standing beyond it, arms folded, his gaze on something on the floor farther along. He heard her coming and moved aside without speaking, to let her see, too.

The passage went a few yards more to the necessarium's door. In the narrow way, bent as if he had slumped down the wall to the floor, Will lay in the pointless ease of death. Propped against the wall, his bright head was resting loosely toward one shoulder; one arm lying across his lap, the other fallen limp to his side. Frevisse could not see his face and she was glad. But there was no way to not see the dagger hilt between his ribs.

"Oh, God in heaven." She crossed herself. "God have mercy on his soul. And I'd thought he might be our murderer."

"What?" Master Naylor jerked his attention away from Will's body to her face. "You thought that?"

"I thought it was a possibility. There were questions I wanted to ask him today."

They regarded the body silently awhile. Then Frevisse said, "Who found him? When?"

"One of the hall servants, just before dawn, when everyone was starting to stir. The first one going to nature's call."

"And no one came in the night?"

"Not that they've said, and someone would have by now if they had."

"So he could have been here all night," Frevisse said. "He doesn't look to have been to bed, though he was maybe readying to go." He was fully dressed except for his boots; only his hosen covered his feet. She edged forward near enough to touch his hand and lift it a little. "He's been dead long enough to be quite cold, and he's stiffening."

She knelt and made herself look into Will's face. It was

nothing; empty of expression; Will was completely gone from it. She shifted her attention to the dagger. "It's thrust in full to the hilt," she said.

"See here." Master Naylor pointed to the wall above the body where a long scar in the plaster ran from the height of a man's chest in a long curve to disappear behind Will's back. "It went full through him and out the back. That's from the point."

"And it was his own dagger, I'd guess." She indicated the empty sheath at his side.

"So it was someone he knew."

"And trusted enough they were able to take his dagger and stab him through before he could cry out or fight back," she agreed. "Any struggle or noise would have roused someone in the hall." The guesthall servants mostly slept on pallets around the great hall at night.

"Or it was someone he didn't so much trust as had no suspicion of," Master Naylor suggested.

"There's that, too," Frevisse agreed. She stood up. "Have Sir Gawyn and Mistress Maryon been told?"

"Mistress Maryon knows. She went in to Sir Gawyn."

"Did she see the body?"

"She didn't want to."

"But I do," Sir Gawyn said behind them from the guarded end of the passage. He had dragged a doublet on roughly over his shirt and hosen. Strained and grim, he leaned on Maryon who was as pale as he was and had her face averted.

Master Naylor said, "Let them by."

Maryon stayed where she was. Sir Gawyn came forward alone with one hand to the wall for balance, and Master Naylor moved aside to let him come to Will's body. Frevisse in the narrow space settled for stepping back instead of trying to pass them both and so could see Sir Gawyn's expression as he looked down at his squire. Of the possible emotions he might have had, he showed none. His eyes were dark and still in a face rigid as stone. He looked at Will for as long as a slow heart might beat twenty, then backed away, still looking, leaning on the wall for support until he turned, reached out for Maryon, and let her help him away along the passage.

When they were gone, Frevisse knelt down and gently straightened Will's body until it lay flat on the floor. She laid his other arm across his chest and raised her gaze to Master Naylor standing at his feet.

"The questions I meant to ask aren't changed, but there are more of them now. And there are ones I need you to ask."

Master Naylor stared at her grimly for a rude while, then said, "What would they be?"

"What I want to know—what I want you to ask everyone outside the cloister—anywhere near the nunnery, come to that—is who saw Colwin and when yesterday afternoon, and if anyone heard him say he was going anywhere or meeting anyone."

"I can ask that and be able to tell you by late afternoon."

"That would do well. And the same about Will. Who saw him where and when and with whom. Were there any guests in hall last night?"

"In neither one."

"So it's someone here then."

"Or someone who came in over the wall," Master Naylor offered. "That would be no great trick."

"But finding Will and killing him and leaving again all unknown and unnoticed—that would be difficult."

"Granted. And we can be sure it was Will he meant to kill. Coming with Colwin's death, it can't be chance. But why? What's so particular about these people that they're so death-haunted? It was no chance attack by outlaws that brought them here, was it?"

Frevisse refused him any answer beyond an ambiguous shake of her head and asked, "Have there been any strangers seen around of late? Have you asked?"

"No one unaccounted for. I've asked and kept an eye out."

"But there have been travelers, some who've stayed here in the guesthall since Sir Gawyn and the others came, even if not last night?"

"Yes."

"And one of them might have suborned one of our people to the murder—the murders—for a price."

"Who among our people would you pick for a hired murderer?" Master Naylor asked scornfully. "The ones you don't know well, I know. How likely do you think it is that one of them could do it and not betray himself?"

"Not very likely. But is any of this likely?"

"Not very, but then I don't know as much about it as you do." His look dared her to change that. She met his stare, refusing him, and finally, grudgingly, he asked, "What else do you want to know?"

"Will said he exercised their horses yesterday afternoon. Do you know when he did that? Or if he did it."

"He didn't," Master Naylor said flatly. "He was never in the stable yard at all in the afternoon, so far as I know, and I'll flat swear he never exercised the horses. There was no need. Colwin did that every day."

"Will told me that he didn't and that's what they had words over yesterday morning."

"Then Will was wrong. Or lying about what they quarreled over."

"The latter seems the more likely, but learning what the

quarrel was truly over will be difficult now, unless someone overheard them."

"I saw them at it. No one was near enough to hear."

A frustrated silence came between them, until Master Naylor bestirred himself and, indicating Will's body, said, "Be as it may, I have to have this seen to, and harry our folk into the fields before the bailiff begins to yelp there's no hope of having the haying done in time. Is there aught else I can find out for you?"

"Not that I can think of now. Have you sent for the crowner yet?"

"A man went yesterday to find him."

So now there would be, probably shortly, Master Montfort to deal with again. But she had remembered another matter. "Ask your stablemen particularly about what they saw of Colwin or knew of between him and Will," she said. "And see what you think of their answers." Another thought came to her. "Who was at the pigsty when the boys were?"

"The sty?" Master Naylor echoed, but then followed where her mind was going. "You think their falling in was no accident?"

"They say it wasn't. It's a dangerous place to fall. If you and Father Henry hadn't had them out of there quickly, they could have been killed."

"You think it was someone turned the rail and dumped them?"

"It could have been, yes. You were there. And Father Henry. Who else? Was Colwin still with you?"

"And Will. And the pig man and a few stable hands who thought they had nothing better to do. Adam and Watkin."

"Do you remember who was where, when the boys fell?"

"I was talking with Father Henry. We'd turned aside. I wasn't noticing anyone that I remember."

"I'm willing to discount you and Father Henry—"

"Thank you."

"—but that still leaves Will and Colwin, the pig man, the two stablemen."

"So I have more questions to ask," Master Naylor said.

"And I'd best go talk to Sir Gawyn now."

Master Naylor moved back to the turn of the passage to give her better room to pass, but asked, "How is it with Domina Edith?"

Frevisse stopped short, remembrance hurting sharply again after the little while she had been free from it. She took a steadying breath and said, "Dame Claire doesn't expect her to wake again. It could be any time now."

Master Naylor crossed himself. "She's a good, blessed lady. God have her in his mercy."

"He surely must," Frevisse said. "Will you ask prayers for her from everyone?"

"She has them already."

As Frevisse had expected, Sir Gawyn and Maryon were together. He was seated on the edge of the bed, hunched over, head down, hands clenched together and clamped between his knees as if to keep them from finding something violent to do.

Maryon stood beside him, her hand resting on his shoulder in a comfort that the whole tense set of his body was refusing to accept. As Frevisse entered, she withdrew her hand but did not move away from him. He barely rose to the courtesy of lifting his head to nod in greeting.

"Dame Frevisse," Maryon said, and even her usually controlled and pleasant voice was a little raw with pain and worry. "Is there any idea of who killed him?"

"Not yet. There are questions being asked that we hope will help. I have to ask you some, Sir Gawyn."

"Go on," he said without looking up.

"What we know is that Will was killed sometime in the night and that no one heard anything. Where did he usually sleep?"

"Here with me. This was where he always slept," Sir Gawyn said.

"His pallet and blankets were there." Maryon indicated the floor along the farther wall. "I—I put them away after we—after we saw—" She gave up trying to finish that and said instead, "The three of us talked together awhile after supper and then I went to my own room, as always. Will saw to Sir Gawyn in the nights."

"After Mistress Maryon had gone," Frevisse asked, "everything was as usual?"

The effort to answer showed in Sir Gawyn's strained voice as he said, "As usual as it's been this while we've been here. He saw to my wound and saw me into bed and we talked awhile, about Colwin mostly." Sir Gawyn paused as his voice unsteadied, gathered himself and continued. "I fell asleep then and slept through the night. When I woke this morning and he wasn't here, I supposed he'd gone out for no more than a moment and would be back."

"How long had he been with you?"

"Close to twenty years," Sir Gawyn said harshly. "He was a half-grown boy and my spurs were hardly cold from my knighting when I took him on. We've been together that long."

"He didn't go to bed last night when you did?"

"I fell asleep while we were talking. He was still dressed and not in bed."

"And you slept without hearing anything all night?"

"All night," he repeated bitterly.

"Gawyn, pray you, lie down," Maryon urged. "You're exhausting yourself the more."

Ignoring her, still talking to his clenched hands, he said,

"And now we can't even leave here. They've found us, and I'm no use to anyone, and Will is dead. There's no one to keep them from the boys."

"The boys will be kept strictly in their room in the cloister from now on," Frevisse said. "They'll not go out of it, and someone will be with them all the time, day and night, and only those we know well will come into the cloister itself until this is settled."

"Will was killed in your own guesthall," Sir Gawyn said. "It was someone who knows the nunnery who did that." He reached to take hold of Maryon's wrist. "You have to go back into the cloister and stay with them. For your own safety and theirs. It isn't much but it's the best place now. The safest."

"And leave you here? I think not." Maryon's refusal was as complete as it was unhesitating.

"Maryon, listen. If they want me dead, they'll have me dead. If Will couldn't stop them, assuredly you can't. Better you be with the boys and keep them as safe as may be. I'm not who matters in this anyway."

"You matter to me!" Maryon cried out softly.

"But not before them. Whatever our feelings between us, we're both pledged otherwise. It can't be helped. You know it. Our words were given."

Another woman might have gone to her knees beside him then, hidden her face against him and begged for him to find a way to help them out of this desperation. Maryon instead turned to Frevisse and demanded, "He has to come into the cloister with me. We need to be all of us together. That's the best thing left now."

Frevisse started a shocked refusal at the idea of a man settled into the cloister, but cut it off. Maryon was right. It would be easier to guard them if they were all together, and the cloister was a more enclosed place than the guesthall.

Master Naylor could put guards at the few doors there were into it. Haying or not, there were men enough for that, especially now that it was so plain that someone was willing to kill and kill again to come at the boys. She changed her protest to, "I'll speak to Dame Claire. I think we can find a way to manage it."

"Why Dame Claire?" Maryon asked. "Why not ask Domina Edith and save time?"

Frevisse stared at her. "You don't know Domina Edith is dying? The while you were in the cloister, you never heard?"

Maryon's face changed. "Ah, that's right. I'd heard that. But that's the way of it when you're old, isn't it? And Dame Claire has the power? She can agree to our coming in?"

Chilled with this reminder that what mattered so deeply to St. Frideswide's mattered very little to the world at large, and understanding that for Maryon the boys' and Sir Gawyn's needs were the most urgent, Frevisse said evenly, "I'll speak to her immediately about it."

"Thank you," Maryon said. Sir Gawyn had taken his hand back from her, had closed again into himself, and only nodded. Despite whatever Maryon had willed herself to believe, he had seemingly very little hope himself.

Chapter

◪ 19 ◪

FREVISSE INTENDED TO return directly to the cloister then, to ask permission for Sir Gawyn and Maryon to refuge there and have them into safety, but at the top of the guesthall stairs down to the yard she paused. Master Naylor must have dealt with sending the gawkers and idlers off to the haying when he came out; the yard was empty except for a little cluster of guesthall servant women whose duties kept them from the haying, but those duties did not include listening with their heads close together at the half-open cloister door. She raised her hands to clap peremptorily at them, then paused, realizing what they were listening to.

The chapter house door must have been left open to the lovely morning air, giving clear scope to Dame Alys's booming voice. At this distance Frevisse could not make out the words—the women at the cloister door were apparently having better luck—but the temper and indignation carried well. Dame Alys was in full cry against something or someone.

Frevisse clapped her hands sharply, once. The women turned toward her with guilty starts, except the one leaning farthest into the opening who had to be jostled by a neighbor

before she joined the others in quick curtsies toward
Frevisse and scuttled away to disappear into the old guesthall the other side of the gateway. When they were gone,
Frevisse hesitated a moment, listening to Dame Alys's voice
go on, fulminating at whatever had aroused her ire. She was
in full cry, not likely to stop soon, and Frevisse turned back
into the guesthall. There was small use in presenting the
need to bring Sir Gawyn into the cloister to the nuns in
chapter with Dame Alys in that mood. Chapter meeting was
open for discussion, and once the matter was given over to
everyone to have their say, it could easily be the hour of
Tierce before they had done with it. It would be better to
wait until after chapter and speak only to Dame Claire.
Persuading her of the necessity would take less time and far
less arguing.

Frevisse's honesty dragged her to admit that avoiding the
general arguing in chapter lay strongly behind her choice,
but it was also true that Dame Claire presenting a completed
decision to the others later was the quickest way to have Sir
Gawyn into safety. Meanwhile there was something she had
meant to do, useless though it seemed to be now.

A quick question to Ela in the guesthall took her down to
the kitchen in search of Nell. From her time as hosteler she
remembered Nell as a wisp of a young woman with a soft
heart and kind ways, clever enough to follow instructions
without having to be told twice and shown how in the
bargain.

Nell was sitting on a stool in the chimney corner where a
slanted shaft of morning light through one of the small, high
windows fell brightly. A sewing basket was on the floor
beside her, but she was not sewing, only sitting, gazing
sadly at the floor, her hands lying in her lap on what
Frevisse guessed was a man's white shirt. Absorbed in her

thoughts, she did not notice Frevisse until, standing in front of her, Frevisse said, "Is that Will's shirt?"

Nell quickly rose and curtsied, the shirt pressed to her bosom now. "Yes, Dame, pardon, I didn't see you come. Yes, it is, please you."

Not wanting Nell too uneased to answer questions readily, Frevisse smiled kindly. "He gave it to you to mend for him?"

"Yes, Dame." Nell held it out to her. "I've finished with it just now. Even though . . ." Her voice trembled away. She said instead, "Are his people wanting it back now?"

"We'll maybe need it to bury him in," Frevisse said. A tear slipped from one of Nell's eyes. It appeared that Will had made a conquest. In surprise, Frevisse asked, "Had you become . . . friends with him?"

"Oh no, Dame! Of course not, I know better than that, him just passing through, not here for long or anything. But . . . he spoke kindly to me. We talked a little, now and again. Nothing more. Was it . . . Did he die . . . Was it horrible?"

Her question was not morbid curiosity but pained concern, and Frevisse answered her, "No. A single stab to his heart. If he felt anything, it was only for a moment. Then he was dead."

Someone had known just where to strike after taking his dagger from him, and had done it with great strength. Not easy, surely, in that small space and with Will already wary from Colwin's death and the attempt on the boys. Someone was very skilled. Or very lucky. And desperate and ruthless to have taken his chance where he could so easily have been heard or seen.

Nell sighed. "That's not so bad then. Though he died unshriven and all, and that's bad, but maybe he had a chance to say Godamercy and that would help, wouldn't it?"

"Assuredly," Frevisse said. "I'll do extra prayers for him, to help."

"And I will, too. I hope they find whoever did it and gibbet him high!" But there was fear as well as anger in Nell's voice, and she added, "They'll catch him soon, won't they, the man who's doing this?"

"Yes, of course. It would be charity to pray for the other man who's dead, too. For Colwin."

"I will, though he wasn't nearly so good as Will. I think he would have bullied a girl if he'd had the chance, would that Colwin fellow. He was more fond of himself than he'd reason to be. Oh my!" She crossed herself. "I'm speaking ill of the dead and him not even buried yet. It's awful, people being killed like this, all of a sudden. And nearer all the time. Nobody wants to sleep here tonight but where could we go and know we're safer, I ask you?"

"I doubt any of you are in peril. It's the people who came with Sir Gawyn who are dying. May I see Will's shirt?"

"What? Oh, surely, indeed, Dame Frevisse. Here."

She held it out readily and Frevisse took it. "You've made a grand mend of it. Where was it ripped?"

Pleased to be praised, Nell showed her. "Here, just along the shoulder seam. A big rip it was."

"Yes, now I can see. How did he do it?"

"He didn't say. He just asked me to mend it and I said I would. I was glad to, he was so pleasant and—"

"Was there anything else wrong with the shirt? Was it wet or anything? Or dirty as if he'd been in a fight or some such thing?"

"Just man-dirty. It's still not been washed. I was going to do that. See, it's grimed around neck and sleeve edges. But no, it wasn't wet."

Frevisse gave it back to her. There was nothing about it to tell her anything except that Will had told the truth at least about it being ripped. But he had lied to her about how, and how would she find out the truth of it, now that Will was dead?

She found chapter meeting had ended when she came out of the guesthall and saw Dame Alys crossing the yard toward her, on her way to her morning bullying of the guesthall servants. Frevisse, when she had been hosteler, had found they worked well enough if an eye was kept on them and an ear given to their troubles, but Dame Alys seemed to find them all a lazy pack of scruff-ridden layabouts, to use her own words, lice-headed fools who needed her constant nagging to do anything at all. By the lowering expression on her face, things were going to go worse than usual for them today, and seeing Frevisse in her way plainly did not help.

"You, Dame!" Dame Alys demanded. "What have you been about that you couldn't be bothered to come to chapter?"

Frevisse braced herself and said, "Master Naylor wanted to see me because the squire Will had been killed in the night in the guesthall's back passage."

Dame Alys sucked in her breath through clenched teeth. "Killed? Murdered, like the other one? In my guesthall? And Naylor summoned you instead of me? That's wrong, Dame! The guesthalls are mine, not yours anymore!"

"It isn't a matter of the guesthall. It's a matter of murder and in that the problem is mine."

"And *that's* wrong!" Dame Alys declared. "You're seeing into what isn't your business. That's Dame Claire's doing and *she's* wrong to let you do it!"

There was never any use in answering Dame Alys's anger with anger; it only drove her to greater excesses. As mildly as she could, Frevisse said, "It's only until the crowner can come. Then—"

"Five men killed hardly a week ago and now two more dead on our doorstep! We're in need of more than the crowner. We're in need of armed men to hunt down whoever is doing this and keep us safe while they do. It's out of hand and ought to be stopped. There's been enough of it, and if Dame Claire doesn't do something now, somebody else ought to!"

"I'm trying to, Dame," Frevisse said evenly.

"But it isn't you who should be trying! It's Dame Claire's friendship for you that's brought us to this. There was never this sort of thing when Domina Edith had her way here. I said as much in chapter this morning and I'll say it again. There are things wrong here, very wrong, and it's clear Dame Claire can't put them right!"

Frevisse abruptly understood it was not the murders that had her in such a rage, or even that Frevisse had been called to the guesthall instead of her this morning. Those were merely sticks to beat the matter she was really angry over—that Dame Claire had authority she did not have, and that when the time came Dame Claire would in all likelihood be elected prioress instead of her. What made it worse was that Dame Alys had an edge of right to what she said. It was not Frevisse's place to be doing what she was doing over the murders, and only Dame Claire's permission allowed it. And there was indeed something very wrong here: something she was deliberately concealing not only from the nuns but very specifically from Dame Claire who had the greatest right to know. Stiffly, knowing that if everything eventually came out in its tangled detail she would be at Dame Alys's mercy, Frevisse said, "I'm sorry you've been offended," and moved away from her.

"There'll be more about this in chapter tomorrow!" Dame Alys declared at her back, loudly enough to be heard from guesthall to cloister.

Head and back held straight, Frevisse went on, refusing her any answer.

She found Dame Claire at her duties as cellarer in the kitchen, waited while she finished discussing what greens there were for dinner, and asked her to come to the slype. Dame Claire gave her a hard, questioning look but came. She was pale from the night spent in prayer in the church, but as Frevisse detailed Will's death her face lost what color it had left. Shaken out of her usual, competent calm, she said, "Another murder? How can this be happening? What are we going to do?"

"Bring Sir Gawyn and Mistress Maryon into the infirmary for their own safety," Frevisse said promptly.

"You can't be serious!"

"A badly injured man is in peril of his life. He can stay in the infirmary and not even be seen."

"Dame Frevisse, have you thought about what you're asking? Bring a *man* into the cloister?"

"And a lady. These people are in danger and unable to help themselves. How can we refuse them the greatest safety that we have?"

"How much safer will they be in here?" Dame Claire returned. "Whoever is doing this is apparently desperate and assuredly bold."

"But the boys have only been attacked when they're outside the cloister, and whoever shoved them in the water yesterday and then killed Colwin didn't attack me. Something holds him back at least that much."

"But if there's no other way to come at his prey—"

"Master Naylor can put a guard at every door."

"There aren't men to spare."

"For this he'll have men."

Dame Claire's chill expression did not change.

Desperately, Frevisse said, quoting from the Rule, " 'Let

all who come to the monastery be welcomed like Christ, for he will say—'"

Dame Claire interrupted her with uncharacteristic impatience, her eyes angry. "Your point is made. But in all its existence, there has never been a man allowed to stay in our cloister."

Frevisse made no reply, only waited.

At last Dame Claire said, "Can this wait at least until Sext so Sir Gawyn can be brought in without any of us seeing him?"

"Yes," Frevisse agreed quickly, relieved and willing to accept nearly any concession so long as he and Maryon could come into safety.

"Then send Master Naylor word of it and that he's to post the guards as he sees fit. But mind, whatever comes, even the end of the world, you're at Sext."

Frevisse bowed her head and curtsied. "Yes, Dame."

Dame Claire made to go, then said instead, angrily, "What is it about these boys? They're the cause of this all, aren't they? Why is this happening?"

Miserably, Frevisse could only shake her head. "I can't tell you."

"What if something happens to you? How will I know what is going on or what's best to do if something happens to you?"

"Domina Edith—"

"—directed me to trust you and I am, as best I may. But she's beyond questions or answering now."

"Then Maryon knows, and Sir Gawyn."

"Who are probably as marked for death as all their men have been."

Dame Claire's blunt, practical mind could be uncomfortable upon occasion. Inwardly flinching, Frevisse answered bluntly back, "That's why it's still better you don't know."

"I begin to doubt that," Dame Claire snapped and again made to leave.

But Frevisse asked, "How is it with Domina Edith?"

To her surprise Dame Claire's anger drained away into a slight, pleasured smile as she said gently, "Very peaceful. Go up to see her if you want. We agreed in chapter to go one by one through the day, as we chose, to see her, pray by her briefly, say good-bye." Behind the smile tears welled up. No matter how peaceful the parting, it was parting forever. Dame Claire tried to say something else, could not, shook her head, and went. Left alone, Frevisse made a short prayer asking for strength and mercy, and then went to find a servant to send in search of Master Naylor.

She waited for him in the cloister and stepped outside the cloister door into the yard to talk with him when he came. He took the orders grimly, made terse agreement to them, and asked bluntly, "Are you sure of what you're doing?"

"No," she said back, and reentered the cloister.

There was only a little while until Sext, and though she would rather have allowed someone else the task, she supposed she should tell the boys of Will's death as well as what else was toward. She turned toward their room, in time to see a flick of child-sized movement disappearing into their doorway. Anger born of frustration clenched in her. Were they such fools they still didn't know their danger and understand they had to stay in their room? And where were Tibby and Jenet with their strict orders to keep them in it?

Grimly, Frevisse went along the walk, rapped sharply on the door frame since the door already stood open, and went in without waiting to be asked. Tibby and Jenet rose to their feet with bobbing curtsies, a little startled at her suddenness. Edmund and Jasper sitting on the rush matting playing at something with straws looked up, ready to be interested in anything new. Lady Adela, standing beside them, dropped in a deep curtsy and said, understanding Frevisse's face before anyone else did, "It was me in the passage, Dame, not them! They've stayed in here just as they were told to."

"And you've only come to keep them company," Frevisse said, no less grim outwardly but her anger dissipated by the child's explanation. "Not lead them out to mischief again?"

"No, Dame." Lady Adela shook her head urgently to show how sincerely she meant it, her fair hair flicking around her shoulders with her vehemence. "We won't go out anymore, ever, until you say we can."

"You promised me that before and you went anyway. Why should I believe you now?" Frevisse included Edmund and Jasper in the accusing question.

"Because we know it's dangerous now and won't do it again. Will we?" Lady Adela asked Edmund and Jasper.

Both boys shook their heads. They seemed none the worse for yesterday, except for a kind of solemnity, a wariness to their watching, that Frevisse had not noticed in them before. Partly she was glad of it; it meant yesterday's terror had left a lesson and they would assuredly be more careful because of it. But it also angered her, because it was a lesson they should not have had to learn so young.

But all she said was, "That's good then. See that you remember it, please." Including Jenet and Tibby in what she had to say next, she went on, "But I'm afraid I have bad news to bring you."

"Colwin is dead," Jasper said sadly. "He was drowned where we nearly were. Dame Perpetua told us."

"She came between breakfast and chapter to tell them," Tibby explained quickly. "She thought it best they know as soon as might be and hear it from her rather than someone else."

"That's well," Frevisse said, sick with what she had to say next. They had seemingly absorbed Colwin's death well enough, but they had known Will better. What his death would mean, coming so close after everything else, she did not know. "But last night sometime—we don't know when yet—Will was killed, too. In the guesthall."

Tibby's mouth dropped open. Jenet shrieked and threw her apron over her face, pressed her hands to it, and began to rock and keen. Lady Adela sank down on her heels between the two boys and put her arms around Jasper. He and Edmund stared up at Frevisse, their eyes huge and shocked.

"I'm sorry," Frevisse said, feeling the words were useless.

Tibby stood up. "I'll bring something to drink from the kitchen. Cider. Something. We need something."

"That would be good," Frevisse agreed, and Tibby left. Frevisse sank down to the children's level, to see their faces directly. Stricken and silent, they stared back at her, nobody heeding Jenet wailing across the room. To the children Frevisse said, "We'll find who did it. We don't know yet but we'll find out."

"How did they kill him?" Edmund asked.

"He was stabbed. In the heart. He would have died almost as it happened."

"Did he fight them?"

"He didn't have a chance to."

"He should have fought them! Jasper and I would have fought them!" Edmund's anger was not enough to stop the tears welling up and sliding down his face. "They won't kill us like that! We'll fight them if they come!"

"Nobody is going to kill you," Frevisse said. "You're safe here."

"They've killed Hery and Hamon and Colwin and Will," Jasper said in a curiously calm voice. He was not crying; he was not doing anything except sitting there and saying the truth with horrible certainty as he stared into nothingness over her shoulder. "They tried to kill us at the pigpen, and they tried to kill us at the pool, and they'll go on trying because they don't want us to be alive anymore."

"Jasper," Frevisse said in agony for the pain and fear he was refusing to show. "Who would want you dead? Why?" Those were the most basic questions of all and she had no answers to them.

But Jasper did. He shifted his eyes and looked at her. "The people my mother is afraid of. She sent us away because she's afraid of what they want to do. She was trying to save us."

Trying to pretend he was not crying, Edmund said, "We thought they'd all been killed when we fought them by the stream, before we came here, but there must be more of them. They'll try to kill Sir Gawyn and Mistress Maryon next!"

"No they won't. We're going to bring Sir Gawyn and Mistress Maryon into the cloister, into the infirmary, and there'll be guards at all the doors. No one will be able to reach them here. Or reach you either." Unable to face Jasper's expression that refused even that little hope, and not knowing what to do about Edmund's tears, Frevisse rose to her feet and snapped, "Jenet, stop wailing! You've done nothing else since you came here and we're all tired of it!" To the three children, more gently, she said, "I have to go see to other things now. Edmund, Jasper, you will stay here, in this room. You understand now? No going out for anything unless I say you may?"

"We'll stay," said Edmund. "We won't go out at all." Jasper nodded.

Frevisse thought Lady Adela would stay with them, but the girl followed her from the room, trotting as best her limp would let her to catch up and then stay beside her as Frevisse went along the cloister walk.

Well away from the boys' room Frevisse stopped. Lady Adela stopped with her. "Do you want something, child?" Frevisse asked. Lady Adela had never sought her company before.

Her hands clasped prayerfully in front of her, her face tipped up to see Frevisse's eyes, Lady Adela asked, "They *will* be all right, won't they? You won't let anyone hurt them?"

"I'm doing all I can to keep them safe, and so are other people. And no one will hurt you, either, so you don't have to be afraid."

"I'm not," Lady Adela said indignantly. "Not for me. It's just that I love Jasper and I mean to marry him, and so no one had better hurt him."

Improbable young love was something Frevisse had no time or patience for just now. "My Lady Adela," she said with what restraint she could manage, "you are Lord Warenne's daughter. I don't think you can go choosing whom you will marry." She refrained from adding, "And especially you should not choose either of these boys."

As much as her soft, sweet face allowed, Lady Adela's expression hardened in unwonted stubbornness. "My father doesn't want me and I'll choose whom I like, no matter what he says."

"Lady Adela—" Frevisse began, then decided this was not an argument she had to participate in, most especially now. Instead she asked, "Why did you break your word and go out yesterday?"

Startled by the change of direction, Lady Adela answered, "An oath given under duress isn't binding. You made us promise not to go out so it didn't count."

"An oath isn't . . . Who told you that?"

"Isn't it true? We thought it was true or we wouldn't have

gone." Lady Adela seemed distressed at the idea her argument might have been wrong.

Frevisse gathered her wits and replied as clearly as she could. "If you're forced to swear an oath because someone is threatening your life, if you're in danger and have to make a promise to save yourself, that's an oath made under duress and you are not bound by it. But it wasn't that way when I asked you to promise, was it?"

"No-o-o," Lady Adela admitted. "I suppose not."

"So who told you about duress?"

"I promised I wouldn't tell."

"Was it someone here?"

"Y-e-s."

"Lately?"

"Y-e-s." Lady Adela had become quite interested in her toe tracing the line of the stone paving in front of her.

"Lady Adela, I think you had best tell me. You love Jasper. He and Edmund are in danger, and I need to know everything I can if they're to be kept safe." With difficulty, Frevisse made her tone mild.

Reluctantly, Lady Adela said, "Now he's dead, he won't mind or be in trouble for it. There's that."

"There's that," Frevisse agreed, holding tightly to her patience. "So please tell me."

"It was one of the men who belong to Edmund and Jasper."

"Will? Sir Gawyn's squire?"

"No. The other one. The one we met at the stables that day. The bigger one. The one who drowned."

Colwin. "Yes," Frevisse said. "I know who you mean." But not what it meant. It was simply another shape among the pieces she was gathering but none of them fit together yet with any sense. "When did you have chance to talk to him about oaths?"

"That day at the sty, before Jasper and Edmund fell in. He was asking what we did all day, shut up in the nunnery, and didn't we ever want to be out. So I told him about how we *had* been out and how you'd made us promise not to do it anymore, and then he told me about oaths made under duress. Only he was lying?"

"He was lying," Frevisse said firmly. "What were Edmund and Jasper doing while you talked with Colwin? Did they talk to him, too?"

"Not then. They mostly talked with Master Naylor."

"Who else was there before the boys fell in?"

"Father Henry and Will and the pig man and some other men from the stables, I don't know their names."

"So there were you and Edmund and Jasper, Father Henry, Master Naylor, Will and Colwin, and the pig man and some men from the stables." She went through the names slowly, ticking them off on her fingers. Lady Adela's head bobbed to each one. "Anyone else?"

Lady Adela's head changed from bobbing to shaking. "No one else."

"And you were talking to Colwin when the boys fell in."

"No, I'd stopped that. I was just standing on the bottom rail of the fence—Master Naylor said I couldn't go up higher because I'm a girl." It was plain she scorned that reasoning. "I was leaning over to watch the piglets. I wasn't talking to anyone."

"Who was standing near the boys when they fell?"

Lady Adela frowned with concentration, then shook her head again. "I don't know. I was looking at the piglets."

Frevisse withheld a sigh. It would be very helpful if someone knew where people were at that moment. She was sure now that it had been the first attempt to kill the boys. The murderer had been there and no one had noticed anything.

Chapter

❧ **20** ❧

AT THE END of Sext, when they had left the church and were gathered in the cloister walk before scattering to their different work, Dame Claire informed the nuns of Will's murder, and told them in the mildest way that while they had been in service Sir Gawyn had been moved into the cloister's infirmary and guards set at all the doors into the cloister, for his safety.

Some word of Will's murder had already begun to spread by way of the servants before then. Frevisse had felt the unease of it among the nuns when they gathered for the office with much looking at one another and small, urgent hand signals. They stirred now as Dame Claire told them, but when she went on to explain about Sir Gawyn they were startled into staring silence at the idea of a man brought deliberately into their midst.

It was Dame Alys who reacted first, pushing red-faced to their fore, looming over Dame Claire and raging, "Without asking? You let a man be brought in here without consulting us? What are we supposed to make of that? It's against the Rule, both doing it and not consulting us. What are we to make of it? A man in cloister!"

Seeming even smaller than she was in front of Dame
Alys's bulk but as strong-willed in her quieter way, Dame
Claire declared coldly back, "This is not the time to discuss
it. You will wait until chapter tomorrow. Besides, there have
been men in our cloister before."

"On business. Or as guest of Domina Edith's parlor and
always one of us there to keep it proper. Not put to bed in
the infirmary! The Rule, Dame! You forget the Rule!"

"And you forget charity! And the Rule that comes before
even St. Benedict's! Do to others as you would have them
do to you!"

"He's a man!"

"He's hurt and he's in danger!" She cut Dame Alys off
with the sign for silence.

Caught with her mouth open, Dame Alys huffed and
purpled, enlarging with frustration and outrage to what
seemed the point of bursting, then spun away, shoved
through the other nuns, and stormed out of the cloister,
presumably to wreak havoc in the guesthall, where no one
could gesture her to silence.

Dame Claire waited for the slam of the door into the yard,
then motioned for the others to go about their business.
Hushed, they obeyed, some more sullenly than others, only
Frevisse staying and so only Frevisse seeing when Dame
Claire let go her show of command and drained suddenly to
weariness. But when Frevisse moved toward her, holding
out a questioning hand to help, Dame Claire drew herself
straight again, made a gesture of refusal that was close to
anger, and went back into the church.

Rebuffed and hurt by it even while understanding that
Dame Claire resented the position she had put her in,
Frevisse sighed and went to see how Sir Gawyn and Maryon
did.

As she passed the door to the boys' room, Edmund leaned out and caught at her skirt.

"Please, Dame, may we go see Sir Gawyn, now that he's here? We'll only go there and come right back. We promise. Jenet will be with us."

Jasper stood behind him, nodding earnest agreement. A luster had come back to him with this chance to see Sir Gawyn again and a hopefulness that Frevisse could not deny.

"Let me see how he does first. He may be too tired just now, after coming from the guesthall. But surely soon Jenet may take you to see him."

Jasper drew a deep, delighted breath. He and his brother were so alike to look at, with their dark red hair and gray eyes and sturdy, graceful build, and so alike in what they did together; but Frevisse had noticed before now that Jasper did not talk or demand as much as Edmund did, perhaps because he had Edmund there to do it for him. But she thought he saw more of what was around him and felt what he saw more deeply than his brother did. Edmund would probably come to charm birds off the trees, as the saying went, and woo his way to anything, but she suspected it would be Jasper who would make true friends and hold them against whatever happened in his life; and he would hurt more over whatever happened to him than his brother did.

Because there was nothing she could do to help that or keep him from any of the pain that would inevitably come to him, any more than she had been able to keep him from the hurts already happening, she smiled past Edmund at him with particular kindness before going on to the infirmary.

Beyond the room where the medicines were made and kept was the longer room with its six beds where, God forbid, ill nuns could come for special rest and care. Living removed from any town and most people, under the stringent balance of the Rule, there were few illnesses in the priory beyond winter rheums, so the room was mostly unused, but it was kept in readiness, and there had been no trouble making up a bed by the door with fresh sheets and blankets for Sir Gawyn.

But he was not lying in it when Frevisse entered. He was at the far end of the room, walking carefully from handhold on the bedpost at the end of one bed to the bedpost of the next, with Maryon hovering, as ever, near at hand. His face was set with concentration, his hair dark with perspiration at the temples. He looked up from his feet when he realized someone was there and, reading her expression rightly, said, "If I do naught but lie in bed, I'll only grow feeble."

"And this way you may exhaust yourself beyond recovery, pushing yourself too hard too soon," Frevisse returned.

"He walked here on his own," Maryon put in.

"Slowly," Sir Gawyn said wryly. "And I think I'm ready to lie down again now."

Maryon took hold of his unhurt arm and helped him back to his bed. The strain of the past days and today showed in her tense movement; her usual grace seemed as exhausted as Sir Gawyn's strength.

When he was lying down again—and admittedly his color was better than it had been; he might be right about the walking, despite what doctors insisted in such matters— Frevisse said, "You understand you're to stay strictly in here?"

"We heard," Sir Gawyn said.

"That was Dame Alys ranting?" Maryon asked.

"Indeed," Frevisse agreed. "The boys are confined to their room, too, but if you like, I'll give permission for Jenet to bring them to see you."

Maryon smiled. "They were at their door as we came along. Yes, it would be good to have them come."

"No," Sir Gawyn said. His eyes were closed. "Not now. Later."

With a worried look at him, Maryon reversed herself and agreed, "Not now. You're tired. Later."

"But you could go see them," Frevisse suggested to her. "I think they'd be glad of that."

"They would, wouldn't they?" Maryon agreed, but not eagerly. How deep was the bond between her and Sir Gawyn, that she was willing to neglect the boys for him? "I'll go now, while you rest, Gawyn."

Not opening his eyes, he nodded.

Frevisse stepped back to let her go first, but as Maryon did, Sir Gawyn said, "Dame Frevisse, would you stay a little?"

Maryon glanced back with a slight frown but went on. Frevisse returned to his bedside. With an effort, Sir Gawyn drew himself up a little on the pillows so he was not lying so helplessly flat and shifted himself, favoring his shoulder, into a better position.

"How badly does it hurt?" she asked.

"Surprisingly little, unless I move it too much." But it was not his shoulder he was concerned with just now. "Has anything more been learned about Will's death? And Colwin's?"

"Master Naylor is asking more questions, to learn where they were yesterday, and when, and if anyone unknown has been seen around here, but I've heard nothing from him so suppose he hasn't found anything new."

"So no one has any idea about their deaths?"

"I have ideas."

Sir Gawyn waited, and when she went no farther, said, "But you're not going to tell me."

"They're too unformed as yet. We're guessing they were killed because they stood between someone and the boys.

And we know someone wants the boys dead because someone has tried twice to kill them."

"Twice?" Sir Gawyn's voice darkened. "What do you mean, twice?"

"Two days ago they fell into a pigsty where there's a fierce sow with piglets. It was thought an accident, that they'd lost their balance. The boys insisted they didn't, and now I agree. I think someone deliberately moved the rail they were sitting on and made them fall."

"And you know who was at the sty when it happened?"

"Colwin and Will and some of our priory folk. No one else."

"So it's someone within the nunnery, not from outside."

"And therefore someone able to enter and leave the guesthall in the night familiarly enough not to disturb anyone or, if he did, not be particularly noticed," Frevisse agreed. "And Will lied about what he did yesterday, but I don't know why yet."

"Lied? About what?"

"About where he was when Colwin was killed. He wasn't with the horses. That isn't how his shirt was torn."

"You're thinking he killed Colwin?"

"He might have." She hated to say it, but the possibility was there.

"He wouldn't have." Sir Gawyn refused the idea flatly. "And if he did, then who killed him?"

"I don't know. The pieces don't make sense yet. But they will. Before I let them go, they will. It's the only way to be sure the boys will be safe. And you and Maryon."

Sir Gawyn did not answer that. His gaze, like his voice, was dark with anger and frustration. And maybe fear, Frevisse thought, because he, like Edmund and Jasper, was helpless, dependent on what others did or did not do.

Frevisse left him, returned to the church for some of her

duties as sacrist, and waited for word from Master Naylor. It came just before None, brought by Ela from the guest-house—and was no use. With the painstaking carefulness of having learned Master Naylor's words by heart, Ela reported, "He's asked everything you wanted asked of everyone who could be asked and no one says more than you already know."

"There've been no strangers seen and unaccounted for? No idea of what Colwin and Will had words over? No one knows where Will was yesterday afternoon?"

"I can only say what Master Naylor said and that's all he said," Ela replied patiently. "There wasn't any more. You want me to tell him something from you back?"

"No. I've nothing to say back. Thank you."

Nothing to say back and nothing new to work with.

At the end of None, with its prayers offered for Domina Edith, she knew she should not put off going to Domina Edith any longer.

The day had grown quite warm, excellent for the haying but uncomfortable for one in long-sleeved gown, wimple and veil. The air on the stairs up to the prioress's chamber was still and hot, but there was no one there except herself and, without meaning to, Frevisse found she had paused in that momentary privacy to gaze out the narrow window there. From here there was a distant view over the nunnery's wall to green grain fields beyond and the forest beyond them, but her mind was nowhere near to what she was seeing.

Someone in St. Frideswide's was a murderer.

The first, unsuccessful attempts to kill had been directed at Edmund and Jasper, but though it had been Colwin and Will who actually died, she still thought the boys were the intended victims. Colwin's and Will's deaths had been happenstance.

At least Colwin's almost assuredly had. But someone had deliberately set out to kill Will. Because he was in the way of the boys' deaths? Because once Colwin was dead, Will needed to be, too? Why? Where had he been yesterday when he was not exercising the horses?

Colwin had used Lady Adela and the oath to lure the boys from the cloister. Had he merely been making mischief to amuse himself, or had there been purpose to it? But if he had made the attempt against the boys there at the pigsty when an unexpected chance offered itself and then again more deliberately at the pool, who had killed him? Or had it been Will who tried both times to kill the boys, and when Colwin had interfered with him, or came on him by accident, killed him for it? But how did that lead to Will's death?

Every possibility ended in the uncertainties of questions she could not answer yet. There were too many pieces missing. Or she was not seeing the pieces she had in their right order. There were answers somewhere, and some way to find them—but they had to be found quickly, before there was more murder.

But first she had to go to Domina Edith, to face a farewell she did not want to make.

Wiping at her damp forehead and the frown drawn tiredly between her eyes, with a wish that she had had more sleep last night, she continued up the stairs.

The parlor was still, empty in the afternoon sunlight beginning to slant through the wide window overlooking the courtyard. In the bedroom beyond it the stillness was almost as deep. Sister Thomasine knelt at the prie-dieu in silent prayer. Sister Lucy sat beside the bed, fanning Domina Edith's face with a sheet of parchment taken from some book. The gentle sway of her hand, the small noise of the parchment moving in the air, were the only sound and movement in the room, and for a dreaded moment Frevisse was unsure that Domina Edith still lived.

But faintly, faintly the sheet over her stirred and her face was not yet graying with death.

Frevisse had meant only to stand in the doorway, make her silent farewell and a prayer and go softly away. She had thought that was all she could bear. But Sister Lucy's face was as wan as Domina Edith's, and Frevisse went forward, silently held out her hand for the parchment.

The elderly nun hesitated. Frevisse made a gesture as if washing her face and stretched her back. Sister Lucy blinked with weary acknowledgment of her need, gave over the parchment, and rose from the stool, hand pressed to the small of her back. She moved aside and Frevisse took her place, beginning to fan Domina Edith's face as Sister Lucy left the room.

Frevisse had thought to pray while she sat there, but she found herself watching Domina Edith's face instead. The gentleness of her dying had taken much of the age from it. She seemed small and smooth-skinned as a child, but the serenity she had lived in showed in her sleeping face with a completeness that only years gave. She was past being old; she was no longer really here at all but well along the way that could only be gone alone, no matter how you went about your dying, no matter how much or little you were loved.

Tenderly, for her own sake even more than Domina Edith's, Frevisse leaned forward and kissed her on the forehead. Gently, as gently as the prioress's breathing there in the summer stillness of the room.

When Sister Lucy returned, Frevisse gave her back her place without comment and went away, her grieving quiet in her for a while.

This time she paused deliberately at the window on the

stairs to look out, over the nunnery wall to the green distance of fields and the forest and the blazing clear sky beyond them all. She had chosen long past to make St. Frideswide's the world to her, closed into it so she could set her mind and heart free in quest of matters beyond the world. But whatever she had chosen, the world beyond the walls was still there with its fears, its dangers, its ambitions.

Its beauties.

Here, from the narrow window, only its beauties could be seen, but that did not mean the fears, dangers, and ambitions were not real. Nor did their reality mean that beauty was a lie.

All of them were real. The error lay in denying the reality of one because the others existed, too.

And there was the trouble with how she had been looking at the pieces of the problem. They had to fit together some way, and she had not yet found it.

Chapter
❧ 21 ❧

THE STAIRWAY'S WARMTH was suddenly too much to bear, and Frevisse went hurriedly down. She needed somewhere else to think. Not the cloister walk, somewhere she would be unlikely to be interrupted. Somewhere . . .

As she came out at the bottom of the stairs, Sister Juliana bustled past her toward the outer door. Sister Juliana was not given to bustling; distracted, Frevisse watched her. And then heard the firm, ongoing knocking at the outer door. A knocking heavy enough she should have heard it herself. By Sister Juliana's sharp glance as she passed, she agreed, but there was no help for it now and Frevisse began to withdraw discreetly from whatever outward business was demanding attention. If she went the other way along the cloister walk . . .

Sister Juliana's alarmed cry echoed along the passage from the outer door. Frevisse spun around and went back to help. But in the passage, as she came in sight of the door now open and Sister Juliana standing there, her step faltered as if suddenly there were insufficient floor under her feet. Nearly filling the doorway—and no way to stop him if he chose to come in—was a man in helmet and breastplate, with a glimpse in the yard beyond him of mounted, armored men.

Quelling an urge to retreat, Frevisse steadied herself and went forward. In a clear, assured, and carrying voice, she said, "What is it, Sister Juliana?"

Sister Juliana turned to face her, eyes wide, mouth working soundlessly. Frevisse laid a gentle hand on her arm and spoke past her to the waiting man. "Can we help you in some way, sir? If you want shelter for the night, I pray you go across the yard to the guesthalls. You and your men will be seen to there."

The man was fumbling at the chin strap of his helmet. As she spoke, he loosed it and pulled his helmet and coif off to show his sweat-matted hair. He was suddenly far less threatening. With a slight bow, he said, "My lady would speak with a Dame Frevisse, said to be in this house. Is it possible?"

"Your . . . lady?" Frevisse asked, her voice level with outward politeness while she tightened her hold on Sister Juliana's arm to keep her silent and hold her there, thinking for a shocked moment he must mean the boy's mother, God forbid, and she did not want to face that alone.

But with a nod across the yard the man said, "The countess of Suffolk."

Frevisse could not stop an audible gasp of relief. She looked past him and aside from the armored men directly in sight of the door to the other riders across the yard. There were perhaps a dozen of them, men and women mostly dressed in the dark blue of the Suffolk household, as the soldiers were under their light armor, she realized now. Some of them had dismounted and one of the women was bringing a filled goblet from the well to the most richly dressed of the women. Still mounted on her tall gray palfrey whose dark blue harness was embossed with the de la Pole

arms of golden leopard heads, Countess Alice took the
goblet with murmured thanks, but her head was already
coming around toward the door, drawn by her name.

Her cousin's loveliness startled Frevisse as it usually did.
With her cream complexion touched with rose and her
finely drawn features and fair hair, Countess Alice was an
ideal of fashionable womanhood. Her houppelande was a
plain-cut one for travel, its sleeves hanging no more than a
foot below her wrists; but it was of rich cloth as deeply
green as the young fields, and while her women wore
wimples and simple veils for riding, her own hair was
gathered up and hidden under a padded roll with liripipe
drawn under her chin and thrown over her left shoulder with
an elegance that bespoke both ease and assurance.

"Frevisse! Cousin!" she called, and waved with her free
hand, not needing to bother with her reins since a squire was
holding to her horse's bridle.

"My Lady Alice," Frevisse returned with a curtsy.

"Your *cousin*?" Sister Juliana breathed beside her, fear
forgotten in wonder. It was known that Alice Chaucer was
Frevisse's cousin, their mothers being sisters, and that she
was married to the earl of Suffolk, but knowing that by way
of priory gossip and actually seeing the countess and her
retinue and guard in St. Frideswide's courtyard were two
vastly different things. "Your cousin," Sister Juliana repeated almost reverently.

Impatiently, Frevisse said, "Yes, I know. You'd best go
tell Dame Claire."

Reminded that hovering in the outer doorway staring
hardly suited with her dignity and the priory's propriety,
Sister Juliana curtsied quickly toward Countess Alice and
retreated out of sight.

Frevisse, her mind running quickly through possible
reasons Alice might be here without warning, waited while

a squire lifted Alice down from her fashionable box saddle and one of her ladies brushed travel dust from her skirts. When the woman, satisfied the countess was presentable, stepped back with a low curtsy, Alice came across the cobbles to Frevisse, hands held out in greeting.

Their lives had gone such widely different ways that they rarely met, but of late an affection that had barely been there when they were girls together had grown between them, partly out of shared memories and affection for Alice's parents, both dead now, and partly out of newly discovered respect for each other, for the women they had become. It was with unfeigned warmth that Frevisse took Alice's hands. Across the yard she could see Dame Alys looming at the top of the guesthall steps and said, "Your folk will be seen to, but you'll come in, won't you?"

"Gladly, Cousin." Smiling, graceful, Alice swept past her into the passageway; but as Frevisse turned from closing the door, Alice said, low-voiced and intent, her smile and light manners gone, "Is there somewhere private we may talk immediately? The prioress's parlor if there's nowhere else?"

Even wary as she already was, Frevisse was disconcerted by her cousin's intensity and said, "Not her parlor. Domina Edith is dying."

Alice's concern was instant and real. "Frevisse, I'm sorry to hear it! Father spoke of her sometimes. He thought very well of her. I'm indeed sorry."

Frevisse shied from the sympathy. "There's the lower parlor, just here at the end of the passage. We can talk there."

All smiles and lightness again, chatting about the warm weather and wasn't it good for the haying—Frevisse had never known her to take particular interest in haying before—Alice followed her into the cloister walk and along it to the parlor door. It was an austere room, kept for the nuns to receive their personal guests, anyone not needing the prioress's attention. There was a bench, a few stools, a table where refreshments might be put, a chair, but neither Frevisse nor Alice sat.

Alice had all the elegant loveliness her own fair features and her and her husband's wealth could provide, but it was her father's intelligence that lived behind the elegance, and as Frevisse closed the parlor door, Alice dropped her lightness and smiles again and said, "Your letter reached me. What have you heard about Queen Katherine that made you so curious you wrote me of her?"

"What's so desperate that you came here because of my letter?" Frevisse returned as quickly.

Countered, Alice paused, her expression revealing how rarely someone met a demand of hers with an answering demand. Then she shifted past annoyance to acceptance of Frevisse's challenge and with a straight-lipped smile nothing like her earlier one answered, "I showed your letter to Bishop Beaufort—"

"Beaufort!" The bishop of Winchester. The duke of Gloucester's great rival in the royal government.

"He and my lord husband are together in all matters around the King now."

"Then why show the letter to him rather than your husband?"

"Because Suffolk is bound for France with the latest muster. Your letter reached me barely in time for me to tell him of it before he sailed. He said Beaufort should know, that I should show it to him, and when I did—"

Frevisse swung away from her, hands clenched together, and paced the small length of the room. "I never thought it would go so far!"

Ignoring her outburst, Alice said, "My lord bishop thinks very well of you, from that matter at my father's funeral."

Frevisse shook her head; she did not want the bishop of Winchester to think of her at all. "He thought, as I did, that there was more than idle curiosity in your letter and that we should know more and immediately. For him to take an open hand in it would be too notable—"

"But for my cousin to come visit me would be a smaller matter."

Alice nodded. "Exactly. Now, why did you write that letter? What do you know here about something that's so far gone barely farther than the lords of the Council?"

It was request and demand both. And a just one.

Frevisse pressed her hands over her face and drew a deep, steadying breath, then tucked her hands quietly into their opposite sleeves, lifted her head, and said, "Queen Katherine's two younger sons are in sanctuary here."

Alice hissed in her breath through her teeth. "Frevisse, this is dangerous."

"That I know," Frevisse agreed tersely, and told her of the attack on the boys' party before they arrived at the priory, explaining in brief how the boys came to be here, ending with, "And now two more of the men who came with them are dead."

"Dead? How?"

"One drowned, the other stabbed. And two attempts have been made to kill the boys."

"Do you know by whom? Or why?"

"No. Ideas but no answers. Alice, are they truly so important that they should be costing men's lives?"

"They're the King's half brothers, and their mother's brother is king of France, for all our government refuses to say so. Yes, they're that important."

"And you mean to take them away. To Bishop Beaufort."

"They're plainly in deadly danger else. Once they're in

my care, under my protection in Suffolk's name, they're safe."

"From whom?"

"Frevisse, you could just let me take them. You might be better not knowing all this."

"There have been a great many dead men on the priory's hands because of whatever this is. Four of the men who were traveling with the boys, the five men who attacked them, whose names we don't even know."

"I know them," Alice said.

"What? Who were they?"

"They were our men. From our household."

"Alice, they tried to kill the children!"

"If they did, it was wholly against orders. No, I think they tried to intercept them, as they had been told to do. They were the ones who were attacked. They had been most strictly told the boys were to be kept safe and brought to me."

"Why?"

Alice drew a deep breath. "Frevisse, this is dangerous."

"I've gathered that," Frevisse said dryly. "So is ignorance and right now I'm very ignorant of what is toward here."

They stared at one another, not in challenge but in assessment—Alice determining how much could be told, Frevisse judging how much truth there would be in it.

"It's this way," Alice said. "We learned the boys were gone almost as soon as their mother sent them away, their brother one direction, these two another. We could guess where they were going and sent men to intercept them if they could."

"How did you know?"

"By a spy in the queen's household," Alice said simply. "The same way we knew about the boys at all."

"How long have you known about them?"

Ruefully Alice admitted, "Barely two months. No one has been concerned about Katherine. She's been living so quietly, away from court, making no trouble for anyone, we thought. Only lately has there been any rumor that that wasn't the truth of it, so only lately did we manage to . . ."

She paused, looking for the word. Frevisse offered, "To insinuate someone into her household?"

"To corrupt someone already there," Alice said. "Their secret depended on their people keeping it. They were very careful of who was around them."

"Not careful enough, it seems."

"There is a point for everyone—" Alice reconsidered. "—for nearly everyone, where the price is high enough to buy their loyalty."

"And you found your person and the price."

"And apparently so did Gloucester."

The duke of Gloucester, the King's uncle, known to resent the limits of his power in the government.

"Do you suppose his agent found the same person your agent did?" Frevisse asked.

"I don't know. I suppose once you begin to be treacherous, you may be indiscriminately so. The point is, Queen Katherine is in deep trouble for marrying one Owen Tudor without the royal Council's permission, and for having royal children by him. It was foolish of her. Careless."

"At least three children's worth of carelessness."

"How did you know there are three?" Alice asked sharply.

"We have two here and you said their brother went another way, meaning at least one other."

"Well, there's going to be a fourth. The queen is pregnant yet again."

It did not seem to Frevisse that four children instead of

three would make the matter much worse, so she simply asked, "What will happen to her for this?"

"She's been put under guard, discreetly, at Hertford for the time being. Tudor has been arrested—"

"For what?"

"Gloucester will think of something. It was his doing. What could be handled quietly he's going to turn into a wide-blown scandal, like the fool he is."

Frevisse almost asked why again but stopped herself. Enough of her curiosity was satisfied, and whatever politics were going on, with Queen Katherine, her husband, and their children as pawns and probably helpless ones, it was not her business. Edmund and Jasper were, and she asked instead, "What do you want with the children?"

"Someone has to have control of them. Better us than Gloucester. Especially since it seems he wants them dead, judging by what you've told me."

Frevisse refrained from asking exactly who "us" might be. Presumably, whoever in the government was presently ranged against Gloucester, and that undoubtedly included the earl of Suffolk. Her letter to Alice had raised trouble she had not counted on. "And if you have control of them?"

"*If?*" Alice questioned.

"They've been given sanctuary here. We have to know what's intended by you or whomever you'll give them over to, before we'll allow them to go with you."

Alice lifted her eyebrows slightly. "Pardon me? I don't know if I understand you."

"I mean that the children are under our protection." Such as it was, but Frevisse did not add that. "We can't simply give them over to you because you've come for them."

"You wrote to me about them."

"In confidence, for advice, and unaware you had so deep

an interest in them. I trust you, but I need to know more. What do you intend for them?"

Alice's momentary haughtiness eased. "You're right. I'm too used to giving commands to those who have to take them without explanation. You won't and you shouldn't. This is the way it is. Gloucester is outraged by this marriage. He sees it as a desecration of royalty and his late brother's memory. He'd execute Owen Tudor if he could, but I think that will be stopped. The queen will be put into honorable confinement in a nunnery, near London probably. Gloucester won't be satisfied with less, and her foolishness has earned it." Alice had never let her own warm heart interfere with her common sense or her ambitions. "As for the children, they're a complication for so many different reasons it can't be said what will become of them eventually, but I purpose to put them into Barking Abbey outside London. My husband's sister is abbess there and they'll be as safe as anywhere, beyond anyone's reach until we know what to do with them. King Henry is gentle-hearted. I think he won't reject them or their mother—his mother—when the matter comes to him."

"But here and now someone is trying to kill them," Frevisse pointed out. "Apparently someone working for Gloucester."

"That would be my guess, too," Alice said. "I think Gloucester would have them put down like cross-bred pups out of a purebred bitch if he had the chance. He assuredly has the wealth and power enough to buy someone for the deed if he wants."

Buy someone. Buy someone desperate enough to face what it might cost to win the reward Gloucester would give.

Neither she nor Master Naylor could believe anyone of the nunnery had been so suborned, that anyone they knew was capable of such killing.

But if, given what she knew so far about the murders, she could not believe that anyone of the nunnery had killed Will and Colwin and was trying to kill the boys, then it had to be someone not of the nunnery.

Someone not of the nunnery—but in it.

Sir Gawyn. Maryon. Jenet.

One of them.

And she had brought them all together, into reach of the children.

"Frevisse?" Alice asked, seeing her mind had gone away somewhere.

"I have to go," Frevisse said abruptly. "Stay here, I pray you, until I come back."

"What is it?"

"I think I see the answer to what's been happening and it's ugly and I have to deal with it now, before— Pray, excuse me." With haste too great for better manners, she left Alice where she stood.

Chapter

◼ **22** ◼

TIBBY AND JENET were together at the table, Tibby's elbows on it, chin in her hands, Jenet twisting her apron's corner, while they talked of their loves—Tibby with plans, Jenet with tearful regrets for her loss.

"Oh yes, we'd hoped to do that. A little house of our own somehow. In Leicester maybe. I've folk in Leicester. Hery, he could turn his hand to anything and I'd maybe raise extra in the garden to sell at market. My uncle, he would have helped us start. But now it's all come to nothing," Jenet mourned.

"My Peter is good at almost anything he puts his hand to, too. He's always saying to me . . ."

It didn't matter what Peter said; they weren't really listening to each other, only talking to keep each other company. Edmund and Jasper had half an ear to them, on the chance they might say something interesting but mostly, taking advantage of the women's distraction, they were busy in the far corner with Edmund's dagger, carefully pricking apart the rush matting for no good reason except they hadn't found anything better to do, though even memorizing Latin prayers for Dame Perpetua was beginning to seem possibly more interesting.

So they raised their heads eagerly to the sound of footsteps outside the door and were already on their feet when Sir Gawyn appeared in the doorway.

"You're better!" Edmund exclaimed.

"Somewhat, yes," Sir Gawyn agreed. His left hand was tucked into his belt, to ease his shoulder, but he had apparently come from the infirmary alone.

Tibby and Jenet sprang to their feet and made deep curtsies. "You." He nodded at Tibby. "Could you bring us something to drink? It's a warm day."

"Yes, sir. As quick as may be," she said readily.

"And have something for yourself along the way," he added.

Tibby smiled more widely at him. "Yes, sir. Thank you, sir."

Sir Gawyn stepped in and aside to let her go out, then leaned against the doorjamb.

"Come and sit," Edmund urged.

"Not just yet," Sir Gawyn said. "Jasper, come here."

Jasper went to him eagerly, ready to help him to the bed or a stool or wherever he wanted to go. Sir Gawyn laid a hand on his shoulder and looking down at him said, "I need you to come with me, out of here."

"Oh," said Jenet coming forward. "Beg your pardon, sir, but Dame Frevisse said they're not to go anywhere, either of them, without she says so, sir. Even with you. She—"

"Jenet, face that way," Sir Gawyn said, pointing to the wall behind her.

Close in front of him now, Jenet blinked at him, bewildered by the order, then obediently turned her back on him. Deftly, too quickly for any warning even if either of the boys had thought to give it, he jerked his dagger from its sheath and, hilt first, struck her hard on the back of her skull. Even through the layers of cloth the crack was audible; she crumpled down into a heap without a sound.

Sir Gawyn did not watch her fall, was already turning toward Edmund. The room was small; Edmund was staring at Jenet, not fully realizing yet what had happened, and did not see in time to move as Sir Gawyn struck again, the knob of the dagger hilt to the back of his head. He collapsed as Jenet had, silently, a small heap on the floor.

Jasper gasped and as Sir Gawyn turned toward him, cringed back. But Sir Gawyn was putting his dagger away, holding out his hand instead. "It's all right. They're only unconscious. They'll be all right. I swear that to you. But this way no one can say they let me escape."

"Escape?" Jasper squeaked.

"We've been found. The people hunting us have found us. They're here with armed men in the yard. They won't hurt Edmund or the women so long as they're in here but they'll kill me. I have to escape and I need you with me. They won't try to hurt me if you're with me."

"But then I won't be safe in here!"

"You'll be safe with me instead. I swear I won't let them hurt you. You've been safe when you're with me, haven't you? Once we're clear of them, we can go back to your mother or on to Wales, whichever way is possible. No one will hurt you, I promise it. My Lord Jasper." Sir Gawyn held out his empty hand. "Come with me."

Jasper hesitated, but Sir Gawyn's need was very real. It showed in his voice and outstretched hand. And how would he ever be a knight himself if he refused another knight his aid, if he refused an adventure when it was offered to him? He put his hand in Sir Gawyn's. The knight grasped it, gave him a tight-lipped smile, and said, "There's my brave man. Come on then. Quickly."

Jasper looked aside to Edmund. "He'll be angry when he wakes up."

"You're smaller. I can handle you more easily," Sir Gawyn said tersely, already going, his grip tight around Jasper's hand, making him come perforce. "Is there a back way out of here to the stables?"

"Past the kitchen and through the side yard, out into the courtyard," Jasper said breathlessly.

"Too long. Too likely to be cut off. We'll go the bold way then."

Jasper wished Sir Gawyn would let loose his hand; he'd said he'd go with him, he didn't have to be dragged.

They were nearly to the outside door unseen, but Dame Frevisse came out of a doorway ahead of them along the cloister walk, directly in their way. Her face showed how startled she was, and so was Sir Gawyn, but on the instant he had swung Jasper to his hurt side, clamped his left arm around his neck and shoulders, and drawn his dagger with his other hand, to lay its point against the side of Jasper's throat as he said, "Let me by and the boy lives. Move aside."

Dame Frevisse moved back into the doorway, hands held empty out in front of her as if to show she meant to do nothing; but she said, "Where's Edmund? Where's Maryon?"

"They're all right. They're unconscious, that's all." Sir Gawyn was pushing Jasper past her as he spoke. His arm was beginning to choke and Jasper dug fingers into his sleeve, trying to loosen it. To his shock, the dagger pricked into his neck and Sir Gawyn said, "Don't struggle." To Dame Frevisse he added, "You go ahead of us. I want one of the horses that's out there and no one to follow us."

"Those are armed men out there, the earl of Suffolk's men."

"I know what's out there. Maryon went to see what was

happening and told me. That's the countess behind you in the room, isn't it?"

Dame Frevisse had begun to back away from them, toward the outer door. Now she stopped and said sharply, "It would be too dangerous to you to take her. Don't even think it!"

"I know that! Jasper will do well enough."

"That's right," Dame Frevisse said harshly. "Children are more your sort of foe. And men who trust you."

"Move!"

"Let him go. You won't be able to escape so many."

"If they want him alive, and I'd guess that's why the countess came, no one will follow me."

Somewhere behind them, Dame Claire called anxiously, "Dame Frevisse!"

Her eyes fixed on Sir Gawyn, Dame Frevisse said back, "You can't help. Keep away."

They had reached the outer door. "Open it," Sir Gawyn said. "Tell them what I want."

She held back momentarily. Sir Gawyn pressed the dagger's tip deeper into Jasper's neck than he had before. Jasper gasped at the unexpected pain; his neck prickled under a thin run of blood. His grip on Sir Gawyn's arm tightened, trying to pull it a little loose. Sir Gawyn did not realize he was hurting him, surely. But the grip around his throat did not loosen at all, was too tight now even for him to speak. Dame Frevisse was looking at him, frightened, he thought, and reaching behind her for the door latch.

"Go on!" Sir Gawyn urged. "I won't hurt him unless I'm made to."

"You're hurting him now," Dame Frevisse said back. "Let him breathe a little, for God's pity."

Sir Gawyn's arm loosed a little, to Jasper's gasped relief. He'd known Sir Gawyn hadn't realized how tightly he was holding him. But more angrily than before, Sir Gawyn ordered, "Go on! Out!" and this time Dame Fervisse turned her back on him to open the door and go out.

There were men in armor and horses and a few women in the yard. All but a few of the men had dismounted, but they all seemed ready to travel again at a moment's notice, though guesthall servants were going among them with pottery mugs of something to drink. Heads swiveled toward them as they came out, and Jasper saw the nearest few men come suddenly alert, hands going to their sword hilts as they realized what they were seeing.

Dame Frevisse held out her hands to them. "Don't do anything! He's sworn he won't harm the boy if we don't do anything! Let him have a horse and let him go."

After a hesitation, all but the closest man faded back; he held out his reins toward Sir Gawyn, with nothing friendly in his face. Jasper, his eyes going rapidly from face to face around them, saw nothing friendly in anyone's; but it was Sir Gawyn they were staring at, not him.

"Dame, take the reins from him. You, go farther off," Sir Gawyn ordered.

Dame Frevisse and the man obeyed, Dame Frevisse taking the reins, the man then stepping backward, farther away, his eyes never off Sir Gawyn.

"Hand Jasper the reins."

Dame Frevisse obeyed. As she did, her gaze dropped to Jasper's face. To his surprise he saw she was not afraid, only sad. To Sir Gawyn she said softly, "Don't do this. Let it end here."

Sir Gawyn drew in a short, harsh breath, as if she had hurt him, but said, as hard-voiced as before, "If no one follows us, I'll let him loose somewhere safe and you can have him back. But only if no one follows us. Stand over there, both of you. Out of the way."

She did, and Jasper knew this was the most dangerous part. Sir Gawyn would have to mount before anyone could reach him to stop him, and it wouldn't be easy with his hurt shoulder.

But he had already thought out the problem. He let Jasper loose and said, "Climb on the horse. Have the reins ready." He gave him boost enough so Jasper could grab the saddle and scramble up, scooting well forward to leave room behind him in the saddle for Sir Gawyn. Jasper took the reins, and Sir Gawyn swung the horse around so it was between him and everyone else. He was on its off side now but from there, able to use only his right hand for it, he would be better able to mount. Slipping his dagger into his left hand, he grasped the cantle with his right and brought himself up into the saddle in a single swift swing, settled behind Jasper, his left arm around him again, across his chest this time, and the reins in his left hand, the dagger back in his right before anyone could close on him.

The man who had given over his horse made one spasmed movement as if to go for Sir Gawyn, but Dame Frevisse put out an arm to hold him back. On the tall horse, Jasper felt more exposed to the stares than he had before, but it was Dame Frevisse he was looking at, even as Sir Gawyn urged the horse forward. Suddenly he wished very, very much he was back in the cloister, that none of this was happening. He was suddenly desperately afraid, more afraid than he had been when Sir Gawyn struck Jenet and then Edmund, almost as afraid as when the riders had attacked them. And part of the fear came from what he saw in Dame Frevisse's face—grief and anger and desperation as she realized there was truly no way to stop Sir Gawyn now.

"Jasper," she said; and she was talking to no one but him in all the crowded courtyard, pleading with him to understand something. "He made Colwin try to kill you and Edmund, and he killed Will. Jasper!"

The last was a cry at their backs as Sir Gawyn dug his heels into the horse and set it into a canter toward the gateway, guiding it more with his legs than the reins.

Trying to twist his head around to see Sir Gawyn's face, Jasper cried out, "You didn't do any of that!"

Sir Gawyn didn't answer. They were through the gate, the canter rising to a gallop across the outer yard for the open gateway beyond. Jasper clung two-handed to the saddle, still straining around to see Sir Gawyn. Why would Dame Frevisse say it if it wasn't true? "You didn't!" he cried again, begging Sir Gawyn to agree. But he didn't, and Jasper's last, "You didn't!" was more with despair than pleading. Sir Gawyn wouldn't say it, and the glimpse Jasper had of his face told him why.

They were through the outer gateway, were making the wide turn into the road that here ran between the nunnery's outer wall and deep ditch with hedge beyond it. There was no one left to stop Sir Gawyn's escape now, and Jasper didn't plan what he did then. It was partly fear, partly outrage at Sir Gawyn's treachery, partly a cold, brilliant anger that came, out of all proportion to his size and years, with the full realization of what Sir Gawyn had done and how Sir Gawyn was using him. He reached left-handed across himself, below Sir Gawyn's arm around him, grabbed his own small dagger from its sheath and stabbed it hard as he could into the horse's shoulder in front of the saddle.

The horse screamed, flung sideways in frenzy away from the pain, and at full gallop was somehow falling, the ground gone from beneath its hooves. The green mass of the hedge smashed toward them from the side and behind him Jasper felt Sir Gawyn twist sideways in a desperate wrench.

And then nothing.

Chapter

⚅ 23 ⚅

THEY CARRIED SIR Gawyn back to the guesthall and laid him on the bed that had been his these days past. By then Dame Claire was there, and Father Henry, but as the men stepped back from the bed it was obvious that it was Father Henry who was needed. Dark, frothed blood oozed from the corner of Sir Gawyn's mouth each time his chest labored at a breath, telling he was badly, badly broken somewhere too deep inside to be helped, so that the bleeding cuts across his face from the hedge did not matter, nor that his shoulder wound had been opened by the fall and bright blood was seeping through his doublet in a spreading stain. He would not live long enough to make tending to them worth anyone's while, even his. Frevisse after showing the men where to lay him went back against the wall beyond the foot of the bed, not wanting to see him but unable to bring herself to leave.

For mercy's sake he should have been unconscious but he was not. As Dame Claire bent to wipe away the blood running from his mouth, his eyes searched past her among the strangers' faces around him. He seemed able to move only his eyes and his hurtfully breathing chest until he whispered, "Jasper," and stirred one hand.

Master Naylor came forward, bent over him so Sir Gawyn could see him clearly, and laid a quieting hand over his. "He's not hurt. He was only stunned and the breath knocked out of him by the fall. He's unhurt. Someone has taken him back to the nunnery."

Sir Gawyn's eyes closed and his lips moved silently in what looked like prayer.

Master Naylor leaned nearer. "You saved him, twisting the way you did to come between him and the hedge. You saved him with that."

Sir Gawyn's eyes opened. "You saw?" he whispered.

"You nearly rode me down by the outer gate. I was there. I saw."

Father Henry had been laying out the necessary things on the table across the room from the box he had run to fetch when he had realized what was happening. Now as he put the stole around his neck and turned toward the bed, his prayers, mumbled in a rapid undertone, became audible if still not comprehensible, and the men around the bed and the crowd of servant faces at the door drew back. They had no place in what was coming and knew enough to leave. In the agony of her own helplessness, Dame Claire hesitated until almost last, then withdrew, too.

But when Frevisse and Master Naylor moved to follow her, Sir Gawyn whispered hoarsely, an odd, thin gurgle to his voice, "No. Dame Frevisse, stay. And—I don't know your name."

"Roger Naylor, the priory's steward."

"Roger Naylor. You and Dame Frevisse. You stay and hear this. Someone should hear. Besides the priest. Someone who can tell . . ."

He began to choke on his own blood. Frevisse went to

him quickly, rolled him on his side and held a cloth to catch what drained from his mouth, wiped his lips clear, and eased him to his back again. Sir Gawyn groaned and, eyes shut, whispered, "I wish to confess my sins," beginning what had to be done before absolution and the last rite could purify his soul.

But it was maybe to Father Henry least of all he spoke, with the need to make someone understand what he had done and why as strong or stronger than the need to save his soul. The words came as broken as his breathing, and his eyes stayed shut, his hand still now, all of what little strength remained in him given over to the words.

"I sold my honor to someone working for the duke of Gloucester. In the queen's household. For money I promised that when the time came I'd do what I could to give the children into his hands. And when the time came, I couldn't keep the promise. I broke it and kept my oath to their lady mother instead. I meant to take them to Wales. We killed those five men at that stream, and Hery and Hamon died, because I kept my promise to her." The cruel, wheezing effort to breathe overtook him, held back the words. No one touched him or spoke. More weakly, but still determined, he went on. "And then they told me my arm was gone. That I wouldn't use it well again. That meant there was nothing . . . left . . . for me . . . except poverty. Except . . . Gloucester would pay . . . to be rid of the children . . . his man had said. He'd said if Gloucester couldn't have them, then they were better . . . dead . . ."

Frevisse wiped blood away again. Master Naylor, because Sir Gawyn seemed unable to go on, said, "So you thought to have them killed."

"Their lives or mine," Sir Gawyn agreed. "I knew . . . Will . . . wouldn't . . ."

"So you told Colwin to do it," Frevisse said.

A slight twitch of Sir Gawyn's head agreed.

"And Will found out." Frevisse said it because she did not think Sir Gawyn could. "He realized Colwin made the boys fall into the pigsty and that's what they quarreled over at the stables, but he couldn't change Colwin's mind. And when Colwin followed the children yesterday, Will followed him but was too late to stop him, struck him unconscious, and when we had left the stream, stripped off his clothes and drowned him in the pool. If I hadn't come, Will would have saved them, but I came and Will stayed hidden, hoping to keep your secret."

"Yes." Sir Gawyn drove the word from himself, struggled for breath, and said, "Prayers for Will."

"As many as I can make," Frevisse said. "I promise." But there was more she had to know. Willing Sir Gawyn to go on answering her, she said, "It wasn't that easy, was it? Colwin regained consciousness enough to fight being drowned and that's how Will's shirt was ripped."

"Yes. He told me . . ."

"He told you what he'd done because he was your squire, you were his knight. He wanted you to stop."

Sir Gawyn's nod was small, painful.

"But now Will was a danger to you as well as a traitor, so you killed him last night. When everyone had settled for the night, you asked him to help you to the necessarium, took his dagger, and killed him there in the passage."

"Yes." Sir Gawyn opened his eyes, fumbled his hand to grasp her sleeve. "But Will wasn't . . . traitor. I . . . was. He . . . was trying to save . . . me from what . . . I'd tried . . . to do. He meant . . . to talk me . . . out of it . . . after Colwin was dead. He . . . tried . . . and I wouldn't . . . listen."

It had not been only Colwin's death that Will had cried for yesterday on the guesthall steps, but for the death of his

belief in his knight's honor. Frevisse hoped that he knew—
that somehow he knew—what Master Naylor had said: that
at the last Sir Gawyn had killed himself to save Jasper in
that crashing fall. And Tibby running from the cloister as
they had carried Sir Gawyn back across the yards had told
her that Edmund, Maryon, and Jenet were alive and coming
conscious. So he had meant it when he said he would not
hurt Jasper if they let him go. He had not killed Edmund;
there would have been no point then in Jasper's death. "But
then why did you change your mind at the last and not kill
them as you escaped?"

Sir Gawyn's hand slipped loose from her sleeve and
knotted with pain into the blanket under him. Eyes shut, he
whispered, "Because it would be known I did it and . . .
everything . . . lost then anyway. So there was no point . . .
anymore . . . if Maryon knew." He labored more heavily at
his breathing and barely managed to force out, "Tell
Maryon . . . sorry." And Frevisse realized they were out of
time. She felt Master Naylor's hand on her arm and let him
draw her aside, leaving Sir Gawyn to Father Henry and the
ending that would come very soon now.

As she and Master Naylor left the room, both of them
silent, distantly the cloister bell began to toll the slow count
of years that marked a death. A stroke for every year
someone had lived.

That was not right, Frevisse thought. Sir Gawyn was not
yet dead.

And then she knew.

The bell was not for him. Not yet.

Tears scalded in her eyes, blurring sight of people all
across the hall going down upon their knees as they realized,
too. Not for Sir Gawyn.

Requiem aeternam dona eis, Domine. The words came to
her from the Office of the Dead without bidding. *Et lux*

perpetua luceat eis. Eternal rest give to them, Lord. And perpetual light shine on them.

In pace, domina, libera.

In peace, my lady, go free.

EXCITING NEW
VOICES IN MYSTERY

BERKLEY PRIME CRIME

__**FRESH KILLS**
by **Carolyn Wheat**
0-425-14921-8/$9.00
"Carolyn Wheat is one of the best new writers in the field."—**Lawrence Block**
When a routine adoption case turns to murder, lawyer Cass Jameson uncovers a web of extortion that caters to the dreams of childless couples. *(Trade Paperback)*

__**DANCE OF THE MONGOOSE**
by **T.J. Phillips** 0-425-14921-8/$9.00
"Crime fiction at its riveting best...sensational."
—**Faye Kellerman**
When writer Joe Wilder's friend is accused of murdering his father, a corrupt judge, Joe begins an investigation that makes him realize that time can tarnish the strongest of childhood loyalties...and even an island paradise hides its share of snakes. *(Trade Paperback)*

__**DEATH ON THE MISSISSIPPI**   *(December)*
by **Peter J. Heck** 0-425-16939-0/$10.00
Broke after a lifetime of poor investments, Mark Twain reemerges with a new and even more daunting title: detective. And when Twain's address is found on a murder victim in New York, he must board a steamboat bound for New Orleans to catch a killer linked to his riverboat days. *(Trade Paperback)*

Payable in U.S. funds. No cash orders accepted. Postage & handling: $1.75 for one book, 75¢ for each additional. Maximum postage $5.50. Prices, postage and handling charges may change without notice. Visa, Amex, MasterCard call 1-800-788-6262, ext. 1, refer to ad # 560

| Or, check above books | Bill my: | ☐ Visa | ☐ MasterCard | ☐ Amex | |
and send this order form to:
The Berkley Publishing Group   Card#_____
390 Murray Hill Pkwy., Dept. B   (expires)
East Rutherford, NJ 07073   Signature_____ ($15 minimum)

Please allow 6 weeks for delivery.   Or enclosed is my: ☐ check   ☐ money order

Name_____   Book Total $_____

Address_____   Postage & Handling $_____

City_____   Applicable Sales Tax $_____
                                      (NY, NJ, PA, CA, GST Can.)
State/ZIP_____   Total Amount Due $_____